Twist...

Cinderella
NINja WARRIOR

Maureen McGowan

Silver Dolphin

San Diego, California

Silver Dolphin Books
An imprint of the Baker & Taylor Publishing Group
10350 Barnes Canyon Road, San Diego, CA 92121
www.silverdolphinbooks.com

Copyright © Silver Dolphin Books, 2011

Interior and cover design by Pauline Molinari.
Cover art by Mike Heath.

ISBN-13: 978-1-60710-255-7
ISBN-10: 1-60710-255-2

Library of Congress Cataloging-in-Publication Data
McGowan, Maureen.
Cinderella : ninja warrior / Maureen McGowan.
p. cm.
Summary: In this twist on the traditional tale, Cinderella trains as a
ninja warrior to help her escape the control of her evil stepmother and
attend a special Magic Festival at the palace. The reader is given chances
throughout the text to choose the direction of the plot.
ISBN-13: 978-1-60710-255-7
ISBN-10: 1-60710-255-2
1. Plot-your-own stories. [1. Ninja--Fiction. 2. Stepmothers--Fiction. 3.
Princes--Fiction. 4. Fairy tales. 5. Plot-your-own stories.] I. Title.
PZ8.M1761Cin 2011
[Fic]--dc22
2010037054

Printed in the United States

1 2 3 4 5 15 14 13 12 11

*For Bev Katz Rosenbaum, who gave me the chance,
and for Catherine Grace, who's as strong and
beautiful as any fairy tale princess.*

taBLe of coNteNts

HOW THIS BOOK WORKS

Welcome to *Cinderella: Ninja Warrior*, a different sort of fairy tale that's twisted two ways. First, it's full of adventure, loaded with danger, heaped with action, and sprinkled with magic. Second, *you* get to control what happens.

At three points during the story, you can put on Cinderella's slippers and decide—if you were her—what you'd do next. By making these choices, you get to determine how her adventure unfolds.

But don't worry—there are no right or wrong decisions, just different ones. As you'll soon discover, Cinderella's a pretty special girl. She's strong and smart and brave, and if she can learn how to believe in herself, she'll figure out how to reach her happy ending, no matter what challenges you throw in her path.

Each time you reach a decision point, you'll be given two choices. Once you make your choice, all you need to do is flip to the next section in the story. When you reach the end of each section, there will be a guide to tell you where to go next.

Have you figured out the best part yet? That's right—you can read this book over and over! In total, there are eight different routes that Cinderella can take to reach the end of her adventure. Eight stories in one! Can you figure out all the possible routes?

Enjoy!

1

Section 1

Home Not-so-sweet Home

Cinderella's shoulders quivered with fatigue as she tipped the twenty-seventh wooden bucket of fresh water into her stepmother's bath. The water, laced with sweet-smelling oils, sloshed up the tub's sides, threatening to spill over the edges and onto the pristine floor that she'd have to mop again if the hot water escaped.

She brushed stray blonde hairs off her lightly freckled face, and then crouched to stoke the fire, which crackled as it heated the tub. Stretching her aching fingers toward the warmth, she rubbed the calluses on her palms and fingers. Along with her many other chores, the countless trips from the cellar to the upstairs bathrooms to fill three tubs twice a day had taken their toll on her body.

Cinderella had just turned eighteen, but her hands looked much older. Her real mother, one of the most powerful wizards in the kingdom, had died at her birth, and five years later her father died too, only days after he remarried. Her stepmother, also a wizard, treated Cinderella more like a servant than a daughter.

Cinderella often wished she were a ninja warrior—no, make that a ninja and a wizard. A wizard could break her stepmother's entrapment spells, and a ninja, well, a ninja could give her stepmother what she deserved.

But hard work and determination carried more power than if-onlys and wishes. Her stepmother's magic was powerful, and it seemed as if she'd thought of everything to keep Cinderella trapped. That was no excuse for Cinderella to sit back and do nothing, though. It was better to practice the few innate magic skills she had inherited from her mother, and to develop her self-taught ninja training. Sometimes the best offense was a good defense.

Enough of this whining, thought Cinderella. There would be no time for training if she lazed about staring at the fire and daydreaming. If captured, real ninja warriors didn't sit around thinking about escaping—they took action. She sprang to her feet and grabbed the empty buckets, ready to make the much easier trip down the three long flights of stairs to her cellar room. Her stepmother had used black magic to cast entrapment spells that kept her confined to the cellar, except to do chores during the day and to garden at night.

Twisting sideways, she squeezed through the tiny entrance at the top of the servants' stairs that were dark and narrow in places.

When her father was alive, she'd been scared to even go near the cellar where she now lived. The few times he'd taken her down there to help fetch jars of pickles or retrieve her sled during the winter, she'd clung to his neck, burying her face in his srong chest. And they'd used the main stairs, which were not scary at all compared to the rickety back stairs that she was forced to climb. Still, she couldn't suppress putting a slight skip into her step as she descended, jumping over the broken fourth step on the second flight and not even breaking her gait on the uneven rises.

On reaching the bottom, she gripped her buckets and moved into a crane stance to prepare for a side kick. "Ha-ya!" she shouted, and then her bare foot struck cleanly against the heavy wooden door.

The door swung open, hitting the stone wall with a bang, to reveal the cold room that doubled as a bedroom for her and storage space for everyone else in the house. She'd moved into the cellar at age five, right after her father died. The damp, chilly room no longer scared Cinderella; she had much scarier things to face every day—like her evil stepmother.

In the opposite corner of the room, her fluffy gray cat lifted his head from the straw-filled burlap sack the two shared as a bed.

"Hello, Max." Cinderella walked toward the iron water pump on the far side of the fireplace and set the wooden pails next to it, ensuring they were lined up perfectly. She'd long ago discovered that the only way to avoid her stepmother's punishments involved a combination of obedience and precision. Being compliant and faultless didn't always work, but she aimed to stay on her stepmother's good side, with hope that she might be released from this prison existence someday.

Who was she kidding? Her stepmother didn't have a good side. Yet Cinderella had to believe she'd gain her freedom someday—without this hope to cling to, she'd go insane.

Max flicked his tail and it struck the corner of her most precious possession—her *Way of the Warrior* book. She dashed over and bent to tuck it back under the bed. It simply would not do if her contraband reading material were discovered. The only books she'd ever been allowed to read were the ones her stepmother selected for her lessons, and since age twelve, when she surpassed her older stepsisters in their studies, she'd been cut off from books altogether. She scratched Max's favorite spot, right under his chin, and he purred and stretched. He was her only friend now; it didn't matter that he wasn't human. Sometimes, she was sure he could understand her words and even guide her actions.

Not long after she'd first discovered him as a tiny stray kitten in the garden, he inexplicably pawed her ninja training book off the enchanted library's bookshelves. Cinderella had dusted those shelves nearly every day, and never had one book even budged. How Max had swiped it off the shelf remained a mystery. At first she'd only read the book to counteract boredom—the exercises seemed too intimidating to try—but every time she'd taken it out, Max had pawed at the pages, drawing her attention to the illustrations. Eventually she tried some, mostly to shut him up.

And it had paid off. The ninja training slowly improved her concentration, strength, and balance, and she soon found that she had other abilities—magical abilities—that required the same basic skills. While training in the garden one cold night a few months ago, she'd focused on the hoe throughout her meditation exercises. Finished, she flicked her hand, and the hoe moved. She and Max danced and skipped around the garden in glee. Well, she could only *assume* Max had been happy for her.

With practice, Cinderella could now move small objects over short distances with her mind—sometimes—and was thrilled she'd inherited even a small portion of her real mother's powers. It was one thing to perform spells with a wand, but only the strongest wizards could perform magic using just their minds—wizards like her real mother. But even raw talent needed training, and with her mother gone, she had no one to teach her.

Max pushed his paw against her leg and stretched while she scratched him.

"You're a clever cat, Maxie. Did you find any mice today?"

He flicked his tail.

"Maybe tomorrow Agatha or Gwendolyn will leave some milk in their porridge bowls and I can give you a treat." He rubbed up against her side. "Speaking of treats, I'm dying of thirst." Max twisted on the bed and pawed at the burlap sack. "Yes, I know I should practice." She put her hands on her hips. "Is it too much to ask if I have a small sip of water first?"

Max meowed and rubbed his back on the rough burlap.

Turning to the cupboard on the wall opposite the fireplace, Cinderella reached a hand toward her pewter goblet on the top shelf, above the beautiful crystal and bone china dishes that were reserved for the rest of her family.

Concentrating, she focused on connecting her hand to the goblet. *Come to me, goblet.*

Her fingers tingled and the goblet wobbled, but it didn't move off the shelf. She dropped her arm in defeat.

Who was she kidding? Her magic wasn't that strong. To do something that purposeful, she needed a wand and instructions.

She carried her stool from the side of the planked table to the cupboard and, after tucking the bottom hem of her torn skirt into the waistband of her pantaloons, climbed onto the stool's scratched seat. Balancing barefoot on the wobbly stool, she stretched up to reach her goblet.

She snagged it, the stool tipped, and she shot one leg and her arms to the sides to catch her balance. Still on one leg, she let the stool tip to one side, then the other, as her body stretched out in all directions.

Striving to keep her balance, she found her center, brought her limbs in, leaped high into the air, tucked her knees into her chest, and executed a perfect somersault, landing on her toes without a sound.

Max raised his head from the bed and meowed to her, his bright green eyes sparkling.

"Why, thank you, Max." She pulled the frayed fabric of her skirt from her pantaloons and curtsied. "It *was* an excellent one-footed backflip, wasn't it?"

She grinned. *There I go again, talking to my cat.* Clearly, she spent too much time alone.

Max pawed at the burlap sack.

"Okay, okay, I'll practice. But it's too dangerous to bring out the book during the day. You know that, Max." Cinderella preferred to wait until everyone else in the house was asleep before trying anything. There was more room to train in the garden, where she worked alone at night. Besides, if her stepmother knew she'd inherited any of her real mother's abilities, she'd make the entrapment spells even more restrictive.

Holding the goblet in front of her, Cinderella bent her legs to lower herself into a crouch, and then spun and leaped, kicking and chopping at an imaginary foe as she crossed the room to reach the pump. Once there, she pushed down on the handle until fresh water flowed from its spout, and then eagerly set her goblet under the stream to catch the crisp, ice-cold water from deep in the well, her reward for the past twelve hours of grueling work.

Not seeing her stepmother or her stepsisters for four hours had been a fine reward, too. It was unusual for them to leave her alone for so long. She glanced at the single window of thick glass that she'd long ago given up trying to break. The pane was too thick and probably enchanted to give it extra strength. Given the angle of the shadows on this long spring evening, she figured there was less than two hours before darkness set in, the back door opened, and the wolves came out.

But what if something had happened to her stepmother? She had been gone a long time. Would the entrapment spells be broken if her stepmother was killed? Maybe one of the doors out of the house would open before nighttime arrived.

Cinderella set down the goblet and dashed to the cellar door that led up the steep, damp stone staircase into the garden. Taking a deep breath, she pulled on the iron handle.

It didn't move an inch—not even a wiggle. The garden door was sealed as it always was when the sun was up, just like every other exit from the house. She slumped against the door. As impossible as it seemed, she believed that someday she'd find a way to escape.

Balanced in a one-armed handstand, Cinderella slowly scissored her legs, concentrating on maintaining her balance. Suddenly, a cackling laugh shattered the peaceful silence of the house. Startled, Cinderella wobbled for a moment before catching her balance, and then stepped out of her handstand.

Her stepsisters, Agatha and Gwendolyn, were home.

She pulled her navy skirt back on over her pantaloons and draped her bibbed apron on top, wrapping the grayed ties twice around her waist before smoothing her hands down the coarsely woven fabric.

The heels of her stepsisters' shoes thumped a hard rhythm above her, making the floorboards groan.

"My feet are killing me." Gwendolyn's shrill voice carried through the floor.

"Mine, too," Agatha said. "Cinderella! Oh, Cinderella!"

Cinderella took a sip of her water.

"Cinderella!" both sisters shouted at once, and the floorboards above her head shook again.

She gave Max one last scratch under his chin before starting up the rickety wooden stairs. Stepping into the parlor, she found Agatha and Gwendolyn sprawled on a pair of matching brocade chairs in front of the fireplace, the mantel of which—like every other surface in the room— was covered with her stepmother's collection of glass animal figurines. Cinderella wasn't entirely convinced that some hadn't once been live animals, and hoped she wouldn't one day find Max sitting on this shelf.

"There you are." Agatha, the younger of the two sisters, wrinkled her nose as she spoke. "Help me with my slippers. They're pinching my dainty little feet."

"Certainly, Sister." Cinderella tried hard not to laugh. Agatha's lush red curls and smooth, peachy complexion were undoubtedly beautiful, but her feet were anything but dainty. Agatha's feet matched the considerable height she'd inherited from her equally statuesque mother.

Agatha's dark red satin dress fit her perfectly, and the ivory ribbon at her bust complemented her pale skin nicely. But any pride Cinderella felt in her own skills as a seamstress was outweighed by resentment. How could she be fully proud of something she'd been forced to make? Especially when she didn't possess one nice dress herself. The only clothes she had, she was wearing.

She silently admonished herself. Envy wouldn't get her anywhere.

"Take mine off first," Gwendolyn said, lifting her silk-covered arms above her head. "You put the wrong size slippers on my poor feet today." She tugged on one of the deep brown ringlets dropping down from the elaborate hairstyle Cinderella had spent an hour on that morning, and then stretched her long, lean limbs forward on the white rug to reveal her huge feet, bent and pinched into pink slippers two sizes too small. Both sets of her sisters' shoes were coated in filth; Cinderella's gaze followed a muddy trail across the room.

More floor scrubbing would be one of her next chores, and it would take hours to clean the muck out of the rug—not to mention the shoes.

She knelt down before Gwendolyn to tackle her first assignment. She searched in vain for one clean spot on the silk shoes that would take hours of meticulous work to turn back to their previous pink, but could find none. She tugged at the heel.

"Careful." Gwendolyn kicked her in the shoulder and Cinderella fell onto her bottom.

"Do you think we'll be invited to the royal ball?" Agatha asked her sister, ignoring Cinderella.

Cinderella pulled herself off the floor and turned her back to Gwendolyn to gain the necessary leverage for prying the shoe from her stepsister's foot. More dirt scattered onto the white rug.

"Of course we will, silly." Gwendolyn's knee bumped Cinderella's back. "Get out of the way, you stupid, ugly girl. Why aren't my shoes off yet?"

"I suppose you're right," Agatha said. "Prince Tiberius needs a wife. Any fine family with unmarried daughters is sure to be invited."

"Especially those families whose daughters are both unmarried and beautiful, such as us," Gwendolyn said, and both girls giggled.

Goosebumps rose on Cinderella's arms. Yes, her stepsisters were beautiful, but what husband would want to live with their ugly laughs?

Cinderella smiled at her own joke as she pulled Gwendolyn's shoes off, and then removed Agatha's. After bundling the shoes into her arms, she stood.

"Cinderella, where's my tonic?" Gwendolyn screeched. "You know if I don't take my tonic soon after my evening meal, I suffer from indigestion." She burped loudly. The strong stench of onions and gas made Cinderella feel faint. On the nights her family ate out, the lack of table scraps meant Cinderella didn't eat a single morsel.

She glanced to the carafe of tonic sitting on the side table not four feet from her stepsister. Would it kill Gwen to stand and pour herself a drink? "I'll fetch your tonic as soon as I take these shoes to the cellar for cleaning." Cinderella started for the door.

"Get it now, you lazy girl!" Gwen stood and pulled Cinderella's blonde hair, yanking her back.

"Ow!" Cinderella dropped one of the shoes and more dirt scattered onto the carpet.

"You clumsy thing." Agatha kicked the shoe out of Cinderella's reach just as she was about to retrieve it and looked up to Gwen, as if seeking approval.

"Clumsy and lazy." Gwendolyn kicked the shoe again. "This room is filthy—look at the trail of mud—and I still don't have my tonic."

Cinderella dropped all the shoes to the floor. "It wasn't me who tracked mud in, it was you. And the tonic's right there. Pour it yourself. Can't you see I'm busy?"

"Busy?" Gwendolyn stood, indignant. "You ungrateful brat. How could you possibly be busy? You stay in this house all day long. Your only responsibility is to do a little tidying, while Agatha and I are tasked with all the important duties."

"Yes," Agatha added. "We do everything."

Towering a good eight inches above Cinderella's diminutive frame, Gwendolyn shoved her. "You have no worries, no serious duties to perform. You have no need to shop, or pick out an outfit each day, or ensure your handbag matches your slippers."

Cinderella bit her tongue. Her stepsisters had terrible taste and relied on her to select their clothes each day. Not that Gwen was likely to admit it out loud.

"Goodness knows she never does anything with her hair," Agatha said, and smiled at Gwen.

"Why bother?" Gwendolyn sneered. "That straight, stringy stuff? It looks like straw." Cinderella fumed as Gwendolyn patted the deep brown hair that Cinderella had spent hours twisting and coiling that morning.

She couldn't help it if her own hair was limp and straight. If she stole a fraction of the time she spent on her stepsisters' hair each morning for herself, her own hair would show a great deal of improvement. The one time she'd managed to sneak some of her stepsisters' hair soap and use hot water, her hair had shone like gold when she passed through a sunbeam.

"Speaking of grooming"—Gwendolyn's lip curled into a sneer— "does she even bathe?"

"Oh, Gwen, you're terrible." Agatha lifted a hand to her lips.

Gwendolyn smiled at her sister. "At least the soot on her cheeks almost covers those hideous freckles." The two stepsisters giggled.

Cinderella drew deep breaths to calm herself, remembering her ninja training. *Sticks and stones*, she thought. *Sticks and stones.*

"No wonder she's never asked to attend the endless luncheons and teas and banquets and balls we frequent," Gwendolyn said.

"I wish *I* could stay home all day." Agatha plopped back onto her chair. "We have so many obligations."

"She has no idea how hard we work." Gwendolyn crossed her arms and glared at Cinderella.

The deep breathing was not working for Cinderella and she wondered if ninjas ever had to deal with people as horrible as her stepsisters. Agatha and Gwendolyn wouldn't recognize work if it stepped up to shake their manicured hands.

"How ungrateful." Gwendolyn picked up one of the shoes and threw it at Cinderella. "In spite of your plain looks and utter uselessness, our mother has generously put a roof over your head."

"This is *my* house," Cinderella muttered under her breath.

"What did you say?" Gwen stepped forward and towered over her much shorter stepsister.

"This house belonged to my father." Cinderella stood her ground, bracing for whatever might come. "I was born in this house."

"Yeah, and killed your mother in the process," Gwendolyn snickered.

Cinderella's throat caught. How dare Gwendolyn be so cruel as to bring up her mother's death? She'd died during childbirth. Her mother's absence weighed like a stone on Cinderella's chest, and the loss had broken her poor father's heart.

"Your father hated you so much for killing your mother"—Gwen examined her nails—"that he had to find new daughters. *Better* daughters." She smiled at Agatha.

"That's not true!" Cinderella's cheeks flushed. "He was sad, but he didn't blame me."

Had he blamed her? She fought to keep her lips from quivering. Her stepsisters had gone several steps beyond mean. "My father loved me. If he were still alive—"

"But he's not, is he?" boomed her stepmother in a deep voice as she entered the room.

Oh, great, thought Cinderella. *As if this day couldn't get any worse.*

The tall, dark-haired woman strode in, wearing a bright blue gown, a scarlet velvet jacket, and a menacing scowl.

"Your father is dead, Cinderella. Get over it already."

Cinderella's insides shook, and she tried not to let the tremors show on her face.

Her stepmother took off her long, scarlet gloves. "It's bad enough the man inconsiderately left me with the costs and responsibilities of maintaining this property. He also saddled me with you." She snapped the gloves against one hand. "Child or not, the day of my thoughtless husband's tragic fall to his death, I should have put you out for the wolves. Perhaps I still should."

"Then do it," Cinderella muttered as she picked up her stepsisters' shoes. "Let me go, please." She hated her stepmother for putting the image of her father's broken body back into her mind.

Her stepmother pursed her lips. "Cinderella, as I've told you many times, you may leave when you learn to behave." She strode up to Cinderella and glared down at her. "Or when you give me what I want."

Cinderella clamped her mouth shut and lowered her gaze. Years ago, she'd given up trying to convince her stepmother that she didn't know where her real mother's wand was hidden. She truly had no idea, but her stepmother's continued suspicion that she did was likely the only thing that was keeping her from throwing Cinderella to the wolves.

The tall woman circled Cinderella like a mountain lion teasing its prey. "Besides, I can't toss you out. That would be cruel. A girl like you, with no skills, who's lived a sheltered life under my protection—you wouldn't survive one day in the real world."

Cinderella drew a deep breath to keep herself from saying anything. She'd talked back enough today. Provoking her stepmother never paid—it cost. Over the years it had cost Cinderella burns and bruises and, three times, broken bones.

And what her stepmother said about her chances of survival outside this house? They had to be better than her chances of surviving in it.

She might not know the ways of the world, she might not have been blessed with great beauty, she might not be able to break a strong wizard's entrapment spells or get past vicious wolves, but she had a secret weapon: determination. If obeying her stepmother didn't earn Cinderella her release, she was determined to obtain a wand—somehow, someway—and with it, master enough magic to burst out from under her stepmother's crushing grip.

Her stepmother looked down. "Cinderella, why is there dirt all over these floors? And why were you chatting with your sisters when clearly there's work to be done?"

"She hasn't fetched my tonic yet," Gwendolyn said. "And I asked her for it ages ago. She's so lazy."

"Lazy, ungrateful girls need to be taught a lesson," her stepmother said as she pulled her shiny black wand from its sleek holder strapped around her waist.

Cinderella braced herself. Would she spend another night as a mouse? Last time that happened, she'd had to hide behind a cupboard to ensure she didn't end up as Max's dinner.

Her stepmother strode around the room, her wand raised high. "When was the last time this room was dusted?"

"Two hours ago." The words had barely left Cinderella's mouth when a thick blanket of black dust landed on every surface except a small circle surrounding Agatha and Gwendolyn, who laughed loudly when they saw Cinderella's new predicament.

"I see you're a liar, too, Cinderella. Either that or you're highly incompetent and should take more care, have a little pride in your work." Her stepmother's eyes narrowed and darkened, and a chill fell over the room. "And if I find even one of my precious statues cracked or broken, you'll pay with a few breaks of your own."

Cinderella's muscles tensed as she glanced around at the hundreds of glass figurines it took her hours to dust each day.

Her stepmother flicked her magic wand and a life-sized parrot sculpture with lifelike feathers etched into crystal tipped off the edge of the stone mantel.

Cinderella leaped straight over her stepsisters in a gravity-defying hurdle, and snatched the delicate sculpture before it smashed into the stone hearth. She barely had time to rise up on her tiptoes to set it carefully back on the mantel before a life-size glass statue of a wolf teetered back and forth on its wooden stand on the other side of the room.

She vaulted over Agatha's brocade chair, narrowly missing Agatha herself, and set the wolf gently on the carpet.

"Clumsy girl." Her stepmother's voice was hard and sharp. "I'll teach you to be more careful with my things."

Cinderella scanned the room, wondering what her next challenge would be. An ornate sculpture of a vulture, with drops of red glass dripping from its beak—one she'd always hated—shifted toward the edge of its pedestal high above the floor.

She raced toward it.

"What a fool."

Her head spun at her stepmother's voice behind her to see her real mother's vase, a simple, elegant, clear glass vessel, hovering in the air.

Cinderella's heart pinched and the air whooshed from her lungs. The vase was the only thing left in this house that once belonged to her mother. If the vase were to fall . . .

The vulture slid another inch, started to tip, and Cinderella sucked in a ragged breath. Her ninja acrobatics could take her only so far. Her speed and agility wouldn't let her save both the vulture and the vase, and her magic skills were too weak.

Even if her magic were stronger, she couldn't let her stepmother know she'd inherited even a tiny amount of her powerful mother's skills—at least not yet.

She lunged to save the vulture, and as she caught it, its sharp-edged beak pierced her hand. She winced in pain and set the vulture on the floor, and bright red blood dripped down her arm.

The sound of her mother's vase smashing into a hundred pieces assaulted her ears and penetrated her heart. Grief grabbed the inside of Cinderella's throat, and she dropped to her knees. Agony gripped her belly, her chest, the backs of her eyes, but she swallowed the instinct to cry. She could not show her stepmother how much she hurt.

"I'll take my bath now," said her stepmother, her voice cold and sharp as an icicle. "And this mess had better be cleaned up by the time I am done."

After cleaning dust and mud from every surface in the sitting room, scrubbing everyone's shoes, and ensuring her stepsisters had at least two clothing choices for the next day—each with perfectly matched slippers and handbags—Cinderella set a half-filled watering can at the edge of her small vegetable patch.

All around the edges of the garden, red eyes glared at her through the darkness.

"Go away, wolves!" she shouted to the vicious animals that encircled the property and kept her from escaping through the woods behind the back garden, or down the road that led to the village. At least her stepmother had enchanted the edges of the property—or perhaps the animals themselves. The wolves never took a step past the edge of the trees, and after a few terrifying escape attempts during which she'd narrowly avoided being eaten, Cinderella had never again stepped into the woods. Without a weapon, her ninja skills were no match for a pack of hungry wolves, and her fledgling magic skills certainly weren't.

Cinderella turned away from the woods and studied her watering can, heavy and glinting in the moonlight. Earlier, she'd used magic to lift the empty container off the ground. It couldn't be that much harder to lift it partly filled, could it?

But she soon found that it was. And after a few unsuccessful attempts, Cinderella was so exhausted she could barely see straight.

She looked up at the moon. Only four hours before she had to rise and draw the water for the morning baths and make breakfast. Her sisters rarely rose before the sun was high in the sky, but her stepmother was less predictable, and Cinderella knew she'd pay a steep price should her stepmother's porridge not be ready at the very moment she called for it. She'd pay an even steeper price should she dare taste a spoonful before the rest of her family had taken their fill.

Max nudged against her leg and meowed his encouragement. If he weren't a cat, she'd swear he was coaching her.

"You're right, Max." She crouched to stroke his back. "If I can clean up that mess in the sitting room in only two hours, I can do this." She rubbed the sleepiness from her eyes and lifted her hand.

Concentrate. Concentrate.

The watering can lifted slowly from the ground, an inch at first, then two, and then three inches. Her mood also lifted with each inch it rose. Every nerve in her body tingled and the feeling trailed out to her fingertips as the watering can continued to rise. Once it reached a foot off the ground, she shifted the angle of her hand and the can tipped. Just another few inches and the water would pour out onto the delicate lettuces below.

A rabbit raced across the garden.

The wolves howled.

Cinderella lost her concentration, and the watering can tumbled into the dirt, spilling water into a puddle.

She sighed, but Max jumped into her arms and licked her chin. "Thanks, Max. I did do better this time."

Most nights it felt as though she'd never develop the skills to escape. She was a puny, untrained, inexperienced girl, lacking even a wand to amplify and hone what little magic she'd inherited from her mother— no match for a powerful and evil wizard like her stepmother. But every day, she became more sure: if she didn't escape soon, her stepmother would eventually kill her.

"Is that dirt under your fingernails?" Gwendolyn's upper lip sneered in disgust as Cinderella stood behind her in front of the ornately carved vanity mirror.

Cinderella glanced down to her hands, holding the ends of a complex pattern of interlocked sections of Gwendolyn's dark hair. It had taken her nearly an hour to get to this point, and if she so much as shifted her hands now, before she fastened the final sections with pins, the entire hairdo would fall apart and she'd have to start over.

"I asked you a question!" Gwendolyn shrieked angrily. Although Gwendolyn was pretty, with her deep brown hair, rose-tinted skin, and flashing green eyes, she could certainly twist her face into expressions that argued with her beauty.

"I'm almost done." Cinderella tightened her hold on the complicated plaits and twists, readying it for the first pin. She wiggled one hand out to grab one.

Gwendolyn yanked away. "Ow! You pulled my hair."

Cinderella's hands dropped to her sides and she drew a deep breath. "Gwen, it was you who pulled away. Now I need to begin again, and if we don't start quickly, you'll never get out of the house today."

"You're not touching me with those hands." Gwendolyn's nose wrinkled. "My hair is filthy now. I need another bath." She shuddered in an exaggerated manner that befit her status as a drama queen, and Cinderella withheld the impulse to roll her eyes.

"My hands aren't dirty." Cinderella looked at her nails. There *was* a tiny line of dirt under the nail of her left index finger. How in the world had Gwendolyn even noticed?

She slipped her hands behind her back. "If you like, I'll scrub them again, but there's no time to rewash and dry your hair. Not if you want it woven into a butterfly pattern today."

Agatha poked her head in from her adjoining bedroom. "Cinderella, what is taking you so long?" she demanded. "Help me with my makeup."

Even with her shiny red hair up in curlers, Agatha, with her lovely, peachy complexion, was genuinely pretty, yet she insisted that Cinderella line her eyes with kohl and adorn her skin with the finest of creams and powders each morning.

"In a moment." Cinderella backed toward the door. "I'm just running down to the cellar to scrub my fingernails."

"What?" Agatha burst into the room, and her hooped pannier frame, without the weight of a dress draped on top, bounced ridiculously with each step. "How could you possibly be so inconsiderate?"

"Inconsiderate?" Who was being inconsiderate? Her stepsisters were wasting her time and a small bubble of irritation rose in her chest. There was no chance that even a speck of dirt had landed on either of her sisters this morning. If her ten minutes with the nail brush before she'd gone to bed last night hadn't dislodged it, no way had working on her sisters' hair or skin done it.

Agatha strode forward and the cagelike undergarment bounced again, almost making Cinderella laugh. "How can you dawdle on a day like today?" Agatha stuck out her lower lip in a serious pout. Toddlers had nothing on the younger of her two stepsisters, who typically followed her older sister's lead.

"What's special about today?" Cinderella asked.

"Idiot! How can you ask such a thing?" Gwendolyn reached forward and poked Cinderella, her long nail nearly piercing the skin just under Cinderella's collarbone. "Today is the most important day of my life."

"Why?"

Gwendolyn rolled her eyes and backed up from her stepsister. "You stupid girl. Today is *the* day. I can't possibly risk not being seen in the village today. What if I'm forgotten?"

"Forgotten?" Cinderella's curiosity grew in spite of her irritation. All this discussion was dragging out the morning dressing ritual even longer than usual. "Who could possibly forget you?" She felt her scant breakfast rise a little in her throat, but flattery was a tool she pulled out of her box of tricks when the occasion warranted.

"Whoever's handing out invitations to the ball, you idiot." Gwendolyn picked through her hair as if she might find evidence of a speck of dirt.

Cinderella furrowed her eyebrows. Last night, while she'd been trying to keep the mud on their shoes from grinding into the white rug, her stepsisters *had* been muttering something about a ball and invitations and the prince, but Cinderella hadn't paid them much attention.

Agatha sat on the edge of Gwendolyn's bed and sank into the feather mattress. "Wouldn't it be dreamy to marry Prince Tiberius?"

"I guess." Cinderella didn't see the immediate appeal, yet felt somewhat excited for her stepsisters if they really thought he'd pick one of them.

Excited for herself, too. If one of her stepsisters became a princess, her stepmother would gain all the power she could possibly want and might even give up on trying to get Cinderella to reveal where her real mother's wand was hidden.

Even if Cinderella knew where the wand was—which she didn't— she'd never give it to her stepmother. With the wand's reputed powers, her stepmother could terrorize not only her, but the whole kingdom.

She refocused on her stepsisters. "You expect the prince to propose marriage today?" Cinderella was pretty sure her stepsisters had never even met the young man.

"No, silly." Agatha leaned back on her elbows, and the hoops rose up around her as if she were lying in a barrel. She kicked her feet, like two huge duck flippers, in front of her.

Gwendolyn spun from where she'd been playing with her hair. "Do you not pay attention at all? He'll propose at the ball, the day of the magic festival. We told you last night."

"There's a magic festival?" Cinderella wouldn't have forgotten that.

"Don't interrupt." Gwendolyn waved a long, slender finger at Cinderella. "The important part of the day is the ball. The prince will choose his bride from among the young ladies in attendance."

"Cinderella," Agatha said as she stood, thrust out her breasts, and ran her hands along imaginary fabric. "You have to sew me the best dress ever, because I plan to be that young lady."

Gwendolyn leaped up. "Well, that's going to be impossible, because he's going to choose me." She flipped her hair over her shoulder. "I hear he has a preference for dark hair."

"You don't know that," Agatha challenged her sister. "Brown hair is so boring. I'll bet as soon as he sees my rich, red curls, he'll fall instantly in love."

Cinderella tapped her foot on the floor and crossed her arms over her chest. Every moment spent dealing with these two was a moment she couldn't spend doing her chores and then training. "So," she interrupted their bickering, "I'm still not sure why today's so important."

"Fool." Gwendolyn returned her attention to her hair. "We need to be seen in the village to be sure we receive invitations."

"Also," Agatha added, "we should buy up all the best fabrics before the other girls get a chance."

Cinderella's eyes ached from the effort of not rolling. Her stepsisters had the worst taste in fabrics, which was something else they'd inherited from their mother. They'd need to purchase every bolt in the store to up their chances of finding the best ones.

"Cinderella, you must help me pick fabrics." Agatha raised her hands to her bust. "I must have the most beautiful gown ever. What do you think would go best with my hair and show off my eyes? A cherry red, perhaps? Lemon yellow? Lime green?"

Gwendolyn stepped in front of Agatha and said, "No, Cinderella, you must reserve the best fabrics for *my* gown."

"Girls, why are you dawdling?"

Cinderella spun, wondering how long her stepmother had been standing in the doorway. "Agatha and Gwendolyn were just telling me how they'll need new gowns for the prince's ball."

"Of course they will," replied her stepmother. Her tone and expression made it clear Cinderella had made the most idiotic comment ever, but Cinderella refused to react. She knew an opportunity when she saw one.

She stood very still, clasped her hands behind her back, and lowered her head slightly, feigning deference. "I should get started on the gowns immediately."

Her stepmother didn't respond.

"Perhaps it would be most efficient if I were to accompany Agatha and Gwendolyn into the village to help select fabrics." It was a long shot, but it was worth a chance.

Cinderella hadn't been into the village since she was nine years old. Back then, she'd enjoyed slightly more freedom. She should've taken advantage when she had the chance, but at the time, she'd been far too fearful to flee.

"Oh, yes," said Agatha, "Cinderella does have good luck picking fabrics. Without her, we usually have to bring home ten or fifteen different bolts of cloth before finding one that's perfect."

One that was passable was more like it, Cinderella thought to herself.

Gwendolyn curled her lips as if she'd tasted something unpleasant. "Agatha does have a point. Cinderella might be useless at so many things, but she does make beautiful gowns and has an eye for fabrics. If I'm to snag the prince, I need the best dress possible."

When her stepmother didn't immediately reject the idea, Cinderella's hopes inched upward, but she kept her head down and her expression neutral. If her stepmother realized how badly Cinderella wanted to go to the village, she'd never let her go.

"Agatha, Gwendolyn," Cinderella said, "thank you for the compliment, but you give me too much credit." She kept her gaze down. "Your fabric selections are always beautiful."

She thought it would be best not to specifically mention some of her stepsisters' previous purchases, like the hideous yellow-and-scarlet upholstery fabric with teapot patterns that Agatha had brought home the last time she'd needed a gown.

If Cinderella played this correctly, she could make her stepmother think it was all her idea to send Cinderella to the village. Even *she* relied on Cinderella's taste in fashion and would realize that sending her stepdaughter to choose fabrics was the best and most efficient way to ensure her real daughters shone at the ball.

Silence filled the room, and Cinderella realized she might have gone too far by hinting at the need for a trip to the village. Her stepmother's hand hovered over her wand, and Cinderella braced herself for whatever punishment she might be forced to endure.

The gong at the front door sounded, and everyone's head turned to the source of the noise.

"Well?" asked her stepmother after no one moved for a few moments. Her voice sounded full of venom.

Cinderella moved her gaze from the wand to look into her stepmother's face.

Her stepmother sneered. "Do you expect the door to answer itself?"

"No, of course not." Feeling slightly giddy that she'd dodged, or at least delayed, whatever bullet had been coming her way, Cinderella skipped down the main stairs in the vaulted front foyer to the door.

She opened the heavy inner door that led to the small entryway separating the main rooms from the outside. It was unbelievably annoying that whoever was outside could easily open the outer door to come in, yet she couldn't open it herself because of her stepmother's entrapment spells.

She stepped forward, determined that this would be the day the front door would not only open for her, but that it would also be the day she'd be able to cross its threshold and leave. She grasped the huge iron handle and, for extra insurance, braced one foot on the stone wall beside the door. Taking a deep breath, she concentrated and pulled.

Nothing happened. She pulled again, and the muscles in her upper back felt as if they were about to tear off her body. It felt pointless to keep trying, but trying was all she had.

She dropped her foot, opened the tiny window in the door, and saw a young man dressed in a suit of burgundy and deep gray velvet; an ostrich feather stuck out jauntily from his floppy black hat. He was undoubtedly a messenger from the castle. She had to admit she was somewhat impressed by his fine uniform.

"The door is unlocked," she told the messenger. "Just give me a moment to back out of the way, and then you can enter." If she were standing within six feet of the door, the spell would prevent its movement.

"You want me to open the door myself?" the messenger asked.

"Yes, my hands are full." Although visitors to the house were rare, she'd worked up a list of excuses over the years.

Even if the cook and grooms employed by her stepmother could see her—which they didn't seem to be able to do, likely the effect of another dark spell—she couldn't ask them for help. If she ever told another soul about the entrapment spells, both she and the person she told would be turned into stone.

The messenger opened the door and stepped inside, his broad shoulders filling a surprising amount of the door's width. His black hat was tilted forward so that it shielded his face from the light and made his features hard to discern. He was tall, and although the uniform was slightly worn and baggy, Cinderella could see the young man had a strong form beneath his broad shoulders.

"Your hands aren't full," he said as he stepped forward.

She stepped back. "I put everything down."

He walked past her into the foyer, glanced around, and, not spotting any evidence of baggage, looked at her curiously. "Where?"

Caught in her lie, Cinderella squirmed under the gaze of his bright blue eyes. Moths fluttered in her belly, as if she had a light in there to which they were drawn.

Mentally swatting the moths away, she squared her shoulders and raised her chin. "Excuse me, but I expect you came here with a purpose. Now that you've barged all the way in, would it be too much to ask what that purpose might be?"

He tipped his head back, as if startled at her question, and she caught another glimpse of his handsome face. Her moths started up again.

He removed his hat and bowed toward her. "My apologies, Miss. This is your home and I'm an intruder. Forgive me."

"Certainly." Her cheeks burned. She hadn't expected him to bow. Men bowed to her stepmother and stepsisters, but not to her. She was nobody.

He straightened and the light struck his smooth cheeks, crisply angled jaw, and blond hair that—now released from under the hat—hung about his face like unruly golden corkscrews.

She sucked in a sharp breath. The messenger, not much older than she, was far more handsome than any man who'd come to their home before. In fact, she hadn't realized this particular combination of ruggedness and good looks was possible in a human being. But it wasn't his looks that struck her most; it was his smile and the glint in his eyes as he studied her with what almost looked like admiration.

An entirely new kind of fluttering started up in her belly.

She swallowed hard before saying, "No, it was I who was rude." It wasn't his fault that she couldn't open the door to her own house, and he'd borne the brunt of her frustration.

His grin widened, revealing dimples on his cheeks. "Shall we put it behind us?"

"Yes, please." Relief flooded through her. "How may I help you?"

He cleared his throat. "Other than yourself, how many unmarried young women reside here?"

"I live here with my stepmother and two stepsisters, Agatha and Gwendolyn. Perhaps you have heard of them. They tell me that their beauty is renowned." She swallowed the shame she felt for poking fun at her stepsisters, even if the messenger might not have sensed her sarcasm. They were pretty, sure, but it was boastful of them to constantly say so.

"Renowned beauties, you say." His eyes flashed mischief. "I'm afraid I've yet had the pleasure to make their acquaintance, but if they're half as beautiful as you are charming, their beauty must be renowned indeed." He stepped back, executed another half bow, and Cinderella's stomach lurched.

She steadied herself and grinned. At least he had a sense of humor.

"Oh." He clasped his hands together. "What a lovely smile."

His voice was soft and deep and reminded Cinderella of how she'd felt the one time she'd tasted chocolate. For a moment, she allowed herself to believe she was beautiful like her stepsisters. She wasn't ugly, she knew that—just plain.

Enough of this, she thought. He was teasing her and eventually her stepmother would expect her back upstairs; there was no sense risking another punishment. "Beyond false flattery," she asked, "do you have a purpose for your visit?"

His body stiffened, and she felt badly that she'd spoken so sharply.

He reached into the leather satchel that was slung over his shoulder and handed her four envelopes. "The king and queen extend their invitation to you and your family and hope you'll attend a ball given in the prince's honor."

She accepted the envelopes, which were made of fine linen paper with gilded edges. Imagine, all that gold used simply to adorn letters.

"Will you attend?" he asked, another smile spreading on his handsome face.

Oh, thought Cinderella with a sense of urgency, *he wanted a response now. Should she respond on everyone's behalf?* "I'm certain my stepsisters will attend."

His smile faded. "Not you?"

Cinderella let out a short burst of laughter, then quickly covered her mouth with her hands.

He looked almost hurt or offended. Ashamed of her outburst, Cinderella cast her eyes down at the floor. He didn't know his suggestion was ridiculous. In fact, he couldn't know *why* it was, or he'd turn to stone. "Do you need our responses right now?" she asked. "Because I can call up to my stepsisters and—"

"That won't be necessary." He returned the cap to his head and tucked all his loose golden curls back under it. "But I do hope you'll come."

Cinderella stammered. "I-I'm not sure that's possible."

"What's not possible?" her stepmother said from the top of the stairs.

A chill invaded the room and Cinderella backed away from the messenger. There was no need to drag him into whatever horrible punishment her stepmother might have in store. She braced herself.

"Good morning, Madam." The messenger bowed again, this time toward her stepmother. "I am here to extend invitations from the palace for you and your three daughters."

Her stepmother smiled, and Cinderella cringed. "For my *three* daughters, you say?"

"Yes," he replied. "I understand there are two other lovely young women at this residence?" The messenger's expression had changed, and so had his voice. It had grown more formal and distant. It was almost as if he could sense the danger that lurked behind her stepmother's smile and upturned lips.

Fighting to keep her hand from shaking, Cinderella climbed a few steps and extended the invitations toward her stepmother. She regretted that she hadn't tucked the fourth one inside her apron. Even if she could never go to the ball, it would've been nice to keep the invitation to serve as a reminder that the possibility of something better lay outside the grounds of her home.

Her stepmother took the envelopes and fanned them out. As she watched and waited to see what the woman might do, it felt to Cinderella as if hours passed. She didn't fear for herself. She was accustomed to her stepmother's cruelty. It was the young messenger she worried about. He didn't deserve to be punished for delivering an extra envelope.

Her stepmother raised her head. "Thank you," she said, her tone making it clear that the messenger was dismissed.

When he bowed a second time to her stepmother, he tossed a quick glance at Cinderella and winked. She raised a hand to her mouth to cover her smile.

As soon as he was out the door, her stepmother dangled one of the invitations between her index finger and thumb, as if it were poisonous. "Well then, Cinderella," her stepmother said, an evil glint in her eye. "It seems you've been invited to the ball. Would you like to attend?"

If you were Cinderella, what would you do?

OPTION A: It must be another of her stepmother's tricks, but what has she got to lose? And on the long shot that her stepmother's question isn't a cruel tease, there's a chance the prince might choose Cinderella to be his bride—her ticket out of servitude. Besides, marrying a prince sounds dreamy. If you think she should say yes, go to section 2: Crystal Clarity (page 39).

OPTION B: Even if her stepmother is serious, what is there to gain from going to a ball? How boring. Not to mention, even if marrying the prince *would* get Cinderella out from under her stepmother's spell, she'd be trapped in a royal marriage with all its pretentious customs and ceremonies. When she chooses a husband, it'll be for love, not money. If you think she should say thanks, but no thanks, go to section 3: Hard Work Rewarded (page 73).

Section 2

〜〜〜

CRYSTAL CLARITY

C inderella tapped her foot on the foyer's inlaid wood floor, anxious to go into the village for the first time in over a decade and feeling as if she'd entered some kind of parallel universe. One where she was allowed to leave the house anytime she wanted, one where her stepmother was more like an actual mother, one where Cinderella was free.

Such a universe was not likely to exist. In this universe, she'd proceed with caution.

Her stepsisters had argued vehemently with their mother about the fabric selection, and their mother finally gave in to her daughters' wishes. Then her stepmother acted as though it had all been her own idea: if Cinderella selected the fabrics, Gwendolyn and Agatha would have a much greater chance of outshining the other girls and snagging the prince.

If one of her daughters married Prince Tiberius—although her stepmother hadn't admitted it—it was clear she believed that, as the mother of a princess and future queen, she'd gain more power.

"Gold? You can't wear gold with your red hair." Gwendolyn and Agatha bickered as they scrambled down the main stairs.

"You're just saying that because *you* want to wear gold." Halfway down, Agatha leaned over the landing's oak banister. "Cinderella, I look better than Gwenny in gold, right?"

Anxious to leave before permission was withdrawn, Cinderella said, "Both of you will look beautiful no matter what color you wear. The prince will have a terrible time deciding which sister to marry."

The two sisters giggled together for a moment and then descended the remainder of the staircase with more decorum. And it was about time they showed more decorum. Now Cinderella needed them to get into their cloaks so they could get out the door. She was still hoping her stepmother wasn't coming.

"What color do you plan to wear to the ball, Cinderella?" Agatha asked as Cinderella helped her put on her bright blue woolen cloak.

"Oh, I haven't decided." Cinderella brushed a piece of lint off her stepsister's shoulder and then turned to help Gwendolyn with her cloak. She still didn't believe her stepmother would actually let her go. "I'm just happy to get the opportunity to attend."

"I guess," Gwendolyn said, not bothering to bend down as Cinderella reached up on her toes to place the cloak on her much taller stepsister's shoulders. "I mean, it's not like you stand a chance at getting a dance with the prince. There will be hundreds of girls at the ball, and maybe only fifteen or twenty open slots on his dance card."

"He'll have a dance card?" Cinderella asked. She had no idea how balls worked and realized that she should have paid more attention to her stepsisters' chatter over the years.

"No, silly," Agatha said as she extended a foot so that Cinderella could stoop to lace up her boot. "It's just a figure of speech. I'm sure he'll have some kind of servant or attendant who'll notify the girls he's chosen."

"Sounds somewhat impersonal." Cinderella turned to lace up Gwendolyn's boots.

"Impersonal?" her stepmother said as she entered the room.

Cinderella's excitement blew up the chimney. Her stepmother had decided to join them, after all.

"We were discussing the ball, Mother." Agatha grinned.

"What about it?" Her stepmother's voice dripped with suspicion.

"How the prince might select girls to dance." Agatha's grin started to waver, as if leery of her mother's mood.

Her stepmother turned toward a blood-red cloak hanging on a wooden peg high on the wall, and Cinderella rushed to take it down and put it over her stepmother's shoulders.

"Agatha and Gwendolyn, for shame. It's cruel to tease your sister with thoughts of dances with the prince."

Cinderella sucked in a sharp breath and closed her eyes for a second. Of course she wasn't really going to the ball. Of course it had been an elaborate tease. Even though she'd assumed as much, it stung anyway. She likely wasn't going to the village today, either.

Her stepmother turned and took Cinderella's chin between her black-gloved fingers, pushing the flesh against her teeth and pulling her face up so high that Cinderella had to lift up on her toes.

"Look at her." Her stepmother kept her eyes on her daughters, and not on the stepdaughter's face she was pinching so hard that she'd probably leave bruises. "Her plain features are so pale and freckled, her drab hair the color of straw—as straight as straw, too—and she possesses no figure to speak of." She barked out a sharp laugh. "Poor thing looks more like a ten-year-old boy than an eighteen-year-old girl. It's cruel to get her hopes up."

"You're so right, Mother," said Gwendolyn, turning up her nose. "It's ridiculous for Cinderella to worry about how the prince will choose dancing partners. No chance will he even notice she's there."

"He'll be too busy looking at me," said Agatha.

"No, me." Gwendolyn pushed her sister, and then the two stuck out their tongues before turning their backs on each other.

Her stepmother released her chin, and Cinderella fought the impulse to rub the throbbing spots.

"Perhaps I'm cruel even to let her go," her stepmother said as she put her hands on her corseted waist. "She'll feel out of place."

Cinderella bit down on her tongue, and wished her stepmother would just admit she'd been playing with her all along and end this charade. And what was with discussing her as if she were invisible? Not to mention the irony of her claiming to care about cruelty. That part chewed away at Cinderella's stomach, but she refused to respond. On the slim chance that leaving the house was still a possibility, acting out wouldn't help.

She didn't really care about the ball as long as she was released from the grounds today. She might be small, but she was strong and fast, and the instant her stepmother's back was turned, she'd make a run for it and never return. Her stepmother would try to stop her with a spell, but if Cinderella was fast and used her ninja skills to leap out of reach, it was possible she could escape.

Her only regret would be Max, sleeping down in the basement. But he'd understand and perhaps one day he'd find her.

"What are you waiting for?" her stepmother snapped.

Cinderella's shoulders jumped, her daydream interrupted by her stepmother's demands.

"Open the door, you stupid girl. Do you think it will open itself?"

Cinderella suppressed a grin as she pulled on the door's heavy iron handle and it swung back. That spell had been temporarily lifted.

Excitement buzzed through her body, making her feel almost giddy. Today was the day she'd escape.

Cinderella quivered with excitement as she closed the gate behind her and she inhaled the crisp spring air. So this was how freedom smelled.

They started off down the road to the village and Cinderella glanced up at the bright blue sky peeking through the canopy of birch leaves. It had been so many years since she'd looked up to the daytime sky.

"Why are we walking?" Agatha whined. "My feet hurt already."

"Exercise is good for your complexion, girls," their mother said. "How can you expect to win the prince's heart if you don't look your best?"

Muttering under their breaths, the two sisters continued to trudge along behind their mother. Cinderella took up the rear, surprised that her stepmother wasn't watching her more closely. Perhaps her stepmother thought Cinderella truly believed she was going to the ball and wouldn't run for that reason, or believed her stepmother's claims that she'd never survive on her own.

She scanned the woods to evaluate her options. If she simply took off at a run down the road, her stepmother would have a clear view of her and be able to stop her with magic, for sure. But if she headed into the woods, she might be able to hide high up in the canopy of branches and avoid a spell. The chance of this plot working was slim, but she had no other ideas.

She studied the tree branches. If she could find a group of branches at the right heights, she could use one branch to swing up to another, then another, and be high in the trees before anyone noticed she was gone. Her stepmother would have to cast a spell on the entire forest to stop her, and she'd never risk that. There was just too much chance someone might detect her illegal use of black magic.

"Ouch!" cried Agatha as she stumbled over her long purple gown and landed on her knees in the dirt.

Ignoring her instinct to help, Cinderella exploited the distraction and leaped to the right, barely grabbing onto the lowest branch of a nearby oak. She arched her back and swung, hoping she could build enough momentum to loop herself up to stand so she could leap from that branch to a higher one.

Her palms scraped on the rough bark, but on the second swing she had enough height. She hoped.

She let go, did a somersault in the air, and landed. The branch bounced beneath her, but she controlled the spring and used the momentum to propel herself higher. She reached up and out toward another branch. She was going to make it.

Just as she began to sense freedom, she slammed at full force into something unseen.

The breath rushed out of her chest and pain spread everywhere. It was as if she'd plowed into an invisible wall between the two branches. She slid down the unseen hard surface to land in a crumpled heap on a pile of dead leaves.

"Stupid girl." Her stepmother strode into the forest and nudged her with her pointed boot. "Do you really think I'd take you off the grounds without taking precautions?"

Dizzy from the impact, Cinderella pulled herself to a sitting position and leaned on her sore arms for support. Her stepmother kicked one of her arms to the side and Cinderella fell back to the ground.

"I think you'll find it quite impossible to go more than thirty feet from me in any direction. Now get up. We have shopping to do."

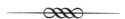

Cinderella's dismay at being stopped on her first escape attempt was soon replaced by a feeling of delight when she caught the sights and sounds and smells of the village. A few feet away, a man dressed in bright orange juggled, tossing fireballs into the air in high, arching loops without getting burned. Cinderella's eyes opened wider and she itched to go closer. He had to be using magic, but what kind? And how had he learned it? A few fireballs might come in handy for her escape. Even if today wasn't escape day, she was still determined to do it one day.

The sweet, cinnamon-tinged scent of freshly baked goods wafted toward her, and she spun around to spot a bakery filled with the most beautiful creations she'd ever imagined. About eight feet away, her stepmother was looking into the window of a hat shop, so Cinderella took the opportunity to dash over to the bakery window for a closer look at the piles of pink-topped cupcakes, bright orange cookies, and cakes with layers so high she couldn't imagine how they didn't topple. Her mouth watered, but she felt a tug on her body and realized her stepmother had moved too far away.

She turned to find her stepmother had crossed the street, and was backing away purposefully, one side of her mouth quirked up in an evil sneer. A horse and carriage hurtled down the roadway from the left, and

Cinderella ran across the street to get closer to her stepmother and avoid getting pulled into the horse's path.

"That's a girl," her stepmother said. "Stay close to me and you won't get hurt." She tipped her head back and laughed.

Cinderella gritted her teeth, but fought off the terrible feelings in her heart. She wouldn't let her stepmother spoil her temporary release from her prison.

Besides, at this point the possibility—however slim—of her attending the ball still existed. Certainly her stepmother wouldn't dare cast a spell on ball night. Her entrapment spells relied on black magic, which was illegal. The most important people in society and all the great wizards would be there, and she doubted her stepmother would risk her black magic being detected. If Cinderella got there, the ball might prove her perfect chance for escape. She'd just have to stay on her stepmother's good side until then.

"Open the door, lazy girl." Her stepmother gestured toward the closed door of the fabric shop. Cinderella pulled it open and followed the woman inside.

As soon as she stepped through the door, Cinderella gasped in awe. Each wall of the store was covered in shelving that reached from floor to ceiling and supported hundreds of bolts of the most beautiful fabrics she'd ever seen.

Until now, her fabric options for her stepsisters' gowns had been constrained by what they'd brought home, and she'd had no idea the magnitude of that limitation. With her eyes open wide, she started around the room, unable to take her eyes of the array of peacock blues, deep ambers, rich reds—every color she'd ever imagined and more—in the shiniest satins, the finest silks, the softest chiffons.

She'd never seen anything so beautiful. How would she ever choose for her stepsisters, never mind for herself?

Just then, she slammed into what she assumed was the edge of her stepmother's range, and not taking her eyes from the fabrics, she backed up a few steps, and then reached out to tentatively touch a deep bronze organza that would bring out the highlights in Agatha's hair.

"Hello?" The voice was male and teasing and familiar, so she drew her eyes from the shelves.

Him. The royal messenger. But he was not dressed as she had seen him earlier; his clothes were dirty and torn. She raised her hand to her lips. "Oh," she said. "Excuse me. Did I plow right into you?"

"A most pleasant collision," he replied. He smiled and his bright blue eyes sparkled, setting off a little buzz inside her.

"Where is your uniform?" she asked, and then hoped her question wasn't rude. "I'm sorry, but I didn't expect to see a royal messenger . . ." Oh, how was she going to explain herself without offending him?

He looked at her from under the rim of his cap. "Surprised I'm dressed in rags?" he asked in a conspiratorial whisper. He ran his hand over the tattered and coarsely woven fabric of his shirt, laced over his broad chest with a well-worn strip of leather.

She shrugged, tipping her head toward her shoulder and smiling. "I'm sorry. Hey, I'm in rags, too." She held up the ragged ends of her gray apron. "But I do love looking at these splendid fabrics."

"Even the most beautiful attire would pale next to you." He tipped his head and smiled, so charming and generous.

She fought the urge to object. Her sisters were beautiful, not her, but she could return his polite compliment without reservation. "Thank you, and you're very handsome." Unbelievably handsome, in fact, even dressed as a beggar. Under the rimmed cap, his blond curls hung about his face and shaded his eyes in the most devilish manner.

"Thank you." He bowed slightly. "Most people can't look past the way someone's dressed to see who's inside." He rested one of his hands on the counter beside them. Cinderella couldn't help but notice his strong-looking fingers. "I'm not really this poor, but I like going about the kingdom dressed as a beggar," he added. "I've run into several people today who know me as the—as the messenger—and you're the only one who's seen through my disguise."

"That's shocking." Cinderella had recognized him the instant she'd seen his bright blue eyes, his curly blond hair, his kind smile.

"I'm Ty, by the way."

She smiled and felt her cheeks burn. "Cinderella."

"That's an unusual name."

"It's a nickname, but it's all I've heard for so many years, I'm not even sure I remember the name I was born with."

"Nice to meet you, Cinderella." He edged a bit closer.

"And you." She stepped an inch back.

"So." He ran his hand along the wooden surface of the counter toward her. "Have you decided?"

To distract herself from his hand, she glanced up at the shelves, and soon spotted a bolt of silvery-blue velvet that might suit Gwendolyn nicely. "Decided what?"

"The ball, of course. Will I see you there?"

She turned to him and cocked her head to the side. "You're going to the ball?"

His head snapped back ever so slightly. "I, well . . ." He looked up and to the side. "No choice. I've got to be at the ball, um, working."

"There are messages to deliver at the ball?"

He looked up and away in amusement. "I'm involved in many areas at the palace."

"Oh." She smiled, warmth spreading inside her. At least she'd find one friendly face in the room. "I'm hoping to go. Perhaps, if you get a break, you might have time to teach me to dance?" She looked down, embarrassed that she'd just asked this young man, Ty, to dance. Working at the palace, he was surely highly skilled at all the court dances, whereas she'd only seen her stepsisters practicing. Why would he want to dance with her?

"I would be honored to share a dance with you," he said. "But won't you be more focused on landing a dance with the prince?" His eyes twinkled mischievously.

"Oh, no," Cinderella said, laughing. She pulled a bolt of silk with golden threads woven through it off the shelf, and he helped her set it on the counter. "The prince won't be interested in dancing with me."

"I wouldn't be so sure." His eyes flashed again, and it was almost as if he knew something she didn't.

Looking into his eyes, Cinderella felt uncomfortable and happy at the same time. "Even if the prince asked me to dance, which he won't, I'm not sure I'd want to."

Ty drew back, startled. "Why not?"

"I didn't mean to offend your employer." She bit her lip and moved her hand closer to his on the counter. "And I certainly didn't want to offend you. It's just that I can't see getting all excited about a dance with someone I don't know, just because he's rich and famous. And the idea that he's going to pick any girl he wants, ask her to marry him, and she's expected to say yes?" She shook her head and leaned back on the counter. "What if the girl he picks doesn't want to get married? What if she doesn't like him? What if she loves someone else? What if she has other plans for her life?"

"Exactly!" Ty laughed and turned to lean against the counter beside her. His arm lightly brushed hers. "I wish there were more girls like you in my kingdom."

"The kingdom is yours?" Cinderella grinned.

Bright spots of red bloomed on his cheeks. "I meant, um, the kingdom belongs to all of us, doesn't it?"

She gave him a sly smile to show that she found his remarks endearing, and then turned to look at the fabrics again, spotting a silk interwoven with threads of silver and mauve that changed colors as it caught the light from different angles.

He helped her take down the bolt. "And I understand what you mean about being expected to marry, whether you want to or not, whether or not you're in love." He leaned his lips closer to her ear. "But I'm starting to believe things might work out for me in the love department."

Cinderella felt a flush rise from deep inside her—and it wasn't unpleasant at all. After she escaped, maybe she'd have a chance to get to know Ty better, but for now, it was best to concentrate on getting to the ball so she could escape.

She turned to search the shop, now bustling with shoppers, to find her stepsisters. If either of them grew angry, it might ruin everything.

She located Agatha tugging at a bolt of cloth, a hideous lemon yellow with bright orange polka dots, from the bottom of a huge stack of fabrics at the back of the store. From the look of the garish colors, it was a tidy stack of bolts no one else wanted to examine, never mind buy. The stack wobbled as Agatha pulled, and Cinderella looked up to the top of the tall pile, where a wooden box of foot-long spindles teetered close to the edge of its perch. If Agatha pulled much harder . . .

Cinderella didn't have time to think. Too many eager girls with their mothers and seamstresses stood between her and Agatha, so Cinderella leaped up onto the counter and then sprang up to grab a wooden beam that ran through the center of the room.

Building up momentum, she arched and swung over the shoppers, let go, and landed on one foot on the edge of a shelf midway up the wall on the opposite side of the store. She pushed off from there, somersaulted over the heads of six shoppers, and landed next to Agatha. "Watch out!" she cried, and pulled Agatha to the side. The box crashed to the floor where her stepsister had been standing. It smashed and the empty wooden spools rolled over the floor in every direction.

One of the shopkeepers ran over and bent to gather the spools. Agatha's face went white and she backed away from Cinderella and looked around the room, as if searching for her mother. Agatha dashed across the room to her mother's side. Apparently, Cinderella wasn't the only one eager to stay in the woman's good graces.

She glanced back through the crowd to spot Ty, who had a huge grin on his face. One of the mothers shoved him, but instead of getting angry, he nodded to the rude woman and stepped aside.

Cinderella suppressed a giggle. If that woman knew Ty worked at the palace, she might not have been so rude. Cinderella loved sharing this little secret with Ty.

He wove his way through the crowd to stand next to her, and even though they weren't touching, she felt his warmth spread through her body. If she didn't know better, she'd think he'd cast a magic spell upon her to make her feel safe and happy and warm yet excited.

He smiled again as he bent toward her, his shaggy curls falling across his face. "Even if you don't go to the ball—which you should—you should definitely enter the magic competition."

"Magic competition?"

"It's part of the festival held the day of the ball."

"Oh, I couldn't." Cinderella poked a finger through a new tear on her skirt she'd have to mend tonight. "I have very little aptitude for magic."

"Speed, strength, agility, not to mention concentration, are major signs of magic aptitude." Ty leaned against the counter. "Almost anyone can learn to cast a few small spells with a wand, but the big stuff, the really powerful magic, takes so much more. It has to come from inside you." He put his hand on his chest. "It's aptitude they look for during the competition, and from what I just saw, you'd have a great chance of winning." The clear admiration in his eyes filled her heart with the most glorious joy.

"But I've never even seen a magic competition." Still, a wave of excitement surged inside her at the thought of entering.

"Doesn't matter," he said. "The royal wizard devises a new set of tests every year."

"The royal wizard will be there?" Her heart raced. She'd only heard her stepsisters whisper about the great wizard's powers.

"Of course," Ty said. "Each year, he grants the winner a year's worth of lessons." He reached forward and his fingers brushed her wrist, his touch like sparks from a fire. "And if the winner is a girl, she's guaranteed at least one dance with the prince."

"What a fabulous prize." She could imagine winning those lessons.

Ty's smile brightened the room and her insides. "So now you want to dance with the prince?" he asked.

"No, silly. You're the only boy I want to dance with." Feeling bold, she lightly slapped his arm just above the elbow. Surprised at the hard muscles she felt on Ty's arm, she pulled her hand back. "I'm excited about the lessons with the royal wizard. If I had training with him, no way could my stepmother—" She stopped herself just in time.

If she mentioned one word about the entrapment spells or her stepmother's illegal use of black magic, both she and the person she told would instantly turn into stone.

"Oh," Ty said. His expression dropped for an instant, but then warmed again. "I am glad you want to compete. Make sure you come with a clear head, and just be yourself."

He pressed his hand to his chest, and smiled at her with genuine sincerity in his eyes. Cinderella felt as if she were floating, as if she were flying, as if no one else were in the room.

How could this day get better? Her new friend Ty liked magic, seemed to like her, and apparently had some insider knowledge of the competition. "Have you entered before?" she asked.

He shook his head. "No, as a royal servant I'm not eligible, but I watch every year. It's highly competitive, but I have a strong feeling you'll do well. I'll certainly be cheering for you to win." He stepped back and bowed, flipping his right hand a few times in an incredibly formal manner that almost made Cinderella want to giggle. Even dressed in rags, the regal gesture seemed to fit her new friend—her only friend unless you counted a cat.

Her heart swelled. She'd found a friend—a handsome and charming young man, to boot. Maybe one day after she escaped ... No, she would not let herself dream of that kind of happiness. The kind that involved true love and happily-ever-afters. Those kinds of dreams were for silly girls like her stepsisters. Once she'd escaped, she'd find her way in the world in a job serving others, but serving them freely, as Ty did in his job at the palace. With her experience, she would certainly be able to find a position as a maid, maybe even in a household where they would feed her something better than table scraps and let her outside during daylight hours.

"Cinderella!"

She jumped and cringed at the sound of her stepmother's voice booming in her ears.

"There you are, you spoiled, selfish girl." Her stepmother grabbed Cinderella by her ear and pulled her forward. "This is how you pay me back for my generosity? Have you forgotten why you're here? Have you forgotten your sisters need help?"

Humiliation and anger rose in Cinderella's chest, but she squashed it down with every ounce of self-control and determination inside her. No way would she do anything to give her stepmother an excuse to withdraw her permission for the ball.

"Get away from her, you rotten beggar boy." Her stepmother shoved Ty with the end of her walking stick. "Can't you see this girl has nothing to give you?"

He tipped his head down in deference. "So sorry, ma'am."

Clearly her stepmother didn't recognize Ty out of his messenger uniform, even though he'd just delivered the invitations yesterday. She thought of telling her stepmother Ty worked at the palace, but even if he were a beggar, it was no excuse for her stepmother's rudeness.

"Now, scat, you filthy street urchin. This young woman is busy, and I'll not have you distracting her. She's lazy enough." She slammed her stick down, narrowly missing Ty's foot.

"Stepmother. Leave him alone, please. He was merely helping me retrieve bolts of cloth that were too high for me to reach."

Ty stole a quick glance from his bowed head position to wink at Cinderella, and she was glad he wasn't too angry about being scolded and threatened.

"All right, then." Her stepmother dug into her purse. "Away with you, now." She tossed Ty a copper coin, and pulled Cinderella by the hair to the other side of the shop.

As soon as she could turn back, Cinderella waved but wasn't sure if he saw, and by the time she'd finished talking Agatha out of a lime-and-pumpkin print, Ty had vanished from the store.

At least she'd have a chance of seeing him again at the magic competition—assuming she could talk her stepmother into letting her compete. It seemed pointless to ask, but she planned to suggest she be allowed to do that instead of attending the ball.

Later that night, Cinderella pulled out her fabrics and laid them on the cellar table. She still found it hard to believe her stepmother would let her go to the ball, but until the opportunity was yanked away, she'd let herself hope. Plus, even if she had no place to wear it, it would be fun to make herself a gown. What she *really* hoped was that her stepmother would let her enter the magic competition, but that was highly unlikely.

She traced her hand over the shimmering, dove-gray velvet she'd selected for her own gown, and then draped the ends of the silver lace and icy pale turquoise chiffon over the heavier fabric. It was nothing short of miraculous that her stepmother had purchased all three and

Cinderella realized she'd been smart to mix them in with the fabrics for her stepsisters so her stepmother couldn't see how nice her choices looked together.

Each fabric alone was unremarkable, but the velvet caught the light when it moved, almost like the inside of an oyster shell, and with pieces of the silver lace and turquoise chiffon on top, the effect was stunning. She'd look like a mermaid, a sea princess emerging from the depths to walk on land for the first time. She wasn't usually one to fuss about clothes or pretty things, but the idea of seeing the look on Ty's face, if he ever saw her in this gown, lit little fires of excitement inside her belly.

Since finding out Ty would be there, her enthusiasm about the ball had multiplied. Even if servants weren't allowed in the main ballroom, she and Ty would dance in the halls. She didn't care, as long as she got the chance to see him again.

She twirled around her cellar room for a moment, and almost tripped over Max. He leaped up into her arms and rubbed his head against her cheek. "Don't worry, Max," she told him. "You'll always be my best friend."

He sprang from her arms and pawed at their bed of burlap sacks stuffed with straw, over the place where her book was hidden.

"Yes, yes, I know, Max." She sat down next to him and scratched under his chin the way he likes. "Just because I've met a new friend doesn't mean I've forgotten my training." Max purred. "And you're right. The magic competition is way more important than the ball." She lowered her voice and whispered in Max's ear, "By the way, I'm planning to escape the day of the ball."

He meowed, jumped out of her arms into the center of the room, and rose onto his hind legs, batting at some imaginary foe.

"You are so ferocious, Max." Cinderella grinned, did a twisting hook kick, and then a series of walking punches. "Just think. The competition and ball are two days away. Can you believe we might be free after that? I'd better get started on my dress."

Max sprawled on the floor and looked the other way, as if he thought her priorities were all wrong.

"Who are you talking to?" a voice demanded from behind her.

She spun to find her stepmother on the bottom stair at the entrance to her room, and reached to gather her fabric. "No one. Just my cat."

"Wait," said her stepmother. "Let me see." She sauntered across the room, her bright green skirt swishing on the stone floor.

Her stepmother dragged her long nails over the fabric, and Cinderella cringed. *Please don't snag it. Please.*

Her stepmother spun. "I'm impressed, Cinderella. Very impressed."

Cinderella swallowed hard. "Impressed" was not what she'd been expecting to hear.

Her stepmother added, "Of course, no gown can make a plain girl like you beautiful." She smiled and shook her head slightly. "With your lack of height, simple bone structure, and the dull nature of your complexion and hair, one can't expect miracles."

Cinderella clasped her hands in front of her apron, every muscle in her body on high alert. Her stepmother never came down here without a good reason—and that reason usually involved some kind of punishment.

"May I help you with anything?" Cinderella asked politely.

Her stepmother kept a fake smile plastered on her face, and Max rubbed up against Cinderella. She slid her foot to the side to push him away. Max normally hid whenever her stepmother came down, and

Cinderella wished he'd hide now. No need to take unnecessary risks with her stepmother's patience.

"We should discuss the day of the ball," her stepmother said. "You will need to complete your chores quickly if you are to have time to wipe the soot off your face before you help your sisters get ready."

Cinderella nodded, still not trusting where this was headed, but hopeful. She was almost starting to believe her stepmother planned to keep her word and let her go.

"You'll be representing this family, and even though the prince will never choose you for a dance, we must have you looking your best." She picked up the silver lace and, holding one corner, unfurled it.

Cinderella's heart seized.

Her stepmother sniffed, handed the lace to Cinderella, and put her hands on her hips.

Cinderella refolded the fabric. She'd never seen her stepmother so amenable. Now was the time to ask. "Stepmother," she began, drying her sweating palms on her apron, "will you and my stepsisters be attending the magic competition?"

Her stepmother's head snapped toward her. "Why?"

Cinderella's mouth was dry, but she pressed on. "I expect my sisters have inherited your talent for magic. Will they be competing?"

"I hadn't really considered it." She slowly strode forward to tower over Cinderella.

She took a tiny step back and said, "I was just thinking . . . I was wondering . . ." She straightened her back. "I'd like to enter."

Her stepmother tipped her head back to expose her long white throat and laughed. "Cinderella, that is the funniest thing I've heard in a very long time."

Anger mingled with fear in Cinderella's chest and she clenched her fists behind her back so her stepmother couldn't see.

"You're a clumsy girl with no aptitude for magic, no matter how powerful your mother was." Her stepmother's eyes narrowed, and her voice returned to its normal icy tone, sending a chill down Cinderella's spine. "She couldn't have been that powerful if a tiny baby killed her."

Cinderella nearly shook with rage, but kept silent.

"Who put this ridiculous notion in your mind?"

"No one," said Cinderella. No need to bring poor Ty into this. "I overheard things in the village."

"Bringing you today was a mistake." Her stepmother paced around the room in long, slow strides. "You're so impressionable and sheltered. Imagine thinking you could enter that competition without a wand or even any training." She spun toward Cinderella and leaned onto the table. "I won't let you bring shame and embarrassment onto our family name. Your father would be mortified."

"My father would be proud of me no matter what."

"You think so, do you?" Her stepmother's eyes shot spikes of ice into Cinderella's chest, but she stood her ground.

Even though most memories of her father involved him being sad, she could remember the smile on his face when she'd learned to read, when she'd drawn him a picture, when she'd sang him a song.

Her stepmother's lips bent up into a sly smile. "I have an idea."

Cinderella braced herself for the worst, wondering what possible torture her stepmother might be contemplating. At least she hadn't reached for her wand . . . yet.

"If you're determined to enter the competition, I insist that you have some training."

Hope rose in Cinderella's chest, pushing back the anger and fear she had felt only moments ago.

Her stepmother leaned on the table, her blood-red nails digging into the wood. "Let's perform a little test to see if you're ready to enter."

"A test?"

Max rubbed against Cinderella's skirts again, meowing loudly, but she couldn't pay attention to her cat. Not now. Not with so much on the line.

"If you pass, you may enter the competition. In fact, I'll buy you the best wand money can buy."

"Really?" A smile burst onto Cinderella's face and she tried to remember when—or if—she'd ever smiled like this in her stepmother's presence. It was so long ago, it might have been never.

"But as with any fair test, failure must have its consequences."

Cinderella's smile shrank, and she felt stupid for believing, even for a second, that her stepmother would let her enter the magic competition. Still, she'd do her best on whatever kind of test her stepmother could devise. The woman didn't know she'd been training, didn't know she'd inherited a little of her mother's abilities as a wizard.

"What consequences?" Cinderella asked, hoping that her voice sounded steadier than it felt.

"If you fail my test, clearly you can't enter the competition." Her stepmother glanced around the room, her expression growing ever more evil as she looked at the fabric, folded neatly on the table. "Not only that, if you fail, you cannot attend the ball."

Cinderella backed up a few steps. The hammer had finally fallen. Her stepmother had just been waiting for an opportunity to deny Cinderella the trip to the ball. No doubt the test would be impossible, and without the ball, she'd lose her best chance to escape. Why had she even asked about the competition?

"What do you say, Cinderella? Will you accept my challenge?"

Cinderella studied her stepmother's face. "And if I choose not to?"

"If you don't accept my challenge, I'll be very disappointed, and how can a girl who's disappointed her stepmother expect to attend a ball?"

Cinderella gritted her teeth. The ball was off the table even if she backed off from entering the competition. How unfair.

Still, she had to try. Winning the competition might be her best chance to develop the skills she needed to escape her stepmother forever. She had no choice but to complete whatever test her stepmother devised.

"Fine," she said, bowing her head. "What is your test?"

Cinderella stared in dismay at the crystal goblets scattered around her on the stone courtyard, and looked up at her stepmother to be sure she was serious. Even by her stepmother's standards, this so-called test seemed impossible.

Her stepmother had used her magic wand to transport every single goblet in the house up the cellar steps and onto the stone courtyard, and now she expected Cinderella to stack them, end on end into a tower, without breaking a single one—without using a wand.

Unbeknownst to her stepmother, Cinderella had moved objects with her mind before, but never with such precision. The completed tower, assuming it was possible to complete it, would be over fifteen feet high, nearly three times her own height. Her stepmother had marked an X on the stone courtyard about eight feet away from the nearest wall, so she couldn't climb the wall in order to reach the top of the tower, or lean the tower against something steady.

The sun had set hours ago, but her stepmother had used a magic spell to cast a bright light on the courtyard, and was sitting at the back of the house in a chair she'd made Cinderella carry out. Her stepmother couldn't use her own magic for the *heavy* lifting, oh no.

Agatha and Gwendolyn were seated beside her, snickering on and off, as Cinderella studied the goblets and tried to devise a plan. Max had disappeared as soon as they'd come outside. Which was just as well; it wasn't as though he could help.

She turned to her stepmother. "May I have more than one goblet on each level?" she asked. A pyramid-type structure might work. Perhaps the challenge was more of a puzzle than anything else.

"Don't be stupid," her stepmother snapped. "I said end on end."

"May I use paste?" If she were granted access to the kitchen, she could make some paste using flour and water. It still wouldn't help build a tower strong enough to climb once its top grew out of reach, but it was her best idea so far.

"I'm losing patience." Her stepmother shot out of her chair. "Are you ready to admit defeat?"

"No." She turned away. There had to be a way to do this.

She glanced across the garden and spotted Max near the edge of the woods. He'd been obsessed with that spot the past few nights. "Max," she called to him, "be careful—the wolves." If he ventured into the trees, the wolves would surely snap him up in a second.

Gwendolyn giggled, and Cinderella tried to hide her anger. Her laughter was cruel, whether it was aimed at her talking to her cat, or at the idea that he might be eaten by wolves.

Max pawed the dirt and then leaped in the air several times, doing somersaults before landing. Crazy cat.

Cinderella transferred her attention to the goblets. Might as well get started. She could think about possible solutions to the problem as she worked. She first selected a water goblet, since they were the largest type, and placed it on the X. Then she picked up a second one. The only way to stack it on top without using other materials in between was to put the second goblet upside down so the narrow round rims of the two goblets touched.

Inhaling to steady herself, she focused with her ninja concentration and added the second goblet. That was easy enough.

Carefully, she placed all the water goblets base to base, rim to rim, until the stack reached her eye level.

A wolf growled, and she snapped her head toward the garden to see Max come running out of the woods.

"Max, come." The silly creature was going to get himself killed. What was it about that particular section of the woods, anyway? He'd been pawing there last night, too. There must be mice or moles living nearby.

She took the first wineglass and set it on the base of the last upside-down goblet, careful to center the smaller base perfectly inside the larger. Another wineglass, and then she'd no longer be able to reach the tower's top.

Still, she wasn't ready to give up.

A wolf snapped in the distance, and she turned to see Max running at the edge of the garden. But instead of coming back toward the house, he shot back into the woods, climbed a few feet up a tree trunk, and then leaped backward, doing a somersault to land on the same spot where he'd started.

The wolves went crazy, snarling and snapping and leaping up to try to catch him as he hit the tree on each pass. If those wolves could take even one step into the garden, they'd have cat for dinner.

Max repeated this bizarre move several times, and Cinderella considered stomping over there to pick him up and move him back into the cellar.

Her eyes opened wide. *Max, you clever cat. That's brilliant!* As crazy as it was to think he'd purposefully offered a suggestion, and as nearly impossible her idea might be, it might prove to be her only chance.

She turned to the wall, about eight feet from her tower, and studied its round stones and mortar. It might just be possible, but only if she kept her focus and concentrated fully. And only if she executed leaps off the wall many feet higher than she'd ever tried before. Best to try a practice run without a goblet in her hand.

She did breathing exercises, using her diaphragm and lifting her arms to pull in more air, then lowering her arms and squeezing her solar plexus to force the air out. She repeated this several times until she felt centered, and then considered the height of her current tower and the distance from the wall.

She ran toward the wall and took a few running steps up the stones before springing up and back. Finding and keeping her eyes focused on the tower, she flew through the air, executing a backflip and ensuring her body was upside down as she passed over the tower of crystal. She landed on the other side of it and crouched, hiding the grin on her face.

She'd have to be lightning-quick. She'd have to concentrate as she'd never concentrated before, but she could do this. Her magic skills might not be well developed, but her secret ninja training would pay off tonight.

"What are you doing, you stupid girl?" Gwendolyn said, jumping up from her chair. "Even if you've given up, you don't need to break the goblets. They cost money, you know."

She ignored her stepsister, picked up a wineglass, drew three deep breaths, and then started off running toward the wall.

One foot planted, two, she scrambled up the wall's surface, then pushed off and flipped back over her tower. She reached her arm down as she passed above the top of the tower, and set the goblet in place. Her task done, she rotated in the air and landed bent-kneed behind the tower. Max, no longer obsessed by the woods, had run back while she was placing the wineglass and now rubbed against her leg.

She glanced over to her stepmother and stepsisters. Agatha was staring at her with wide eyes, astounded, but both Gwendolyn and her stepmother scowled, more angry than impressed. With eight more wineglasses to add to the tower, she couldn't allow any distractions.

Over and over, she added more wineglasses to the tower, end on end, until she was ready to move on to the smallest glasses of all, those for cordials. The diameter of each cordial glass was little more than an inch, and her movements would have to be that much more precise.

Her stepmother was now wringing a handkerchief in her lap as if she wanted it dead. Clearly she hadn't expected to find Cinderella a mere six cordial glasses away from success.

The tower was more than twice her height now. She'd have to run faster to build up more speed, take more steps up the wall, and spring from it with more force and careful aim than before.

It was hard to believe she could do it, but what did she have to lose? The worst that could happen would be broken glasses, some cuts and bruises, maybe a twisted ankle if she landed badly.

She picked up a cordial glass, looked up at the tower sparkling in the light of her stepmother's illumination spell, and then started off at a quick run.

After one, two, three, four, five scrambling steps up the wall, she threw herself up and back, eyes focused on her target, visualizing herself placing the base of the small goblet delicately in the center of the last wineglass she'd placed upside down. She floated through the air, strong, confident, centered.

And then the snowstorm started.

Huge flakes of snow clouded her vision and struck her face, melting as they landed. She ignored the white spots and concentrated on her objective, placing the cordial glass cleanly before completing her backflip's rotation and landing once more on the courtyard surface.

She spun toward her stepmother, who was now standing up, her wand outstretched, a sneer on her lips. "You didn't think I would make this easy, did you?" Her cackle carried like sleet through the night air. "I'm only doing it for your own good. How are you going to learn if you're never challenged? The royal wizard will devise many tests even more challenging than this."

Cinderella heard a wolf yelp and glanced over to the woods. Max had returned to his pawing, in the same place just inside the trees. What had gotten into that cat? He'd been acting strangely ever since the invitation from the palace had arrived, but she couldn't worry about him right now. She had to complete the tower of glass or she'd never have the chance to win the lessons with the royal wizard.

She picked up the second cordial glass and held it, ready to set its rim on top of the one she'd just placed. Given the height she'd achieved and her success despite the short blizzard, the same velocity and trajectory of her last leap should do it. She prepared herself, visualized her objective, and ran as fast as she could.

This time, as she sprang off the wall, a driving wind slammed into her and pushed her off course. She adjusted in midair, flinging her arm across her body to spin herself laterally, and after twisting her body around twice as she passed the tower, she landed on the grass next to the stone courtyard—the cordial glass still in her hand.

She stomped toward her evil spectators. "That's not fair," she told her stepmother. "This isn't the test you set out. We had a deal."

"How dare you." Her stepmother stood, wand raised. "I don't make deals with insolent, badly behaved girls." Her stepmother's eyes glinted red in their centers and bore into Cinderella's heart, filling her with fear.

This was no longer about completing this test. If she angered her stepmother further, it might be about saving her own life. Never before had she felt so certain that her stepmother was capable of murder.

Agatha rose from her chair and said, "Mother, you did agree."

Her stepmother spun toward her daughter and an unseen force pushed Agatha back down into her chair. Agatha ducked her head as if protecting herself from further punishment, and Gwen shook her head and rolled her eyes, as if disgusted with her sister's behavior.

"Go on then," her stepmother said. She waved her hand at Cinderella. "Or do you give up?"

Cinderella tamed her rage and got back to work. One by one, she added the cordial glasses, focusing intensely on her task so that nothing her stepmother threw at her interfered. She merely adjusted her speed and height to compensate for the wind, the rain, the flashes of lightning—and now a swarm of moths. Only once was she forced to abort her flip and not place a glass.

When Cinderella placed the next-to-last cordial glass on the tower, her hair brushed the glass below it. She squeezed her eyes shut, but did not hear a crash. After landing, she squinted one eye open.

She'd done it. Only one more.

Fighting the pride and excitement threatening to distract her, she picked up the last glass and ran toward the wall at full speed, then leaped high toward the top of the tower. Surprised that there were no added challenges, she carefully placed the last glass and then stretched her body out straight, preparing to land.

But the instant that her feet touched down, the ground trembled beneath them.

An earthquake.

The tower shook, swayed from side to side, and then crashed, every goblet shattering into tiny pieces.

She turned to her stepmother. "I did it. Agatha, you saw, right? It's not fair to cause an earthquake to knock it down *after* I finish."

Agatha looked away. Her stepmother rose and shook her head. "So unfortunate, Cinderella. I thought you might have finally overcome your clumsiness, but it looks as though you won't be going to the competition—or the ball."

Can Cinderella change her stepmother's mind?
If not, can she figure out a way to escape
the entrapment spells?
Will she ever see Ty again?

To find out, turn to section 4: Unexpected Assistance (page 107).

Section 3

---❦---

Hard
Work
Rewarded

C inderella carefully set the two gowns onto the dress forms in her stepsisters' shared dressing room that spanned the space between their grand bedrooms. She felt light, more alive and happy than she'd been in a very long time.

It had been smart to say no to the ball, even if it had been impossible at the time to tell if her answer had pleased her stepmother. Since then, she'd worked hard to complete every task and chore she'd been given, like always. But completing these gowns was different, and her stepmother was going to be both shocked and pleased. Although Cinderella knew it was wrong to expect a reward, she certainly deserved and hoped for something—maybe a few hours outside during daylight.

Hearing the clack of her stepmother's and stepsisters' high heels coming up the stairs and crossing the wooden floor, she stepped out to greet them. "I have a surprise," she announced.

"Oh, goody." Agatha clapped her hands, but then Gwendolyn bumped her sister with her hip and Agatha wiped the smile from her face and said, "Yeah, whatever."

Cinderella couldn't let her sisters spoil this moment, for her or for them. As soon as they saw the dresses, they'd squeal with glee, and her stepmother would marvel at her speed and skill. After buying dresses in town for the girls, her stepmother had handed Cinderella huge sacks of beads and sequins and feathers yesterday with an evil glint in her eyes and had insisted she sew every single embellishment onto her daughters' dresses by tomorrow, the day before the ball. By staying up all night, Cinderella had finished a day early.

At first, Cinderella had cringed when she saw all the beads and feathers and sequins. Not so much because sewing on every single item would be tremendously hard work, but because she didn't want to ruin her stepsisters' ball gowns with all that sparkle. But she'd figured out a way to save the dresses.

"Well?" Her stepmother frowned and then snapped, "We don't have all day, girl. What is your so-called surprise?"

Cinderella flung open the doors to the dressing room to reveal the gowns she'd spent all night embellishing. The light from the window across the hall and the skylights above caught the crystal beading and sent sparkles shooting everywhere. She lifted the fabric of one of the skirts to show how lightly she'd applied the tiny feathers to the hem and how ethereal they'd make Gwendolyn appear as she glided across the dance floor.

"Oh!" cried Agatha, who ran forward to touch the beading at the bodice of her dress. Her face was beaming, but then she turned and glanced at Gwendolyn for guidance.

Gwendolyn's eyes narrowed as if she thought Cinderella was trying to play some kind of trick. Of what sort, Cinderella could not imagine.

Her stepmother walked into the dressing room and slowly circled the dresses, her face frozen and expressionless. She examined the dresses carefully, even checking inside, and grunted when she saw Cinderella's even stitching and the lining she'd added under the intricate beading to protect the threads and ensure that not a single bead could get snagged.

Cinderella had never felt more confident in her own work and although she knew it was conceited to be so incredibly proud, she was. She'd worked all night and had the bandages on her pricked and sore fingers to show for it.

Still, in spite of her utter confidence that this was good work, her mouth dried and her smile grew heavy. Her stepmother hadn't uttered a word, and the woman's silence and scrutiny chilled the air.

Suddenly, her stepmother raised her head. Cinderella jumped and clasped her hands in front of her apron.

Her stepmother stepped forward, towering above Cinderella like a hammer over a nail, ready to strike. "Where is it?"

"What?" Cinderella backed up, fear flooding every crevice previously occupied by pride and joy, not to mention the hope that she might be offered a reward.

"The wand." Her stepmother clenched her hands. "To do this so quickly, you must have used magic."

"No, I didn't." She *wished* she had her mother's wand or possessed the powers to have done this with magic. Then she'd have been able to catch a few moments of sleep last night.

"You expect me to believe that you completed all this in one night?" her stepmother asked, her voice hard and spiked. "Without magic?"

Cinderella nodded and swallowed hard.

"Let me see your hands."

Cinderella offered her hands to her stepmother, who yanked them forward, hard, pulling Cinderella off balance. Her stepmother wound the bandages off her hands and then frowned and grunted when she saw the pricks and blisters from the needle and the redness on the sides of her fingers where the chafing fabric had rubbed Cinderella's skin raw.

Her stepmother twisted Cinderella's hands, flipping them over and over, studying them as if they weren't even attached to her arms.

When she finally dropped them and stepped back, her expression had molded into a smile of sorts, but this new expression injected more terror into Cinderella than any scowl. Cinderella knew that smile. Long ago, she'd learned never to accept it at face value.

No longer expecting a reward, Cinderella wondered how her stepmother would punish her and what excuse she'd devise to make her punishment seem just.

"I'm impressed, Cinderella," her stepmother said, stepping back and keeping the hard smile on her face.

Cinderella knew staring at her stepmother was beyond rude, but she had to wonder if she'd lost her touch at interpreting the woman's expressions. There was no punishment yet.

"When I saw the completed dresses and how you'd used every single bead," her stepmother continued, her voice even and calm, "I assumed you'd used a wand, or the services of a powerful wizard to finish this in a single night. But now I see you used only your hands and your patience to complete this difficult task."

Cinderella waited for the "but." When her stepmother doled out praise, there was always a "but," and experience had taught her to expect a big one at a time like this.

Her stepmother turned to Agatha and Gwendolyn, who looked confused. "What do you think of your dresses, girls?"

Gwen looked to her mother for clues as to how she should respond, while Agatha's attention vacillated between the dresses and Gwen.

"Fine work, wouldn't you say?" her stepmother asked.

"Oh, yes!" Agatha ran her fingers over the beading again before stepping back to admire her dress. "I think they're absolutely beautiful. The prince won't be able to resist us." She turned to Gwendolyn and grabbed her hands. "Don't you think so, Sister?"

Gwendolyn lifted one of the feathered sleeves of her dress, and her lips twitched as if she were fighting to keep a smile down. "They're all right, I suppose."

"Tsk, tsk, tsk," her stepmother said.

Cinderella's insides froze.

"You've created a big problem for your sisters, Cinderella."

Her mind spun with the possible problems. "But the beading is lined," she said, "and I made sure the feathers don't fall too far down, so neither Gwen nor Agatha will trip while waltzing with the prince." What problem could she have neglected to anticipate?

"Slippers. Handbags. Hair adornments." Her stepmother shook her head as if she were talking to a child who couldn't remember that seven came after six. "After what you've done, nothing the girls own will do, and with my other engagements today, I cannot make time to shop with them." She pursed her lips together.

"You're right, Mother." Gwendolyn turned up her nose as if smelling sour milk. "My slippers are covered with brushed silver threads, but they won't do with this gown. Under the feathered hem, they'll look plain and everyone will laugh."

Cinderella suppressed a cry of protest. She agreed that the slippers Gwendolyn had planned to wear would be inappropriate with the gown, but not for the same reason. A much simpler pair of slippers would be better—ones of a soft dove gray, or the palest of pale pinks.

"What will we do about this, girls?" her stepmother asked, crossing her arms over her bosom.

"Tear off the beading and feathers?" Gwendolyn suggested, which made Cinderella's stomach feel as if it were about to expel the few bites of porridge that had been left for her to eat after the others had finished.

All her work torn apart? Even her stepmother would never be that cruel. Would she?

"Mother." Agatha stepped forward. "Given we have only today to shop, perhaps Cinderella should accompany Gwen and me to the village to help us pick out new slippers."

"That's actually a good idea," remarked Gwendolyn, running her hand over the beading on her dress. She turned to her mother with a forced smile on her face. Agatha beamed at the praise from her sister.

Cinderella took a deep breath and tried to keep her expression neutral. She was thrilled at the idea of going to the village, even though her sisters were motivated purely by self-interest. They would do everything they could to look their best at the ball, and although Gwen wouldn't admit it, she and her sister relied completely on Cinderella for fashion advice.

Her stepmother's eyebrows drew more closely together and Cinderella wished she could read the evil woman's mind. She wanted to feel hopeful that her stepmother was at least considering her daughters' suggestion, but Cinderella couldn't fully let herself believe it.

"It *is* important that you stand out at the ball," her stepmother said. She approached her daughters and cupped their cheeks, almost affectionately. "It's imperative that one of you end up married to the prince. Imagine the power." Her voice lowered and the silence crept over Cinderella like a cluster of spiders.

Her stepmother spun around and said, "Fine. Take Cinderella to the village if it will increase your chances of catching the prince's eye. If Cinderella can't find anything acceptable, she can certainly bead your shoes, bags, and combs as easily as she did these gowns." She glared at Cinderella as she offered the challenge. "Can't you?"

Excitement rushed through Cinderella at the thought of getting off the grounds for the first time in nine years. Her breath caught in her throat. Even if her reward for doing her work quickly was yet more work—pushing the ultrathin beading needle through leather would be a challenge—she was going to the village.

"And, Cinderella," her stepmother said, rubbing her finger and thumb over her chin.

"Yes, Stepmother?" She fought to keep her voice even.

"Your hard work deserves a reward." She turned to the others. "Don't you agree, girls?"

Filled with anticipation, Cinderella could hardly stand still, but her stepmother's voice was tinged with deceit, as if she were hiding something behind her back even though her hands remained in plain sight.

Cinderella's heart raced. Her insides buzzed. Would her stepmother let her buy fabric to replace the rags she now wore?

The evil woman reached for the small black pouch she had dangling from her belt and pulled out a coin. "Cinderella, purchase something for yourself. A new broom would be useful, I think."

Cinderella grinned. It wasn't a great reward, but she did need a new broom, and her stepmother couldn't crush the happy feelings floating through her. She hadn't been to the village, or off the grounds at all, since she was nine years old. Unless this was some kind of trick, it was the best reward she could've hoped for.

She fought to hide her building excitement. Could she use this trip to the village to escape? Her stepmother would have to release the entrapment spells, and she could certainly outrun her stepsisters.

It would mean leaving without Max, and never returning to the home her real parents had shared, but she was ready. As soon as they were out of sight of the house, she'd ditch her stepsisters and escape.

Cinderella drew in a breath of the fresh spring air. The scent of wildflowers and damp earth compounded her joy. In just minutes, she'd be walking through the iron gate at the end of the path and would be on the road to the village. Excitement churned inside her and she almost felt as if she could fly.

Outside in the daylight, the sun felt so warm on her arms and face—much better than it did when it was filtered through a thick windowpane.

She looked back at the house she'd lived in her whole life. It had been so much cheerier when the shutters were painted butter-yellow instead of black, but she'd still cherish her few good memories: her father tickling her and telling her how her laugh was just like her mother's, the day she'd found Max in the garden, and the fun times she and her cat had practicing her ninja skills—even on the days when her training sessions had made her muscles ache and scream in pain.

With the thought of pain, ugly memories attempted to overtake the good but she refused to let them win. Today, nothing would spoil her mood. Today she'd escape.

"Oh, girls," her stepmother called as they reached the gate.

Dread filled Cinderella's belly as she turned to see her stepmother at the front door, her wand raised high in the air. She knew this moment had been coming. The trip to the village had been too much to hope for. She wouldn't be going to the village as a young woman. Instead, her stepmother would send her as a donkey, a cow, maybe even a rat.

Cinderella braced herself as her stepmother flicked her wand, then looked down at her clothing and body to see what spell her stepmother had cast.

Same torn apron, same navy blue skirt with its frayed hem that no amount of mending could repair, same threadbare linen blouse. She grasped at her hair—still there—and tentatively pulled a piece around to check the color. Still blonde. Was it possible her stepmother hadn't cast a spell?

"Have a good time," her stepmother called out. The woman's cheery voice made Cinderella feel as if she could've been knocked over by a speck of dust.

She opened the gate and her stepsisters walked through. Expecting a strong wind, or an invisible wall, or a pit of quicksand to stop her, Cinderella held her breath and took a long step through the gate.

But no pain struck, so she rubbed her hands over her arms, patted her neck, and ran her fingers through her hair. Nothing. She was outside the property's grounds, on the road to the village. It didn't seem possible.

Feeling giddy, she started to skip down the path. "Come on," she called back to Gwendolyn and Agatha. "Hurry up, slowpokes." A little company might be fun for the first part of the trip. It would be best to wait until she was farther from the house before making her escape.

Agatha started forward, a skip in her step, too, but Gwendolyn grabbed her sister and held her back. Gwen stood still and then crossed her arms over the pink velvet fabric of the dainty jacket she wore over her deep red dress.

Cinderella paused for a second. Let them dawdle if they wanted to. Escape would be even easier than she'd expected. Her heart was so filled with joy, she thought it might burst.

Skipping forward, she kicked a pebble in her way, and then leaped into the air and spun in two full circles before landing. Freedom felt great. Freedom felt wonderful. Freedom was even better than that tiny crumb of chocolate Agatha had secretly passed to her one winter day.

Freedom was—burning!

"Aah!" Cinderella cried as smoke suddenly wafted off her fingertips, flames licked the edges of her slippers, and the already-frayed hem of her skirt smoldered as if she'd stepped too close to the fire while heating the bathwater.

Cinderella staggered back a few steps and the burning stopped, but her nostrils filled with the acrid scent of smoldering fibers.

She spun toward her sisters. Agatha's eyes were wide with alarm and she ran toward Cinderella, but Gwendolyn sauntered forward slowly, a grin on her face that closely matched the one her mother had worn earlier. Cinderella's hope and happiness iced over.

"That will teach you," Gwendolyn said when she got closer.

Agatha turned toward her sister. "What happened?"

"Mother knew Cinderella was too foolish to be trusted off the property." Gwendolyn's evil grin was even more terrifying up close. "These woods are dangerous, Cinderella," she said in a pedantic tone. "Stay close. There are thieves and wolves everywhere."

Cinderella squared her stance. "The wolves only come out at night."

"True," Gwendolyn said, "but they're only one of many dangers lurking in this forest. A girl like you, with no experience, no magic, no way to defend yourself, you can't be running off on your own. You'd never survive." Gwendolyn touched Cinderella's arm, pretending she actually cared, but her hand was cold and heavy.

Cinderella shrugged it off.

"Mother cast a little spell to *protect* you, that's all." Gwendolyn continued to sport a most disingenuous smile.

"Protect me? I nearly caught on fire!"

"Yes, and if you get more than fifty feet from either of us, you'll start smoldering again. More than a hundred feet and you'll burst completely into flames."

Agatha raised a hand to her mouth to cover a gasp, but Cinderella only stared at Gwendolyn, her rage fuming in her eyes. She should have known that total freedom was too much to expect.

Apparently she wouldn't be escaping today—not unless she wanted to burst into flames. She stomped along behind her stepsisters, but soon realized it was no use moping. Even if today's escape hopes were dashed, she could still enjoy the way the sun filtered through the leaves, and how the blue jays and cardinals battled for territory in the treetops.

She kept track of more important details, too. Even if she couldn't escape, it would help to know which trees had branches low enough to jump onto, which areas had thicker or thinner underbrush, which sections of the forest were riddled with poison oak.

About half a mile from the house, she heard the sound of a brook through the trees and her breath quickened as memories of her father flooded in. The summer before he died, he'd taken her to that brook, they'd thrown rocks into the water, and she had delighted at the plopping sound as each stone hit. She had been four years old at the time.

Gathering strength and love from the memory, a warm feeling flowed through her, and she reached up to the branch of an apple tree bending over the path. Her hand singed the leaf.

She spun around and saw that her stepsisters had opened up a gap and were now fifty feet ahead of her on the road. Gwendolyn was laughing. Next to her, Agatha stared at the ground. Gwendolyn set off at a run, and Cinderella had no choice but to race to catch up. Who knew Gwen was capable of moving so quickly?

Within a few long strides, Cinderella had passed Agatha, and as she continued to chase Gwendolyn, she started to worry that there might not be any way to win this sadistic game. If Gwen had been right about the parameters of the spell, the smoldering would start as soon as she was fifty feet from either sister, so if Agatha couldn't keep up, it wouldn't matter if Cinderella caught up with Gwen, the faster and meaner of the two.

She glanced over her shoulder and saw that Agatha had figured out this little detail as well, and didn't want to witness her stepsister become engulfed in flames.

Agatha was dressed in a heavy lavender velvet skirt, under which she wore about twenty layers of crinoline over hoops. She struggled clumsily as she tried to close the distance, but Gwendolyn showed no signs of slowing.

Cinderella stopped and gestured for Agatha to hurry. If she carried her, at least she'd only have to worry about keeping up with Gwen. Agatha tried to pick up her pace, caught up with Cinderella, and bent over, gasping from the effort.

"Hop on my back," Cinderella said, turning and bending down to indicate that she planned to give Agatha a piggyback ride.

Agatha looked horrified. "I can't," she said. "It's not dignified. What if someone should—" She stopped short as Cinderella's dress started to smolder at the hem.

Cinderella spun to see that Gwen had stopped, too, and was bent over, panting, but kept her eyes closely on Cinderella. Each time Cinderella took a step forward, dragging the out-of-breath Agatha with her, Gwendolyn took another step back, keeping Cinderella right on the fringes of smoke.

"Please," Cinderella said, appealing to Agatha with her outstretched arms. She saw something in her stepsister's face that she never saw when Gwen was around. It was a speck of sympathy, a crumb of regret, an ounce of apology.

Cinderella turned again, bent down to offer her back, and this time Agatha hopped on. Cinderella tucked her arms under Agatha's legs and ran toward Gwen.

Gwen straightened up and opened her mouth as if to yell at Agatha, whose arms and legs were clamped around Cinderella's chest and belly like the hoop on a barrel. But instead of shouting at her sister, Gwen turned and resumed running.

Cinderella did her best to close the distance between them, but as slender as Agatha was, she was at least seven inches taller than Cinderella and twenty pounds heavier—with at least half of those pounds coming from her dress. Yet Cinderella had no choice. She had to keep up. If she didn't catch Gwendolyn, she'd go up in flames, and that was a thought too horrible to contemplate.

She would not give up and burn. And she wouldn't give up her plans for escape, either. Even if her stepmother's tales of the world's dangers were true, even if she were attacked by wolves or robbed by thieves, or even if she were simply unable to find work or shelter or enough to eat, at least she'd have tried. At least she wouldn't die a victim of her stepmother's and stepsisters' cruelty. At least she'd have done something to make her life better.

A man dropped from the trees and landed directly in front of Gwendolyn, who stopped in her tracks and screamed, "Aah! Thief!"

Cinderella could clearly see this was no thief, yet a man dropping out of the forest could not be a good thing. Gwendolyn ran away from the man and sprinted back to hide behind Cinderella, who tried to let Agatha down from her back, but the girl's grip was so tight, Cinderella no longer needed to hold her legs.

But assuming this man planned to rob them, she couldn't mount a defense with someone literally holding her back, so she tried to shake Agatha off.

From his size and gait, the man was young and he slowly walked toward them, hands up, palms forward. She'd never seen a thief, but this man looked more like a hunter, dressed as he was in a leather vest over a shirt only partially tucked into well-worn leather breeches. He had a bow and a quiver of arrows slung across his broad chest.

She stared in recognition. The messenger? "That's not a thief," she said to Gwendolyn, and then walked toward the man.

Agatha squeaked, let go of her death grip on Cinderella, and slipped to the path behind her. Cinderella didn't even turn to see whether Agatha had landed on her feet.

"It's you," she said to the royal messenger, who was easily recognizable. His unruly blond curls were loose and caught the patches of sunlight that broke through the leaves above. "You're a hunter and a messenger?" She imagined the freedom.

He bowed to her and smiled broadly.

"Cinderella," Gwendolyn yelled in a scolding tone, "you stupid girl! Why are you talking to that villain? I'm sure the rest of his gang will be here any minute and we'll be robbed and killed."

"If we're robbed and killed, we can't go to the ball," Agatha said, her voice quavering.

Both Cinderella and the young man rolled their eyes at the same time and then started to laugh.

It was time to put her stepsisters out of their terror. She turned to the messenger. "I'll tell them who you—"

The messenger held a finger in front of his lips to silence her, a mischievous glint in his eyes. Mischievous, a little mysterious, but not dangerous. No way did he mean them harm. "I'd rather stay incognito," he said.

Cinderella wondered why and then smiled. "If people know you work at the palace, do they ask a lot of questions about the ball and which girl you think the prince might choose?"

"Um, yes," he replied. "You could say that." He nodded slowly, as if thinking about it.

Gwendolyn, clearly deciding that the danger had passed, was stomping toward them, pulling Agatha behind her. The messenger turned to the two sisters and bowed, his hat shading his face. "I'm not a thief, but a simple hunter. I do apologize for startling you lovely ladies."

"Well, you did," Gwendolyn snapped. "What business do you have falling out of trees to terrify innocent women? My sister here"—she put her hand around Agatha's waist—"might have fainted from the shock."

"I do apologize," the young man said. "I was simply curious about your game and wondered if I could play, too."

"Game?" Gwendolyn asked. "You insolent . . . Oh, off with you!"

Even though her sisters had seen the messenger just a few days ago, it was clear that neither of them recognized him now. They wouldn't dare treat someone who worked at the palace this way.

"Perhaps you might let me escort you into the village," he said. "These woods can be dangerous." He bowed again.

"Hogwash," Gwendolyn said. She purposefully let her heavy handbag bump against his bowed head as she strode past. "Get lost."

Agatha skittered behind her sister.

Cinderella stepped up to the young man. "Are you okay?"

He grinned and said, "Fine. I've had worse lumps than that one."

"I'm glad. I apologize for my stepsisters. They can be . . . well, I'm sorry." It would be incredibly impolite to say anything against her family in front of this relative stranger.

Her cheeks burned under the bright light of the boy's gaze. Something about him made her feel both comfortable and nervous at the same time, as if she were wrapped in warm blankets, awaiting an exciting surprise. It was the way she'd felt the night before the winter festival each year before her father had died, knowing she'd wake in the morning to find treats in the sock hung at the end of her bed.

"Do you mind if I walk with you a while?" he asked.

"I don't mind, but would it be proper?" Feeling silly about her question, she looked down. Her real concern was whether her stepsisters would tell their mother, but what was the point of living in fear?

"Do I frighten you?" The messenger shaped his hands into claws, let out a playful growl, and then smiled.

She laughed. "No, you don't *frighten* me." Frighten wasn't the word that came to mind when it came to this boy.

"My name's Ty," he said.

"I'm Cinderella."

"What were you doing before I interrupted? It looked like you were playing a game of tag."

Just then, the hem of her skirt started to smolder. Cinderella skipped forward quickly and then picked up the pace to close the distance between her and her stepsisters. "They were just teasing me."

"Really?" He fell in stride beside her. "Hey, what's up with that?" He pointed to the blackened hem of her skirt.

"Oh ..." She kept her voice light. "I'm sometimes careless when I tend the fire."

He nodded.

She wasn't sure he believed her, but at least he was kind enough not to press her for more details. It was too embarrassing to reveal the power her stepsisters held over her, and besides, revealing the spell or anything about her stepmother's illegal use of black magic would turn both of them to stone.

"Do you travel this road on foot often?" he asked.

"Not in years."

"Usually in a grand carriage?" He smiled slyly and her heart skipped a beat.

"Something like that."

Gwendolyn glanced over her shoulder, scowled, and then quickened her pace. Cinderella sped up to close the distance.

"Just a moment," Ty said, stepping into the underbrush at the side of the path.

Cinderella stopped too, praying he'd return before the girls got too far ahead.

"Did you decide?" he called out from the woods.

"Decide what?" She kept her eyes on Gwendolyn, who hadn't yet noticed she'd stopped.

"About the ball." Ty was bent over, reaching for something from the forest floor. Cinderella was growing anxious.

"I'm not going," she said.

"That's too bad," Ty said as he came out of the woods with a beautiful bouquet of bluebells and daisies. He handed them to her, and as she accepted them, she felt her cheeks redden.

"Thank you," she said as she took in the scent of the flowers. "I'm not much for balls. All that fancy stuff really isn't me."

"No?" he said. "I was hoping to see you there."

"You'll be at the ball?"

He nodded.

She glanced up to Gwendolyn, who turned to see that they'd stopped. Seizing the moment, Gwendolyn grabbed Agatha by the arm and set off at a run. Cinderella's fingers started to smoke and, before the bouquet could catch fire, she dashed off after her stepsisters.

"What's going on?" Ty asked as he ran to keep up.

"It's hard to explain." More like she *couldn't* explain. "I need to keep up with my sisters, that's all."

"I'm not sure what's going on here," he said. "But if you do need someone to save you from something, perhaps I can help?"

"Thanks, but I don't need saving. Really." She did need saving, but she planned to save herself.

Cinderella noticed that Gwen had slowed her pace, clearly overtaken by fatigue as she was huffing and puffing, so she slowed to a walk, but kept Gwen in sight.

She put her nose to the bouquet and inhaled the sweet scent. He was so charming, but hard to understand. "Do you really work at the palace?" she asked Ty. "I'm starting to think you stole that uniform and the invitations from the real messenger."

"How could you think that of me?" He dashed ahead a few steps and then turned around to walk backward, a grin on his handsome, tanned face. "I assure you, I work at the palace. In fact, um, I'm involved in many areas of palace operations." He was about to fall over a stone in the road.

"Careful!" she said, but he sprang up and glided smoothly over the stone before the warning was out of her mouth. "How did you know that was there?" she asked, dumbfounded.

"The stone?"

She nodded.

He shrugged and said, "I know this path like the back of my hand."

Such concentration. But she realized it was the same kind of skill she'd been teaching herself. "Have you studied martial arts or magic?"

Ty strode alongside her. "Both. I'm training to become a wizard."

"Me, too." She raised a hand to her lips, realizing she'd told him something she didn't want her stepsisters to know. Plus, she'd exaggerated the extent of her education. Practicing her magic and ninja skills with a cat coach hardly counted as wizard training.

"You must have a wise teacher if he or she is including martial arts in your training," Ty said. "It really focuses the mind and body and helps them work together." He turned to her. "What wizard school have you been attending?"

To avoid answering, she checked that her stepsisters weren't watching, and then, still holding the flowers, did an aerial cartwheel.

"Nice. I've learned some acrobatics, too." Ty leaped up, did a twisting somersault, and landed right beside her without breaking stride.

"Impressive," she said, her belly getting strangely warmer.

She wanted to show Ty more of her skills, and ask him about his training, but she'd already been foolishly bold. Plus, since he'd arrived, she'd forgotten to pay attention to her surroundings. In fact, except for making sure she didn't catch on fire, she hadn't paid attention to anything but Ty. She was letting the opportunity to scope out escape routes slip through her fingers, all for a boy. Still, on the chance she ever did escape from her stepmother's spells—and she had to believe she would, somehow, someday—she'd like the opportunity to know Ty better.

"Are you planning to enter the magic competition the day of the ball?" he asked.

"There's a magic competition?"

"Yes, and the winner gets a year's training with the royal wizard."

"Really?" Her heart pounded with excitement. If she won, her stepmother couldn't stop her from taking the lessons without exposing her illegal use of black magic—she hoped. This could be her ticket out, if only she could figure out a way to enter the competition and win. "Lessons with the royal wizard?"

"Yup, and this year, there's another prize, something even better than that." His sleeve brushed against hers.

"Better?" She couldn't imagine anything better.

"If the winner's a girl," Ty continued, "she gets at least one dance with the prince at the ball." He turned to her as if he expected her to jump up and down and squeal with glee.

Cinderella gave Ty a mocking look and said, "Funny. I thought you said *better*."

"You're not interested in dancing with the prince?" He looked oddly hurt. "There aren't that many spots on his dance card, and girls are expected to fight over them."

"Not me. Why would I want to dance with the prince? I've never even laid eyes on him." She jumped over a rock. "If you get a break from your duties, I'd much rather dance with you."

He quickly turned to look at her, and his gaze was so intense, she felt heat rise in her chest and face. She checked to make sure she hadn't fallen too far behind her sisters again, but her flush was caused by a different kind of fire.

"I'd like that." He reached over and took her fingers in his, lightly, as if testing to see if she'd pull away.

She didn't, and when he wrapped his hand around hers more firmly, warmth shot everywhere inside her, spreading like the sparks in the fireplace after she'd used the bellows.

She looked up into his face and this time there was something more in his eyes, something she couldn't quite place, but liked. It seemed he wanted to hold her hand forever, and frankly, she'd be okay with that, even though his touch made her light-headed—as if she'd been spinning in circles or doing too many backflips in a row.

His eyes gleamed bright blue and the curls of his blond hair danced wildly behind him in the light breeze to stroke his neck, almost as if they were beckoning her to do the same. Her breath hitched, and she realized they'd stopped running. Not only that, they were standing closer together—so close that she could feel his body's heat, smell his spicy scent, and hear his breaths hitching, too. For a moment, it was as if the past thirteen years of her life hadn't happened, as if her father hadn't died and remarried, as if she'd lived a normal life like any other girl.

"Cinderella! Come here right now!" Gwendolyn cried.

Her stepsister's voice pierced through Cinderella's happy bubble, bringing her back to reality. She stepped back and dropped Ty's hand.

"Get away from that forest scum!" Gwendolyn's voice grew louder. "And drop those weeds. We're nearly at the gates to the village. It's embarrassing enough that Agatha and I must be seen with you, but if you're mooning around with this common rodent? I won't have it."

Cinderella stepped toward her stepsisters. "Just a moment," she called to Gwendolyn.

Gwendolyn's shouted, "If you don't come this instant, I'll—"

Cinderella knew exactly what that threat held. She gave the flowers back to Ty and, keeping her eyes on him, she walked toward her stepsisters. "I've got to go."

"Don't forget," he said, gesturing with the bouquet as if he were holding a magic wand. "I have a strong feeling you'll do very well. And either way, please come to the ball. I have a feeling you'll enjoy dancing with the prince more than you expect."

"I'll try," she said, and then turned to race after her stepsisters.

Try? She could try all she wanted, but there was no chance her stepmother would let her enter that magic competition or go to the ball. She'd missed that chance.

The woods were eerily silent as they made their way home from the village, and the stillness caused the hairs on Cinderella's neck and arms to raise. Something wasn't right, and she wished Ty were here. Someone who knew magic might come in handy in case of an attack.

She adjusted the new broom handle resting on her neck and shoulders, careful to ensure that the eight sacks of shoes and bags and beads she'd slung over the ends of the sturdy stick wouldn't slip off. The single coin her stepmother had given her had only been enough for the handle part of the broom, but it was no matter—she could attach fresh straw to the end.

The sun was low in the sky now, and created long shadows that stretched and bent in the evening breeze. At least Gwendolyn and Agatha were sticking close to her, but it wasn't clear whether this was because they, too, sensed danger in the woods, or because they didn't want their purchases to go up in flames. Their reasons didn't matter. Not having to keep a constant watch on them after that morning's chase was a relief.

"We should have hired a carriage," said Agatha, her voice trembling.

"Mother said you need exercise and fresh air to look your best for the prince," Gwendolyn replied, but she looked about her, as if she too sensed something wasn't quite right.

"Have you ever encountered trouble on this path?" Cinderella asked her stepsisters.

"Never," Gwendolyn said. "Thieves wouldn't dare attack fine young ladies such as ourselves."

"Why not?" When Ty had dropped from the trees this morning, Gwen had first thought he was a thief, so Cinderella sensed her stepsister was covering her fear.

"Don't worry," Agatha said when Gwendolyn didn't respond. Agatha leaned nearer to Cinderella and whispered, "Mother made up all of those thief stories when you were little, to scare you and make sure you didn't run away."

"Really?" She turned to Gwendolyn for reassurance, but her stepsister looked even more worried now. The color drained from her face, her jaw was tight with tension, and her lip trembled.

Cinderella took a long, cleansing breath to calm herself. No way would she let herself be scared. Not on the day she'd bought her first new possession in a decade. Not on the day she'd left the house in daylight. Not on the day she'd found a new friend—her only human friend.

Her heart warmed as she thought of Ty, and she wondered when she might see him again. When she got home, she'd tell her stepmother she'd made a mistake by declining the invitation to the ball. Even if the magic competition sounded better, she'd go to either if it meant another chance to see Ty. Given that her stepmother had let her out today, perhaps she would again.

Her steps feeling lighter, she picked up her pace, hoping her stepsisters would get the hint and match her speed. The faster they walked, the sooner they'd be out of these woods.

A swishing sound came from behind the trees, and the girls froze in their tracks. Cinderella spun to locate the source of the noise. Three masked figures with long swords in their hands landed on the path in front of them.

Thieves—real ones this time! Two in front and one behind. They were surrounded.

"Hand over your money and sacks," the tallest one growled through a black mask that covered his entire face. His tunic was also black, loose-fitting and belted around his waist with a red sash. The sword he brandished hummed as it cut through the air when he moved threateningly toward her.

Cinderella gasped. She and her sisters were doomed.

"Go away, you brutes! Gwendolyn shouted, squaring her stance and putting her hands on her hips. Her skirt vibrated slightly, revealing her trembling knees, yet Cinderella had to admire her bravery. Perhaps being mean came with an upside.

One of the thieves ran forward, leaped right over Gwendolyn's head, and landed behind her. He wrapped his arms around Gwen's body from behind, trapping her.

She stomped her foot, but the thief was quick and moved his foot, covered in a soft leather boot, out of the way in time.

Agatha started to cry.

Cinderella gripped the broom handle, still slung across her shoulders with sacks hanging off either end. Her heart thumped at an outrageous speed and she took long breaths to slow it.

Step one: gain control over her nerves. Step two: attack the thieves.

A broom handle was a poor substitute for a sword, but she could wield it like one. They wouldn't expect her to have any skills, so best to look defenseless to maintain her advantage of surprise. She bent over slightly, pretending that the burden on her shoulders was harder to carry than it was. With the pails of water she carried each day, the eight bags suspended from the broom handle were nothing.

Another thief grabbed Agatha, whose face was now red and streaming with tears.

"Bind their hands," the tallest one said to the other two. His voice was rough, as if he'd been drinking gravel. "I'll take care of the servant."

Cinderella kept her head bowed but her eyes observant, every sense alert to her environment.

The lead thief stepped forward and raised Cinderella's chin with a leather-gloved hand. Under his mask, all she could see was the glint of his eyes, flashing malice. "She's plain, and dirty," he said. "Still, perhaps we should keep her."

Cinderella bent to one side and let the bags drop off one end of the broom handle. As the bags on the other side slid toward her head, she crouched, swung the stick quickly, and knocked the man off his feet.

He landed on his back, and his sword fell from his hand. The second thief pushed Agatha to the ground and leaped forward just as the leader retrieved his sword and scrambled back to his feet.

Cinderella slid the other bags off the broom handle and, leaving it on her shoulders, she swiveled and spun, striking the second thief in the lower legs and the leader in the upper arm. His sword flew out of his hands and disappeared into the woods.

Both thieves backed away.

She transferred the broom handle to her hands, struck a warrior stance, and twirled the stick as she'd practiced so many times with her garden hoe. The broom handle was better balanced and made of stronger wood. If she could control the rapid beating of her heart and the fear threatening to freeze her muscles, she might be able to defeat the thieves.

The one who'd bound Gwen lifted his blade, so Cinderella struck his forearm with her stick to knock it away. Then she spun, twirling the stick. The lead thief lunged toward her, and she jumped, used his shoulder as a springboard, and executed a somersault, landing right between the other two.

Catching them off guard, she bent forward and spun the stick low, knocking them both off their feet. She raised the stick above her head and the two thieves cowered and scrambled away from her on all fours, like oversized crabs.

The leader retrieved his sword, lunged toward Cinderella, and she jumped to the side just in time to avoid his blade.

Another man landed on the road from the trees, and she braced for another attack. But it wasn't another thief—it was Ty!

After bracing himself, Ty leaped in a perfectly executed side kick, and his foot landed right in the lead thief's chest, sending him onto his back in the dirt. He shot Cinderella a quick smile and they positioned themselves back to back, circling, watching, and waiting. Cinderella twirled her broom handle, ready to defend against the next attack.

The lead thief stood and whistled. When he caught the attention of the others, he turned away and dashed into the woods at full speed without looking back. The other two followed.

Her heart racing with adrenaline, Cinderella dropped her stick, then turned and embraced Ty. His body felt warm and strong against hers. As she pressed her cheek against the linen shirt covering his chest, she heard his heart beating.

Self-conscious, she released him and stepped back, her breaths coming too quickly, her cheeks burning.

"You saved us," Agatha said from where she sat at the edge of the path, and Cinderella wondered if she was talking to her or to Ty. It didn't matter—they'd worked together and the thieves were gone.

"Untie me, you idiot!" Gwendolyn snapped.

The sound of horses' hooves came from down the path and Cinderella spun toward it.

"Get off the road!" she yelled at her stepsisters.

She helped Agatha while Ty helped Gwendolyn, who struggled against him.

"You brute!" Gwen said. "Unhand me, you dirty forest rodent."

The horses came into view and Cinderella heaved a sigh of relief. It was her stepmother's carriage, driven by her groom, who looked through Cinderella as if he didn't see her. Whether he was enchanted or not, none of the paid servants would ever make the mistake of actually speaking to her, lest they be turned into toads or mice or, as in one horrible instance six years ago, a doormat. Her stepmother took great pleasure at rubbing her feet on the mat that had once been her groom.

The carriage drew to a stop and her stepmother emerged, her wand drawn and pointed at Ty.

"Wait!" Cinderella stepped in the way. "He helped fight off thieves."

Ty finished untying Gwendolyn's hands, and she yanked herself away from him as if his touch was vile and much worse than being tied up.

Agatha ran to her mother's side and pressed her face into the bright purple fabric of her heavy dress. "It's true, Mother. It was so scary, but Cinderella and this hunter saved us."

"Get away!" Her stepmother waved her hand at Ty as if he were an ant climbing on her picnic lunch. "Scat, you dirty thing! Get away from my daughters. One of them is going to marry Prince Tiberius, I'll have you know."

"I'm sorry, Madam." He bowed with exaggeration, clearly fighting a grin. "I didn't realize I was in the presence of future royalty."

"Get lost!" Her stepmother raised her wand again.

Ty jumped up to grab a branch and then swung himself up to land on it. He tipped his head toward Cinderella and winked before leaping to another branch, then another, until he was well into the forest.

The brief warmth she'd felt at his wink disappeared when she thought of the thieves—not to mention the wolves—and she hoped that Ty would get himself out of the forest safely.

Cinderella turned to her stepmother, who was comforting a trembling Agatha, and boldness built inside her. If she wanted to gain permission to enter the magic competition, now was the best time to ask. It was possible Agatha might even back her up.

She cleared her throat. "Stepmother, I want to apologize for declining your generous offer to allow me to attend the royal ball, and I've reconsidered. I very much would like to attend the day's festivities, perhaps not the ball, but with your permission, I'd like to enter the magic competition." Hands sweating, she rubbed them on her apron.

Gwendolyn grunted, and pointed down at the bags Cinderella had slid off the broom handle when they'd been attacked. "Pick up our things, Cinderella. You're so careless." She stomped over to the carriage and got in.

Agatha pulled back from her mother, and looked back and forth between the wizard and Cinderella as if trying to gauge the situation. "She did save us, Mother."

Cinderella studied her stepmother, but the woman's face was an impenetrable wall, her emotions and thoughts buried in stone. Cinderella's insides trembled with twin threads of excitement and apprehension. She'd just saved her stepsisters from being attacked and robbed. How could her stepmother refuse such a seemingly simple request, especially since not days ago she'd offered to let her go to the ball?

Her stepmother turned to Agatha. "Get in the carriage, darling, the darkness is almost upon us." She turned to Cinderella and said, "Pick up those bags. I can't believe you could be so careless with your sisters' things, or their lives."

"I had to drop the bags to fight off the thieves."

"Silence."

Fear trembled through Cinderella's bones.

"You're foolish if you expect me to believe you fought off thieves. More likely you told them when and where to attack."

"No—"

Her stepmother raised her hand to silence her. "Only an ungrateful girl would put her sisters in the path of danger, or let them be touched by vermin like that boy who pretended to save them. More likely you and he planned the entire thing." She shook her head. "If I hadn't been worried you were so late and arrived when I did . . ."

Cinderella's lips trembled with the anger building inside her. Just how did her stepmother think she and Ty could have planned anything? She never had contact with the outside world. Even for her stepmother, this was beyond unreasonable, beyond unfair.

"Pick up those bags and grab onto the back of the carriage." Her stepmother got inside and leaned out the window. "Home, driver."

As the carriage turned, Cinderella scrambled to pick up the bags and her new broom handle, but before she'd finished, the carriage set off.

"And, Cinderella," her stepmother yelled out the carriage window, "you'd best hurry. You wouldn't want to get burned."

Will Cinderella find a way to enter the contest?
Will she ever see Ty again?

To find out, turn to section 4: Unexpected Assistance (page 107).

Section 4

———❦———

unexpected
assistance

Cinderella's jaw dropped open in disbelief. She never—ever—should have mentioned the magic competition. Now her stepmother had purchased magic wands for both Agatha and Gwendolyn, and the pair planned to enter to up their chances of impressing the prince.

"Let me try again." Gwendolyn pushed Agatha aside and raised her wand, a beautiful instrument handcrafted from ash. Gwen pointed it at a melon balanced on the edge of the foyer table, and the large fruit exploded, spraying seeds and flesh all over the table and floor.

Agatha clapped and squealed, "Great job, Gwen! You almost had it that time."

Cinderella crossed her arms and slumped against the paneled wall. Not only did she have to witness her stepsisters practicing magic and see the fabulous wands their mother had purchased, but she was the one who'd have to clean up this mess. It simply wasn't fair.

And as used to unfairness as Cinderella had become, now that she'd had a taste of life outside the confines of her prisonlike house, now that she'd learned lessons with the royal wizard were on the line, now that she'd met Ty, she'd uncovered entirely new depths to unfairness.

She couldn't lose hope, though. Since her trip to the village, she'd spent more time thinking of escape ideas than she had all of last year. But so far she hadn't come up with a plan that would actually work. She needed a real solution.

If only she had a wand, perhaps she could take her fledgling magic skills to the pro level. There was only so much magic one could do with one's mind. Maybe she could sneak into one of her stepsisters' rooms the next time they went to the village and borrow a wand.

She silently scolded herself for the thought.

Agatha raised her wand, pointed it at a melon, and the orb rose a few inches off the table. Cinderella was shocked at the concentration and determination in her stepsister's face as she raised it higher.

Gwendolyn coughed loudly, Agatha blinked, and the melon fell, smashing onto the inlaid wood floor, creating yet another mess for Cinderella to clean up.

Her stepmother appeared in the doorway. "Well done, girls, well done. At least someone in this family has some aptitude for magic." She cast a sneer at Cinderella, then turned to her daughters and added, "Now go get yourselves bathed. You need to try on your gowns again."

Her stepsisters looked at each other, grinned with glee, and Agatha clapped excitedly, like a toddler. "Just imagine if he picks me!"

"He won't. He'll pick me," said Gwendolyn, pushing Agatha aside as they raced up the stairs.

Her stepmother turned toward Cinderella. "What are you waiting for, you lazy girl? Clean this mess up at once."

"Might be easier if I had a wand," Cinderella muttered.

"What?" Her stepmother straightened her back, glared at Cinderella, and it seemed to Cinderella as if the woman had grown at least another four inches. She towered over her like a mountain of rocks about to tumble down.

"Nothing." Cinderella picked up some of the pieces of melon rind.

"You ungrateful brat."

Cinderella's hands stung, and she dropped the melon rinds. It felt as if the juice were suddenly laced with acid. She rubbed the burning juice onto her apron, and was relieved when it didn't eat away at the cloth.

Against Cinderella's will, her hands flew up above her head, and then her entire body was lifted and slammed high up on the foyer's paneled wall, nearly level with the second-floor landing. Cinderella was at the same height as the chandelier—the one she had to use pulleys to lower about twenty feet once a week so that it could be polished.

Her stepmother stood below, pointing her wand menacingly. Cinderella had seen plenty of rage on the woman's face, but nothing compared to this. Her features were twisted and distorted so that she looked more monster than human.

"After what your father did, how dare you mention that wand!"

Cinderella's insides trembled in fear. "What wand?" Her voice felt strained, but she took pride that it didn't waver.

Her stepmother's eyes narrowed. "You know very well the wand I am talking about. Your father stole a wand that was mine."

"My father was not a thief." Cinderella tried to pull one arm off the wall, but it was no use; it was as if her limbs had been cemented there.

"Oh, but he was. And a con artist of the worst kind, too." Looking up at Cinderella, her stepmother paced around the foyer, her forest-green skirts swishing on the floor. "He had no use for that wand. No magic at all. After we married, by rights it was mine. He tricked me into marrying him and then stole what belonged to me."

"There's no way my father would use any sort of magic to trick you into marrying him."

"He didn't cast spells, you idiot girl. He used your mother's wand to lure me into marriage, and then refused to hand it over."

"He wouldn't do that." Cinderella kept her voice calm.

"The man deserved to die." Her stepmother shot a bolt of energy at the opposite wall, and the portrait of Cinderella's father fell and crashed into the floor.

Cinderella's heart squeezed and she slipped a few inches down the wall. She forced herself to ignore her emotions so she could concentrate on struggling against the spell while her stepmother was distracted. She slipped another few inches.

Her stepmother spun, pointed her wand straight at Cinderella, and her eyes flashed with red sparks.

Cinderella felt a sting, then a churning in her belly. Her stepmother's magic was getting stronger, and she was becoming more vicious. Never before had she hurt Cinderella internally.

"You do know where it is, don't you?" her stepmother screamed.

"I didn't even know my mother had a magic wand," Cinderella said, forcing the lie from her lips. "How could I possibly know where it would be hidden?"

She felt her throat start to close, as if huge, invisible hands were wrapped around her neck.

This was it. Her stepmother had gone completely mad and was going to kill her. Cinderella closed her eyes and summoned every ounce of concentration she had. Using her mind, she lifted one of the melons off the railing and braced herself, gathering the power to hurl it at her stepmother's head.

Max meowed loudly and Cinderella opened her eyes. He leaped at her stepmother and slammed into her arm, breaking the hold that the wand held over Cinderella.

Cinderella slipped down to the floor, reacting instinctively and landing in a controlled ninja crouch. The melon smashed onto the ground.

Her stepmother flung Max off her arm and fine red lines appeared on her neck where he'd scratched her. She raised her wand again.

"Run, Max!" Cinderella shouted as she flung herself forward to block whatever heinous spell her stepmother was aiming at her defenseless cat. But she didn't get there in time, and her heart nearly stopped when she heard a loud crack and smelled smoke.

She spun toward the smoldering door to the sitting room. *No, please. Please let Max have escaped in time.*

Cinderella ran toward the door.

"Where do you think you're going?"

Cinderella spun around and stared into her stepmother's evil face. "He's just a poor, innocent cat! How could you be so cruel?" Hot tears of anger rose in the backs of her eyes. "Do what you want to me, but don't hurt my cat. I've told you a thousand times, I don't know where the wand is, and even if I did, do you think I'd give it to you now?" If she found it, she'd use it to break free.

Her stepmother narrowed her eyes, then strode from the foyer. Cinderella let out a long breath, realizing she'd escaped further punishment for the moment. Max, seemingly unscathed, peeked around the corner. Hope inched its way back into her heart as she formed a new plan for escape. She had to find her mother's wand, and find it tonight.

That afternoon, her stepmother and stepsisters went to a tea party to strategize with other girls who hoped to dance with the prince the next night. Their absence gave Cinderella her first chance to properly search the house.

Grunting as she finished pushing Gwendolyn's bedroom armoire back against the wall, Cinderella slumped to the floor of the room that had been hers as a child. She'd failed to locate a secret compartment or a lost piece of baseboard behind the huge piece of furniture, and was running out of possible hiding places to check for the wand.

She hadn't bothered searching her stepmother's room. The armoire and a chest of drawers in there, which had once been her parents', were sealed shut by magic in the same way the books in the library couldn't be moved, but it was unlikely her father would have hidden the wand there, anyway. Not if, as Cinderella now hoped, he'd hid it from his new wife.

The gong sounded to signal that someone was at the door, and Cinderella brushed her stray hairs out of her face. Deliveries typically went to the side entrance, where the cook could receive them directly into the main kitchen. A guest at the front door was most unusual. And now there had been two in one week.

The gong sounded again and she stepped out into the long hall that led to the stairs down to the foyer and front door. It sounded a third time. Apparently the visitor wasn't one to give up.

She shrugged. There were no more hiding spots here to search, anyway. She cartwheeled down the hall, performed a twisting back somersault, and landed on the post at the corner of the banister leading down to the foyer. Stepping onto the highly polished, sloping beam of wood, she put her arms out for balance and slid down the banister, one foot in front of the other. When she reached the landing, she leaped off the next post, somersaulted and twisted, pushed her feet off the opposite wall, and then landed on the next section of banister in a perfect handstand.

Carefully maintaining her balance, she walked on her hands down the sloping bar of wood to the next post and then pushed off to the side to land on the final flight of stairs.

And from behind her, she heard vigorous clapping.

She snapped her head around and spotted Ty standing in the foyer, dressed once again in the royal messenger uniform. He removed his plumed velvet cap and bowed.

"What are you doing here?" Her heart raced and her cheeks flushed.

"There was no answer, so—"

"So you just barged right on in?" She stomped down the last flight of stairs. "Who do you think you are, the crown prince?"

He backed up a few steps, clearly startled at her reaction, and she realized that her anger had been misdirected. She'd only been surprised and embarrassed to be observed without her knowledge, and had momentarily forgotten that Ty already knew she had these skills. It wasn't as if he was going to tell her stepmother. She trusted him.

"If you're here to deliver another message about the ball," she said more calmly, "my stepmother and stepsisters aren't at home."

"I'm glad, because I wanted to see you." He looked down, clearly ashamed about his breach of etiquette. "Forgive me," he said, tipping his head down. "I shouldn't have walked in just because you invited me to open the door myself last time."

She stepped forward, to be closer to him. "That's okay. I imagine working for the royal family, you're surrounded by people who have a sense of entitlement."

He lifted his sharply angled chin. "What do you mean by that?"

"I'm sorry." *Oh no,* she thought, *I've offended him.* She ran her hands down her apron and said, "It's wrong of me to think you'd be as conceited as the royal family just because you work for them."

He rocked back on his heels and crossed his arms over his chest. "They aren't so conceited, you know."

"Who?"

"The royal family." He relaxed his arms and put his hands out. "Yes, there are traditions which must be followed, certain protocols, but when you get down to it, the members of the royal family are just people."

She shrugged, not really caring about the royals and silently scolding herself for being rude to the only person who'd ever offered her something resembling friendship. "Can I get you something to eat or drink?" she asked. She immediately regretted what she said, realizing she'd just offered more than she could deliver. Everything consumable was locked up and so closely guarded by black magic, she couldn't offer him anything but water from the well.

"No, but I've got something for you," he said, and dug into the satchel slung over his broad chest.

"Really?"

He pulled out some papers. "Entry forms for the magic competition. It saves time on the day of the event if you fill them in beforehand."

She took the forms and excitement buzzed inside her for an instant, but it was quickly replaced by regret. "Thank you, but I don't think I'll enter the competition."

"Why not?" He removed the satchel and set it on the floor close to the door.

"It's hard to explain." She glanced at the pile of papers. "Why do some of these say beauty competition?"

"Winning that is a second way to guarantee a dance with the prince. I brought those in case your sisters might be interested. They seemed like the type."

Cinderella felt a sharp stab of jealousy and fought to shake it off. She'd never cared that her stepsisters were more beautiful than she was. In fact, she suspected her lack of beauty had made her life slightly easier, but Ty blatantly acknowledging the disparity hurt her in a way she barely understood.

"Yes," she said. "I'm sure they'd do well, as opposed to me."

Ty put up his hands. "Oh, that's not what I meant at all." He stepped forward, his expression earnest. "If I was judging, you'd win the beauty competition in a heartbeat. I just meant I thought magic was more your thing. That you'd enjoy that competition more, and I knew you wanted to win the lessons with the royal wizard."

She blushed. He was charming, she'd give him that. Clearly, he was just being polite about her looks. Still, something in the intensity of his admiring gaze hinted that he might be sincere.

Too embarrassed to ask, she set the forms on the circular table in the center of the room. "My sisters have decided to enter the magic competition," she told him. "My stepmother even bought them wands."

"But not you?" He stepped closer. His smile was so sharp and bright that it almost penetrated her skin.

She shook her head. "No, I didn't get a wand." She tried to make her voice light and airy, as if she could care less about the competition when, really, it was the most important thing in the world. But if she told him she wasn't allowed to enter, he'd want to know why—and she couldn't possibly explain without risking both of their lives.

"You really don't need a wand," he said. "They've got two separate groups, depending on whether you've had prior wand training or not. The no-wand group, in particular, involves testing for magic aptitude, and based on your acrobatic skills—"

Cinderella cut him off sharply and said, "I can't enter, okay?" Cheeks burning, she regretted that the heat was showing up in her voice too, and quickly tried to change her demeanor.

"It's just that you seemed so interested the other day." He reached toward her hand, but dropped back before adding, "I hope you will change your mind."

She wanted to compete more than anything, but she couldn't tell him that without leading them both into a dangerous area of conversation, so she turned and stacked the entry forms again.

Maybe she'd hide the magic ones downstairs, just in case, and leave the beauty pageant forms here for Gwendolyn and Agatha. They'd have a better chance in that competition, anyway.

"How long until everyone gets back?" he asked.

"I'm not sure. My family tends to be unpredictable."

"Why aren't you with them today?"

"Teas aren't my thing."

"No balls, no teas, no royalty—what *is* your thing, Cinderella?" He stepped forward.

He was even taller than her stepmother, and she had to tip her head back to keep contact with the bright, flashing blue eyes that showed genuine interest in her answer.

"Magic, martial arts, gardening." A smile that she'd felt building from deep inside her made its way to the surface and landed on her lips.

"You should really get some formal training," Ty said. "If it's a matter of money, I'm sure a scholarship could be arranged. With your raw talent—"

She backed away from him, her bottom hitting the edge of the foyer table, and the huge crystal vase of flowers on it tipped toward the opposite side.

They both lunged across the large table at the same time and prevented the vase from tipping over onto the floor. Cinderella ended up lying on her back on the table, with Ty bent over her.

"That was close," he said with a grin. "Would've made a huge mess."

He didn't know the half of it. Breaking the vase would've caused more problems for her than cleaning up a simple mess.

His muscular arm was bent, resting near her head on the table, and she'd never felt so self-conscious before. She felt as if she were totally exposed and he could see things about her that no one else could see, which made her uncomfortable.

"Can you show me some magic?" she asked, trying to figure out if she could wiggle out from under him without their bodies touching—and then wondering what it would feel like, should their bodies touch. "I've never had a real teacher."

"I'd love to." He pushed back to stand up and then offered his hand to help her down from the table.

She declined, and instead swung her legs down and slipped off.

"Let's go outside," Ty said, motioning toward the inner door.

She shook her head. "I'd rather stay in here, if you don't mind."

"Why?"

Her stomach tightened. She couldn't tell him that she was unable to go outside, because it would lead to questions she didn't want him to ask. "I, uh . . . don't want to get a sunburn." She looked out the window, relieved to see that the sun was out, making her excuse plausible.

"You are very fair-skinned." He reached his hand forward, as if he planned to touch her face.

She froze, not sure whether she wanted him to touch her or not. No one had touched her face in years, except in anger.

Ty dropped his hand, but her skin tingled as if he'd actually made contact. Who knew that something other than magic could make her cheek tingle? She backed away a few steps. "You were going to show me some of the things you do in your magic training?"

"Of course, but we can't do as much inside." He reached inside his coat and pulled out a thin white wand. "I do have this to help me, though."

Time passed quickly as they completed a few concentration and balance exercises and then performed the few acrobatic tricks they could do safely within the confines of the foyer. As she was the shorter of the two, she could pull off more tricks than he could, even without a wand.

"I know what we can do!" exclaimed Ty, reaching for one of the extra entry forms. He ripped it into narrow strips.

"What are you doing?" she asked.

"Wait and see." He placed the pile of paper scraps on the floor near her feet and looked up into her eyes.

She felt heat from his gaze. "What are you going to do with those?" She pointed to the pile of paper scraps. If even one of those wasn't picked up when her stepmother came home . . .

Before she could finish her thought, he'd raised his wand and the pieces of paper rose, too. First in a random grouping, and then, as she watched, amazed, he gathered them together into a tight ball in the air and scattered them everywhere.

They filled the entire foyer up to the vaulted ceiling, but none landed on any of the surfaces. Instead, the hundred or so small scraps of paper drifted like snowflakes through the room. She spun, delighted by the beautiful effect.

"It's wonderful!" she said as she turned to Ty and smiled. He returned her smile, then circled his wand above his head.

The scraps organized into lines, spiraling up and down through the room, snaking up along the railing of the banister to the top of the stairs, dancing around the skylight and then diving back down to spin circles around her.

"How do you do it?" she asked. "Can you teach me?"

He lowered his wand and the papers fell to the floor, but she was no longer thinking about her clean-up duties. She wanted to learn.

"It took me ages to master," he said. "But I was never able to move objects without a wand. The roy—the wizard who trains me, he made me try to move objects without the wand for almost eight years before he'd let me try it this way." He flicked the end of his wand.

"I can move objects, too," Cinderella said.

"You can?" His face brightened, startled by her revelation, but he also seemed proud of her.

"Sometimes." She stared at a few of the paper scraps and directed her open hand toward them. They rose off the floor, but she wondered if she could control their movement.

She circled her wrist and excitement built inside her as the scraps of paper circled, too. Their movements weren't as controlled as when Ty had done it, but still, she was just learning.

"That's fabulous," he said. "Fabulous!" He stepped up toward her and laid his hand on her shoulder. "I can't imagine how well you'd do with some formal training. You really must reconsider entering the contest."

The sound of a carriage outside infiltrated the room and Cinderella's warm, fuzzy feelings turned cold and prickly. "It's my stepmother," she said. "You've got to go."

She started to gather all the scraps of paper from the floor, panicking when she saw that some were caught up in the brass chandelier.

"Let me," Ty said. He raised his wand and all the scraps of paper gathered together and landed in a small pile on the table.

"Thank you." She grabbed them and stuffed them into her apron pocket, hoping that none would sneak through the small hole at the bottom she'd been meaning to mend.

"Listen," he said as he stepped toward her, "there's something I need to tell you, about me, but I'm not sure where to start." He fidgeted with his hands, and almost looked nervous.

She heard the carriage draw nearer and looked anxiously toward the front door.

"I suppose now isn't the time." He looked down, stashed his wand inside his satchel, then looked back toward her again. "Please change your mind about the competition and the ball. I'd really like a chance to dance with you." He bent down and pressed a light kiss on her cheek, and a wave of heat and joy, combined with terror at her stepmother's imminent arrival, rushed through her.

He put his messenger cap back on, tucked in his curls, and pulled the brim down to shade his face. "Until next time, Cinderella." He opened the door and looked out to the carriage just pulling through the gate. "I'll stall them. I'll tell them I only just arrived and no one answered, so

I left the forms on the foyer table. I'll flatter your sisters into entering the beauty competition. I have a feeling you'll be more likely to enter the magic competition if your sisters don't?"

He was right about that, thought Cinderella. "Thank you," she said.

As he went outside, she grabbed one of the forms for the magic competition and raced down to the cellar.

That night, as soon as she was sure her stepmother was sleeping, Cinderella yanked open the door to the back garden. Max brushed past her on the damp stone stairs as she ran up and into the garden.

If her father had hidden the wand, he'd hidden it well, and she felt almost foolish thinking she'd find it in one day, when her stepmother had searched for thirteen years. She'd searched the entire house now, including her own room. Not that she'd expected to find it down there. Her father hiding the wand in the cellar didn't make sense, given her fear of the place. Not if he'd wanted her to find it one day, as she'd started to hope. He couldn't have foreseen that his new wife would force his only daughter underground after he died.

Right now, her best strategy was to practice her skills. If by some miracle she figured out a way to escape and enter the competition, she wanted to be sharp. However, in the more likely event that she missed the competition entirely, and the stronger her magic and ninja skills were, the more chance she'd have of eventually breaking free from her stepmother's grasp.

At least her stepsisters were no longer entering the magic competition. As Ty had suspected, they'd fallen for his flattery and jumped all over the beauty pageant option. They'd practiced their smiles and walks and spins for the rest of the day.

She spotted her garden hoe leaning against the wall of the potting shed and, instead of walking over to grab it, she extended her arm toward it and concentrated on the hoe, imagining it lifting up and floating toward her.

Come to me, she thought. *Come.* Magic energy flowed through her, starting as a tingle and building in heat and strength and power, making her feel happy and alive and as if anything were possible.

The hoe lifted from the ground . . . one inch . . . two inches . . . three.

She maintained her focus and felt the energy flow out from her hand toward the garden tool.

Max screeched, a wolf howled, but she stayed focused, and, foot by foot, the hoe moved toward her, as joy and confidence increased her power. This was the farthest she'd ever moved the hoe, and it flew the last few inches into her hand. She jumped in glee.

A wolf snarled and snapped, and she turned to see Max pawing in the distance at that same place near the edge of the forest he'd been so focused on these past few days. He seemed to be going crazy. He was spinning and jumping and pawing at the dirt, as if he'd discovered a hidden cache of catnip.

"Max," she said as she walked toward him, carrying the hoe. "What's going on? First you attack my stepmother and nearly get crisped, and now you're taunting wolves?"

He turned to her, made eye contact, and then ran into the forest.

Cinderella froze, her entire body seized in terror, and then she ran. "Max!" If her cat were to be eaten by wolves, she couldn't handle the loneliness, not after all that had happened to her recently.

She plunged into the forest to find him pawing at the dirt about twelve feet in, at a spot in the center of a circle of six tall oak trees. He'd been pawing so hard, he'd already managed to dig a hole about three inches deep.

"Max!" She scolded him in a hushed tone as she picked him up with one hand, her hoe in the other. She quickly spun around, on the lookout for wolves.

He jumped from her arms to dig again, and she glanced into the forest and spotted a few pairs of red eyes in the distance, creeping forward, stalking, and no doubt preparing to attack.

She bent to pick up her cat again, but he writhed and twisted in her grasp. What could he possibly be digging for? It was almost as if he thought something was buried in that place.

And then she wondered, *Could it be the wand?* A ripple of hope flowed through her, which she quickly quashed. It made no sense. How could a stray cat know where her father had hidden her mother's precious wand so long ago?

Still, she was curious. She glanced up. The wolves were taking their time, strategizing, ensuring they were in a tight circle before they attacked. Escape seemed impossible, unless . . . unless there were a wand buried there.

"Out of the way, Max," she said as she raised the hoe. Max jumped aside to let her dig. She stuck the hoe's sharp edge into the hard dirt over and over, flicking dirt out of the way in a hurry, until the hole was nearly a foot deep.

She looked around. The wolves were much closer, only twelve feet away, their circle growing tighter. Even if she did find something hidden in this hole, how would she and Max ever escape the wolves?

Her hoe struck something hard and she fell to her knees, scraped the remaining dirt away with her hands, and found something wrapped in a heavy cloth. She pulled it out of the dirt and Max jumped onto her shoulder and meowed. Cinderella unwrapped the cloth to find an old box underneath.

Six wolves stepped into the circle of trees. There was no time to open the box.

Pressing the treasure into her belly, she pulled her apron up and around it to make a pouch, and tied her apron's strings tightly over the box—which she hoped contained the wand.

She snatched her hoe, the closest thing she had to a ninja sword. Max jumped down and stood next to her.

Planting her feet in a sideways stance, she held the hoe in front of her, her other arm bent back above her head for balance. She started to twist and rotate the hoe with her wrist, making large figure-eights in the air. She revolved slowly, warning each of the wolves with her eyes as she turned toward them. If they attacked, they'd get a strike to the head from her hoe.

Undeterred but cautious, the wolves crept forward slowly, their red eyes glowing, the silvery-gray fur on their backs rising. Condensation from the wolves' breathing fogged the air and drops of drool dripped from their razor-sharp teeth. As much as these wolves had kept her trapped all these years, she had been kept alive due to her stepmother's spell that prevented them from entering the garden.

But not tonight—not unless she got back inside the protective barrier of her stepmother's spell.

Still twirling the hoe, she spun more quickly, wanting to keep sight of all the wolves at once, but careful to keep her focus directly on her hand, so as not to get dizzy. Faster and faster she spun, faster and faster she twirled the hoe, faster and faster the trees moved across her vision until both the trees and the wolves became a single blur.

She slowed for a moment, but the blur remained. Max rubbed up against one of her legs. Cinderella gasped. It was almost as if she'd created a wall of air in the form of a swirling funnel to encircle both her and Max.

One of the wolves lunged forward, but he slammed violently into the tornado she'd created and was flung away, smacking into one of the trees. The wolf stood up slowly, whimpered, and limped away, somewhere deep into the forest.

She spun again, twirling the hoe, her feet burning from the friction against the forest floor. If she wasn't careful, the underbrush at her feet might ignite.

Another wolf lunged forward, mouth open, its huge teeth ready to bite, but again the wall of wind flung it off and into the woods.

This might actually save them. She felt Max rub against her calf and, still spinning, she started to step back, moving the circle of air toward the edge of the forest and the safety of the garden.

Another wolf tried to break through, then another, but her circle held, tossing each wolf aside in turn.

Her apron slipped. The box was going to fall. She lowered her arm to catch it and the circle broke down, dissipating into the night air.

Max jumped onto her shoulder and she ran. She ran as she'd never run before. Feeling the heat of a wolf's breath snapping at her heels, she took a giant leap and landed on the grassy surface of the garden. As soon as she hit the grass, she tumbled over several times, finally coming to rest on her back. Max pounced onto her chest and licked her chin.

She heaved, trying to catch her breath, and slowly turned to see three wolves peering out at her from the edge of the woods. They snapped and snarled, but could not take one step into the garden.

Breathing heavily, she sat, but dizziness took over and she fell back. Max returned to her chest, curled up in a ball, and purred.

He was right. She deserved a short rest.

Early the next afternoon, Cinderella stood at the front window of the house and watched the carriage carrying her stepmother and stepsisters pull through the garden gate and head down the path to the palace. They were off to the beauty pageant and then to the ball, and would not be back until the wee hours of the morning.

Even Cinderella had to admit her sisters would look beautiful in their ball gowns, which she'd packed into big boxes with endless sheets of fine tissue paper so they wouldn't sustain a single wrinkle on their way to the palace.

As soon as she was sure the carriage wasn't going to turn back, she raced down the cellar stairs. The magic competition started in less than two hours, and she still had to crack the mystery of that box—her last hope. She'd stayed up almost all night trying to make it open.

Lifting up the corner of her bed, she reached deep into the straw. Sleeping on the box the few hours she'd allowed herself to rest last night hadn't been comfortable, but it was better to feel the edges of the box digging into her side than to risk her stepmother discovering it.

She set the box on her lap. It was old and simple but beautiful, the joins in the cherry wood barely visible at the corners. A fine carpenter had crafted this box. Perhaps her father?

Now she remembered. The box had sat on her father's bedside table when she'd been very young. The wood's worn patina told her it was a well-loved, well-used box. It was darker in the spot where she'd pressed it last night, as if someone else's—her mother's?—fingers had pressed there many times.

Presumably, those fingers had managed to get it open. Her own attempts to do so hadn't worked. Clearly, the box required magic in order to open it, and in spite of Ty's encouragement, she obviously lacked the proper skills. She heaved a deep sigh. Max jumped up onto her shoulder and batted her head with his paw.

"Stop it, Max. You're distracting me."

He batted her head again.

"What, Max?"

Using her head, concentrating—that was it! "Maybe I need to visualize the box opening."

Max jumped off her shoulder and rubbed against her side, purring. She closed her eyes to focus and drew in a deep breath until she felt her heartbeat slow and a calmness enter her mind.

Open, she thought. *I want the box to open.* Tamping down her anxiety, she pressed her thumbs against the lid and pressed.

It opened, and so did her eyes—wide.

The box was lined with red velvet and had two compartments. She opened the long, thin compartment and saw what she'd been hoping to find—what her stepmother had so clearly been trying to find. It was her mother's wand, it just had to be.

She ran an eager finger along its pale wood surface. Was it pine, or perhaps birch? She wasn't sure, based on the grain and color. It might even be willow.

She lifted the wand and her fingers tingled. Max was going crazy, doing loops in and out and around her legs, brushing and meowing and jumping.

"Yes, Max, you're right. I should try it out."

She pointed the wand at her stool with its wobbly leg, not really sure what she was doing, but thinking that surely her mother's wand should be powerful enough to mend a stool leg. The stool fell over onto the floor. Well, that had not exactly been her objective, but she'd managed to make something happen. She might as well go for the gusto and try to escape.

She ran toward the garden door, which never opened while the sun was up, and concentrated.

Cinderella focused on the handle, then raised the wand and flicked it, saying, "Open, sesame."

A spark flew from the wand and struck the door. She was thrown off her feet onto the floor, and a charred streak appeared on the wood of the door. She jumped up, dashed over, and pulled on the handle. It was as sealed as it ever had been.

Max wound his way between her legs again, insistent and annoying. Maybe there were instructions somewhere in that box? She'd only opened the one compartment, so she tried the other and found a velvet pouch with something weighty inside it. She loosened the silk drawstring at the top and slid the pouch's contents into her hand. Her fingers caressed a beautiful golden necklace.

A heart pendant hung from a chain that was so fine she couldn't see actual links. She examined the pendant and saw a crack along its edge: a locket. Maybe the wand instructions were inside. She dug her thumbnail into the crack, but it wouldn't budge.

Max landed on her lap and she jumped. It was as though the cat had been drinking bowls of coffee. He lunged for the wand, trying to grab it in his mouth, so she tucked it into her apron pocket where he couldn't reach it.

She scratched his back. "Thank you for helping me find the box, Max. I don't know how you picked that spot to dig." The box must have emitted some kind of signal only cats could hear.

Max stretched up to place his paws on her shoulders, then retracted his claws and batted her chin with his paw until she looked down.

Cinderella shook her head. Sometimes she saw something in Max's eyes that resembled intelligence, but today he was being more of a pest. She picked him up and placed him on the floor. The contest was starting so soon and, without the wand, she lacked the power to break her stepmother's spell and escape the grounds. And if she didn't get out, she might never see Ty again.

Based on what Agatha had told her, her stepmother had threatened Ty yesterday when he'd tried to stall them upon their arrival home, so he was unlikely to return to the property. For his safety, she hoped Ty took her stepmother's threats seriously.

She pictured Ty's sparkling blue eyes, his shaggy blond curls, his strong jaw and lips, and imagined the teasing tone in his voice. Her belly stirred and she felt a stab of longing in her chest. At the same moment, the locket sprang open.

Gasping, she checked inside. It was another heart—solid, forged from metal and painted in deep red enamel. The beautiful object fit perfectly inside the locket. But as nice as it was, her heart sank. She hadn't found instructions on how to operate the wand. She placed the red heart back inside the locket and strung the chain around her neck.

She felt around the box for a hidden compartment, but found none.

Ah! The wand itself could have the answer. Perhaps she was supposed to use the wand to extract the instructions from the box. At this point, no idea was too silly.

Leaving the box on the bed, she took the wand from her pocket, backed away a few steps, and lifted the wand. Yes, this would work.

Concentrating, she bent her wrist to prepare.

Max jumped onto her arm. She jumped, and the bolt of magic energy hit the corner of the bed instead of the box. The straw sizzled and burst into flames.

"Ah!" She scrambled around her bed to grab a bucket of water. She doused the flames and then turned to pick up the wand, but Max had the wand in his mouth and was spinning around in tight circles.

"Silly cat!" she said. She tried to grab him, but he wouldn't stop. "Max, give me that. You're going to ruin it."

He spun two more times, backed up a few feet, and then, still holding the wand, he jumped into her arms and passed the wand to her.

Cinderella dropped Max to the floor, wiped the cat spittle off the beautiful wood, and then held it up to the light from the window. At least he'd been careful—it didn't look as if he'd left any tooth marks.

What could she try next?

Max jumped around her again, and she shooed him away. "Get lost, Max. Can't you see I'm busy?" She brushed her wand hand over the misbehaving cat.

On the third flick of her wand, a flash appeared above Max's head.

Cinderella froze.

Her cat disappeared under a searing blue-white light that flew from the wand and turned to smoke.

She'd killed her cat. Her heart clenched. *Please,* she thought, *please let him be okay.*

Drawing a deep breath, she fanned the air with her free hand as the smoke continued to build. There was so much smoke, but it was of a kind she'd never seen before. It was somehow lit from within. It glinted and sparkled and didn't smell the way smoke usually did. It smelled like cloves and vanilla and chocolate. It smelled like . . . magic.

Realizing that casting more accidental spells was not a great idea, she tucked her wand into the pocket of her apron, then waved at the smoke to find Max. It started to clear, but not in the way smoke normally cleared. It didn't spread and dissipate into the air. Instead, it gathered, became more solid, and took form.

She blinked a few times and tried to wave the smoke away, wondering if her eyes were playing tricks on her. The smoke looked as if it were forming into the shape of a person.

A moment later, a short, stout man appeared; he had silvery-gray hair and bright, flashing green eyes, and was dressed in an elegant suit of gray velvet with scarlet trim. A shiny black belt was wrapped around his ample middle. Bits of his hair shot out like tiny wings over his ears. He licked the back of his hand and rubbed it over his cheek, as if he were cleaning whiskers.

She staggered back, tripped over the toppled stool, caught her balance, and then gathered her courage. "Who are you?" Her voice was too soft, too timid. She pulled herself up, struck a warrior pose and this time demanded, "Who are you? Where did you come from? And what have you done with my cat?

The man looked down at his body in amazement and then up at Cinderella with a huge grin on his round, jolly face. He spun around in a circle, almost as if he expected to see something on his bottom. Then he looked back to Cinderella and smiled.

"You did it!" he said, sounding surprised. "I didn't know if you were ready to hold a wand, but under the circumstances, well, I thought it was worth the risk."

Cinderella gave him a stern look. "Where is my cat?" she asked.

"Cinderella," the man said, "it's me. Your godfather."

"I don't have godfather."

"Yes, you do. And thanks for digging up my wand."

"*Your* wand?" She gripped the edge of the table, wondering how long it would take her to reach the kettle hanging over the fire, the only object visible that could serve as a weapon. "That's my mother's wand!"

"It *was* your mother's." The man bent his legs a few times, as if testing them out, and then put his hands on the floor and stretched his backside up. His actions were remarkably similar to a cat's.

Something cracked. He winced as he stood and grabbed his back. "Oh, that's better." He winked. "After your mother died, the wand became your father's, but before he remarried, he gave it to me for safekeeping."

He tipped his head to the side in a slight rolling motion, and pawed his cheek with the back of his right hand. He continued, "That is, until you grew up."

"So, it's my wand?" She was so confused.

"Not yet." The man who called himself her godfather stretched out his fingers, pulsing them a few times, and then drew his nails along the top of the wooden table. Looking as if he'd suddenly remembered something, he cracked his knuckles and smiled. "I'd forgotten how good that feels."

He turned toward her. "I'm the wand's official guardian, and it's up to me to decide when you're ready. It's very dangerous for a fledgling wizard to use a wand without training, especially a fledgling wizard with such strong innate powers." He tipped his head to the side in a weird swooping manner. It was almost as if he were impersonating a cat.

"Still"—he jumped onto her bed, hands first, legs following—"it's impressive how you managed to control the wand. You helped me alter your stepmother's spell."

Cinderella backed away, gripping the wand tightly, wondering if she could use it to keep this strange, catlike man from attacking her. "Who—what are you?"

"Don't you recognize me?" He stepped off the bed, his arms spread as if he planned to hug her. "I'm your godfather, Fred."

"Stay away." She circled the table until it was between her and the man. "Are you a fairy?" She'd heard of such creatures living in the neighboring kingdoms, but had assumed they were just silly stories.

"A fairy godfather?" He laughed. "That's funny. No, Cinderella. I'm your *real-life* godfather, Fred. I came to visit you not long after your father . . ." he hesitated and bowed his head, then continued, ". . . not long after your father passed away." He took a step forward. "I could tell instantly that your stepmother was evil. She'd torn the house apart looking for your mother's wand, not knowing that your father had entrusted it to me before he married."

Cinderella sucked in a sharp breath. "Where's my cat?" She knew she was stammering, but under the circumstances, she decided to give herself a break.

"I saw how your stepmother was treating you, and told her I'd ask the king to grant you ownership of this house, even though you were barely five years old. Failing that, I planned to take you away from this place, forever."

Cinderella had a flash of memory. She *had* seen this man before, but his hair hadn't been quite so gray then. She'd giggled in his arms. He'd brought her candies and chocolate.

"I remember." Her breaths were shallow, but her body warmed and she instantly felt safer than she had in a long time. "What happened? Where have you been?"

"I turned into Max," he said. "Well, I didn't do it on purpose. Your stepmother tried to get me to tell her where I'd hidden the wand, and when I refused, she turned me into a mouse."

"But . . ." Cinderella shook her head. She'd been starting to believe him, but he was clearly crazy. She pushed herself along the edge of the table to keep it between them. "Max is a cat, not a mouse, and you still haven't told me what you did to him."

He laughed and held his belly. "I'm a wizard, you know. I was very powerful in my time. Not quite like your mother was, but good. I did a little tinkering with your stepmother's spell." He leaned onto the table and his fingers kept pulsing, almost as if he were kneading the table.

"Tinkering?" she asked, still suspicious.

"I didn't have enough experience combating black magic—no one does, it's been outlawed for decades—so I couldn't block your stepmother's spell, but I was able to alter it."

"I don't understand."

"Your stepmother turned me into a mouse, but the moment she left the room, I twisted her magic to turn myself into a cat." He swooped his head to the side and then batted at his head in a very Max-like gesture. "Cinderella, I'm Max." He pushed down on the table and jumped up to land on all fours. "Boy, that's not as easy as it used to be."

She looked into his eyes. Crazy as it was, it was true. She whispered, "Max . . ." and then stepped toward him. "Or do I call you Fred?"

He jumped back to the floor, rounded the table, and affectionately squeezed her upper arm. "You can still call me Max. I'm used to it now—and I kind of like it."

She dove into his warm embrace, his strong arms like a blanket wrapped around her. "Oh, Max. I'm so glad you're okay."

They embraced for a few moments, but then Max pulled back to hold her by the shoulders. "I'd love to have a nice long reunion, but we don't have much time."

The magic competition—she had almost forgotten! She glanced out the window to judge the angle of the sun. "I think I'm already too late." She reached up to touch the pretty gold heart.

"I see you found the locket," he said. "Your father gave it to your mother as a symbol of his love." Max smiled softly. "I cared for her, too, and hoped . . ." His voice trailed off and he paused for a moment. "Two wizards joined by the power of love are much stronger than the sum of their parts—but she didn't love me, and it was so clear your parents were very much in love."

An image of Ty's face flashed through her mind and tightened her chest, filling her with happy apprehension that stirred the nerves in her belly and made her swoon. Could what she felt for Ty be love? It didn't seem possible, but, she suddenly realized, the locket had opened when she'd thought about him.

But what did it matter if she were falling in love? Even if he felt the same way, they could never be together. Not with her stepmother's spell hanging over her.

She shook her head. Where had that thought come from, anyhow? Her only concern if she got free was forging a life for herself. And winning the magic competition was the first crucial step in that plan. "I wanted to win magic lessons today," she told Max. "But now I'm too late to compete." Not to mention still trapped.

"Nonsense," Max said. "You might miss part of the opening ceremonies, but you can still make it."

"Do you mean it?" She pressed her hand against her galloping heart. "Can you break my stepmother's entrapment spells?" Hope and joy buzzed around inside her. She was finally free.

Max licked the back of his hand, and wiped his hair back.

Her heart dropped. "I guess you can't."

"I can't *break* them." He held her arm. "The best I can do is temporarily suspend them." He paced around the room. "This has a better chance of working if I define a set time limit and link that to the cost."

"The cost?"

"There's always a cost when you alter black magic, but let me worry about that." He looked away, as if thinking, then turned back to her. "I can release you long enough to go to the magic competition and ball, but if you're not back home by midnight . . ." He twisted his lips. "Let's just say it'll be bad."

"Bad? How bad? What will happen? You have to tell me. Will I turn into a pumpkin or something?"

He shook his head and chuckled. "There are no orange gourds involved, my dear." His tone turned serious, "But the consequences will be bad—for both of us."

"What are the consequences?"

He paused for a moment to think, running the back of his hand over his cheek and then, as if suddenly realizing the feline nature of this gesture, he turned his hand over to rub his chin the way humans did, using his fingers.

"If you're not back by midnight, your stepmother's entrapment spells will become stronger, nearly impossible to break, and I"—he lowered his voice and looked down to the ground, hesitating before continuing with the truth—"I'll turn back into a mouse." He spoke so quietly she could barely hear him. "Forever."

Her chest nearly imploded. "Forever? Is that the cost?" She considered the weight of this cost.

He nodded and looked away, and she got the impression there was more he wasn't telling her. She grabbed his hand. "Then I can't go. The risk is too high. I can't have you turn into a mouse forever. What if I can't get back here in time?"

He brushed a stray hair off her cheek. "It's worth the risk, Cinderella. And you'll be back in time, I'm sure of it. I have faith in you."

"Do you have time to teach me how to use this?" She held up the magic wand.

"Oh, you won't be needing that." He reached for it.

"Yes, I will. I barely know any magic." She smiled sheepishly. "Well, you know that, don't you?" She shook her head, realizing how Max had been guiding her training, even in his cat form. "You've seen my limitations. I won't have a chance without a wand."

"Cinderella," he said, "you're bound to make mistakes if you use a powerful instrument like this wand."

"But I changed you from a cat to a person!"

"On purpose?" He put his hands on his hips.

She looked down. "Well, not exactly."

"That's because I did most of it, Cinderella. I put the magic into the wand. All you did was wave it over me."

Her heart dropped. "Oh."

He squeezed her arm. "You helped. You do have real magic inside you. Not everyone would have been able to complete my spell." A fleck of dust floated in front of him in the sunbeam and he batted at it like a cat. Then, looking embarrassed, he turned to her. "Trust yourself, Cinderella. The most powerful magic isn't inside a wand, it's inside *you*."

Is Max serious?

Cinderella's barely a beginner at magic. How in the world can she compete against others who've trained with less, um, feline wizards, and had wands their whole lives? Then again, Max seems to know a lot about magic, and even as a cat, he helped her a lot.

If you were Cinderella, what would you do?

OPTION A: Insist that Max give Cinderella the wand and then dash off to the competition. If he were that great at magic, he'd have turned himself back into a human years ago. He needed Cinderella's help for that, even if all she did was some timely wand-waving. She needs to win those lessons, and her mother's wand is her best chance to stand out from the crowd. Cinderella will be back by midnight to free him from the spell. If you think this is her best choice, go to section 5: Firestorm (page 143).

OPTION B: Cinderella should follow Max's advice and leave the wand behind. Even if he's still acting a bit feline, he's right. She has talent as a wizard, and can even move things with her mind. Cinderella can win without the wand. If not, she will have done her best. If you think she should give it a try, without the wand, go to section 6: Balancing Act (page 177).

Section 5

firestorm

"**D**on't be such a worrywart, Max. If my stepsisters can lift melons off a railing the same day they buy wands, then certainly after all you made me do in the garden I can do a lot better than that."

She hoped.

Max beamed at her acknowledgment of his help, but then his expression turned serious. "Decide for yourself, Cinderella. Magic is in your blood, but I trained with a wizard for three years, working on concentration and body control, before I was allowed to even touch a magic wand."

"But I've trained with you for longer than that." She wondered if training with a cat counted. "Besides, one way or another, I need to get out of this place. The competition is starting soon, and even if I run, it will take me at least thirty minutes to get down the forest path to the village. Unless . . ." She looked at Max and a sheepish smile spread across her face as she considered using her new wand to conjure a carriage and horses to take her.

She realized she was getting way too ahead of herself. She wasn't even out of the house yet. "Are you sure you can get me out off the grounds?"

"Yes, I can," he said. "But remember, be back by midnight, and not a moment later."

She nodded and tucked the locket inside her dress. It felt warm and heavy next to her skin.

"Now, give me the wand," Max said.

"No." She put it behind her back. "I'm using it to compete." She'd decided. Using the wand had its risks, but it was her best chance.

He put his hands on his hips. "If I don't alter your stepmother's spell to break you out of here, you won't get to the competition."

"Oh." She reluctantly pulled the wand out and handed it over. "You'll give it back, right?"

Max nodded, but he didn't look pleased at her insinuation. He backed up a few feet, cleared his throat, and adjusted the shiny black belt over his round belly. The look on his face told her he was more perplexed than confident.

She was suddenly apprehensive. "Are you sure you can do this?"

He licked the back of his hand and wiped it over his forehead, pushing his hair back. "Shh. Give me a moment. It's been a few years since I've tried anything this big."

"You could do magic as a cat?"

"Some. How do you think I got that book off the shelf?" His bushy eyebrows pulled together in concentration.

To give him space, she backed over to the side of the room in front of the cupboard. She didn't want to get her hopes up too high, but the past hour had been the most incredible of her life. She'd finally found her mother's wand, helped turn her cat into her godfather, and now he was breaking her stepmother's entrapment spells! Even if the break was only temporary, it was the freedom was exhilirating!

Max lifted the wand, then sniffed around the room, occasionally bending to put his ear up against a piece of furniture.

A look of defeat on his face, he lowered the wand. Then, eyes widening, he raised it in triumph, only to lower it once more. He repeated this curious motion several times.

Cinderella's hopes dove up and down with his wand, and she fidgeted, pulling at a loose thread on her apron, resisting the temptation to stamp her foot and insist that he hurry. Before she even reached the competition, she had a long run into the village ahead of her. And thieves in the forest might slow her down.

"Ah," he said after resting his hand softly on the handle of the door to the garden. He backed up and then turned in a slow circle, raising and lowering the wand.

As he turned, pink sparks came off the wand and transformed into an undulating trail of sparkling waves. Max muttered as he turned, but Cinderella couldn't make out his words. It sounded like nonsense. If this was how one used a wand, how in the world was she going to win the competition? She didn't know the words for the spells.

She studied Max carefully, paying attention to every detail, hoping to pick up some clues and remember, but whatever he was doing was far too advanced. Even with her little fire-starting incident, she hadn't made the wand spark. Not like that. She hoped the competition judges wouldn't expect her to do these kinds of things, but if Max didn't pull this off, she'd never have the chance to find out.

The sparkling pink waves now surrounded Max, as if he were spinning inside a shimmering veil, and just when she thought he'd wear a hole in the flagstones from turning so much, he stopped abruptly and raised both arms in the air.

The waves flowed out from Max and slammed into the walls and ceiling and floor, then rippled back to the room's center before heading directly for her. She pulled in a breath and braced herself, expecting the usual pain that accompanied her stepmother's spells. As the energy swirled around her, every hair on her skin rose and tingled.

Tiny sparks—pink and silver and gold—traced their way up and down her arms, her legs, her entire body.

Something slammed into her, and her body tensed. An invisible force tightened around her ribs, but it wasn't painful; it was more like a giant hug, and in spite of the magical embrace, fear crept through her excitement and amazement. She suddenly became nervous and wondered what Max was doing. What if his spell alterations got all mixed up and *she* turned into a mouse?

The sparks consolidated into a long line, circled her five times, then trailed and swirled back into the wand. Max flicked the wand again, hard, toward the cellar door, and then lowered his arms.

His face was bright red and he bent over, panting.

She ran to his side. "Are you okay?" She rested her hand on his heaving back, resisting the urge to scratch at the gray velvet as if it were fur. "Please tell me you're going to be okay. I don't care if I can't compete. It's not worth it if it's going to hurt you."

Still bent over, he raised his hand and pointed toward the cellar door. A cool breeze blew in, carrying a few dandelion seeds to dance over the stone floor.

She gasped with a breath full of joy and hope.

The door was open.

She clapped her hands and twirled, happier than she'd felt since before her father had died—maybe ever.

"You did it!"

He straightened and smiled, but he looked a little tired. "Can you get me the stool?"

She fetched it and held his arm as he sat. "Careful, Max. It has a wobbly leg."

"I know. I've been living here, too." After sitting down, he held her hand and guided her to stand squarely in front of him. He examined her dress and squinted his eyes. "Now, about clothes. You're going to need a gown and slippers for that ball."

"No." She shook her head. "There isn't time. Besides, all I care about is the competition."

"You should go to the ball, Cinderella. A girl like you deserves a little fun in her life."

The idea was tempting, especially if she got a chance to see Ty, but she had to focus. "Max, if I don't get going, I won't make it to the competition."

He squeezed her hands. "Okay, then let's get you something to wear for that."

She stepped back and he got up to cast another spell. Within moments she was no longer dressed in her rags; she was dressed in a sleek white top and trousers, belted at the waist. She leaned and kicked to one side and then to the other. Perfect. It was similar to a ninja outfit, except white, and offered much freer movement than would have in her skirt—let alone a fancy dress.

Max took her hand. "At midnight, no matter what you're wearing, you'll find yourself back in your normal clothes. In fact, at midnight, *everything* goes back the way it was, even—" He stopped himself midsentence and looked down.

"Even what?" There *was* something he wasn't telling her, maybe some other element to the cost.

"Never you mind," he said. "Just be back by midnight."

"I won't let you down." Midnight was no problem. It was too bad she couldn't keep this great outfit to train in, but she had no place to hide it anyway. And as for changing back into rags, as long as these clothes lasted until the competition ended and she caught a few moments with Ty, she would be happy.

Even if her dreams to escape today had been quashed by the need to get home to save Max, as long as she won those lessons, escape would be in her future, somehow. Surely her stepmother couldn't stop the royal wizard if he wanted to train her.

She picked up the wand and tucked it into a narrow pocket along the chest of the jacket, clearly designed for that purpose. She pressed her hand into her chest, glad to find the locket still there after Max's spell.

"Are you still determined to compete with the wand?" Max asked.

She nodded, nerves scrambling her confidence. "Yes. I mean, look what you did with it. I know I don't have your training or experience, but even so, it's clearly very powerful." Plus, it did belong to her mother, so it should match her innate powers. She'd ignore the fact that while using it, she'd tipped over the stool, scorched the door, and nearly set fire to her bed. Instead she'd concentrate on how she'd helped to turn a cat back into a man. It was all about confidence.

Max shook his head, but smiled in a way that made her think of her father. No wonder the two had been friends.

"The power of the magic is not in the wand, Cinderella. The power is inside *you*." He pulled her toward the open door. "Now, let's talk about your transportation."

Clutching her wand, Cinderella ran toward the guard standing in front of the competitors' door to the arena. The horse and carriage Max had miraculously made for her from bits and pieces he'd gathered in the garden had gotten her here fast, but not fast enough. Too bad it was only a one-way ride, but she could easily run home.

Max had wasted too much time trying to talk her out of using the wand. Although still nervous about her decision, she figured she needed all the help she could get. And as the daughter of the wizard who'd owned and trained with this wand, surely she'd be able to harness its power.

"I'd like to enter the magic competition," she told the guard.

"You're too late," he replied coldly, widening his stance. His huge body blocked the entire entranceway.

The chatter of a crowd of young people floated through the dark passageway behind him, beyond which she could see the glow of a brightly lit room, or perhaps it was the sunshine gleaming from the arena floor itself.

Maybe she should duck through his legs? No, that might get her in, but it wouldn't get her entered, and to win she needed to be officially entered. "I've got the application filled out," she told the guard, and pulled it from the back pocket of her trousers.

"Still too late," he said.

"Please." She stepped back and bowed her head slightly in front of the man. "You wouldn't believe what I went through to get here. Entering this competition is a matter of life or death."

"Life or death? Yeah, right." He slanted one side of his mouth up in obvious skepticism.

"Yes. Life or death." Because clearly she'd die one day at her stepmother's hands if she couldn't break free of her spells.

"Listen, lass." The guard's face softened at her earnestness, but his stance did not. "Hundreds of pretty young things like yourself want to win a dance with Prince Tiberius, but they showed up on time. Why should I make an exception for you?"

Cinderella bit down on her lip. He had made a good point. She wasn't anyone special, and asking for exceptional treatment, well, that was just wrong.

Her heart sank. Max had taken such a risk in breaking the entrapment spells for the day, and she'd wasted it. Now she'd have no chance to win the lessons and she certainly couldn't go to the ball dressed in this outfit. She took a long breath to force out her disappointment. "Is it too late to go in to watch?" She would make the most of it, and maybe learn some new magic by observing.

And even though she couldn't compete, she had until midnight to get home. Might as well take advantage of her freedom, however short-lived it might be. Ty told her he watched the competition every year, so there was a chance she'd find him inside.

The guard gestured to the right with his head. "Spectators' entrance is that way. Don't know if you'll find an empty seat at this time, but you can give it a go."

"Thank you." She curtsied to the guard, and then turned to head for the other entrance.

"Wait a moment there, lass!" the guard called after her.

Cinderella's heart froze along with her feet, and she slowly turned. He was probably going to tell her she needed money to get in, or wasn't allowed into the stands with her wand. She should have kept it hidden.

"Here." He raised his hand and flipped his thumb. A coin floated toward her and she reached out to catch it. A silver coin! She'd seen them, but never touched one before.

"Buy something to eat," he said. "Looks like you need it."

Cinderella's face broke out into a huge smile and warmth filled her chest. Her belly, especially pleased at the man's generosity, grumbled. "Thank you. You're very kind. Someday I'll find a way to repay you." She had no idea how—after tonight she'd be trapped in the cellar again—but she meant what she said.

"No need." He smiled and waved her on. "Now get in there and enjoy the show."

Cinderella walked up the long, winding tunnel into the arena, hearing and feeling the electricity and excitement before she could see anything, and when she burst out into the light, her breath whooshed out of her chest. There were so many people!

Brightly colored banners waved, and cheers rose from the rows upon rows of seats in the round arena that reached up toward the sky like open palms. The vibrant colors were like nothing she'd ever seen, nothing she'd ever even imagined.

And the smells—sweet and spicy and hot—from vendors who milled through the crowds, offering treats that made her mouth water. She quickly selected a sausage on a fresh roll and a mug of spiced pomegranate juice, and after eating her food way too quickly—it was so much better than any of the scraps left on her stepsisters' plates—she stepped up to a railing and searched the stands below for an empty seat, but found none. She turned to look up. It didn't look as though she'd have much luck higher up in the stands, either. People were crammed into the seats like pickles in a jar.

Wandering along the circular walkway, halfway up the stands, she searched for an empty seat. She spotted one just behind where she'd bought her food, but then saw it had a purple satin cushion and was much more spacious than the hard stone seats everyone else seemed to have. It had to be reserved for a member of the royal family, perhaps even Prince Tiberius.

She checked over her shoulder to see if she was blocking anyone's view—there were advantages to being short—and then leaned over the railing to look down to the arena floor. Maybe she could stand here for a while, before one of the guards asked her to find a real seat.

The opening ceremonies were nearly over, and the royal wizard was in the center of the vast arena, dressed in a flowing robe that looked as though it were made of water. It flowed and rippled around him. As he swung his arms, the fabric shimmered in the sunlight, creating the illusion of icicles. Then it changed again, turned white, and thousands of tiny birds flew forth, spiraled up into the air, and evaporated. It was spectacular, but the wizard himself was smaller and younger than Cinderella had expected.

The royal wizard flew up to a chair high above the field. The announcer raised his hands. A hush fell over the crowd.

"It is time for the competition to begin," the announcer said. "The first event will be for contestants competing without wands."

Cinderella twirled her wand in her fingers and felt its heat and energy flow through her. What she wouldn't give to get down on that floor.

A hand landed on her shoulder and she jumped.

It was Ty! She threw her arms around him, but, embarrassed, quickly let go and backed up a few steps. Her heart beat rapidly and her cheeks, she was sure, screamed with redness.

"You came," he said with a smile. "Aren't you competing?"

"I couldn't get here in time."

Ty was dressed in his messenger uniform again, but this time it didn't fit well. It was as though he was wearing an entirely different set of clothing. His pants were too short and too wide. He had cinched them at the waist with a beautiful gold cord that didn't match the rest of his outfit. Once again, his cap covered his curls and shadowed his face.

But even shaded, his blue eyes flashed, and her belly flipped. To calm it, she focused on the action down on the arena floor.

He moved beside her, so close that their arms brushed, and bent toward her so that his lips were right next to her ear. "If you don't enter, how will you win a dance with the prince?"

"As if I could go to a ball dressed like this."

"If you win, I'm sure the prince will arrange something suitable." His voice was deep, but instead of calming her belly, it made it dance. He seemed to know a lot about the prince.

She kept her eyes down on the field where the first set of ten contestants were walking across a tightrope ten feet off the ground while wizards below them threw balls of fire at their feet.

"Oh." Her heart rose to her throat as one of the contestants, a gangly teenage boy, fell off the rope and landed on his side on the ground. "That must have hurt." One of the wizards rushed to his side, but it appeared the boy was out of the competition. She glanced up to the scoreboard, and one of the numbers, listed in shimmering lights, disappeared.

"Don't worry," Ty said. "That wizard is a healer. The boy will be fine."

"I hope so. He must be so disappointed."

"Doesn't look like the prince's type." Ty chuckled and bumped her hip softly with hers.

"What's with you and your prince obsession?" Cinderella asked. "I only wanted to enter to win the lessons with the royal wizard. I told you, I don't care about a dance with the prince."

Ty's head twitched. "It's not *just* a dance, you know. The prince will be choosing his bride."

"Like marriage is such a great prize." Cinderella gasped as two competitors were knocked off the tightrope, one after being hit in the side by a huge fireball.

"Don't you want to get married?" Ty ran his hand along the railing. "I mean, someday?"

He sounded hurt, and the expression on his face matched, so she turned her attention from the competition to him. "Of course I do. Someday. I'd love to be a mother." And she'd love her children and treat them with respect. "I suppose it'd be nice to have a partner in life, too, but I plan to have some say in choosing him. No way do I want to be plucked out of a field of other girls, like a piece of fruit at the market. Don't you think it's kind of insulting?"

He crossed his arms over his chest. "Maybe it wasn't the prince's idea. Maybe he's being forced into it."

"That would be very sad for him."

Ty's face brightened, their eyes met, and she felt as though they were the only two people in the arena. The noises and sounds and smells fell away and she felt strong and confident, as if she could accomplish anything she set her mind to do.

If only she could see Ty every day, she'd surely find a way to escape. Just looking into his eyes made her feel stronger, yet nervous, all at the same time. Confused as she was by her conflicting emotions, she liked the strange feeling and never wanted it to end.

"Hey, you two!" called a voice from behind them. They turned to see a big, burly guard lumbering in their direction. "You can't stand there."

Ty took her hand. "Come this way. I know one of the organizers. I want to watch you win those magic lessons."

Cinderella stood with her back to the wall in the backstage area and waited. The room was filled with dozens of young people, all holding wands at the ready and some studying spells in huge books. Her stomach stirred with excitement as Ty approached the wizard in charge, and she hoped he didn't get kicked out of the arena for trying to help her—or worse, lose his job as a palace servant.

The wizard frowned for a moment, and a perplexed look formed on her round face, but then she smiled and nodded. It almost looked as if the wizard was about to curtsy, but then Ty reached out his hand and she stopped.

Odd—but the ways of the world outside her home were all strange and new.

Ty turned and motioned for Cinderella to approach. "You're in, but you've got to hurry." He handed her a piece of white cloth with the number 43 painted on it in bright red. "The tightrope event for the no-wand group is almost over."

"Oh." Cinderella held up her wand. "I've got a wand."

"I see that." Ty took her arm, bent down, and spoke softly. "How much experience do you have with that?"

"Not much, but it belonged to my mother. My real mother. And she was a very powerful wizard."

"I'm sure she was." Ty nodded. "You are full of surprises, Cinderella. I'll get you a number for the other group, if you're sure."

"I am." There was no sense in going back on her decision now.

Ty turned back to the wizard in charge and she handed over another number, this time with 98 painted on it. He helped her pin the number on the back of her shirt. "It's not too late to change to the other group, you know. Are you sure you don't want to?"

As she turned, his fingers grazed her waist and he blushed.

Her entire body tingled. "No, I'm sure."

She wasn't sure. Not of even one thing, and nerves buzzed inside her like bees in a hive. But having the wand in her hand felt like having her mother's support. Besides, she told herself, using the wand, she'd turned Max from a cat into a man, and that was *huge*. Even if he'd helped, and it had been a bit of an accident.

Uncomfortable with her choice, she looked into Ty's blue eyes and instantly felt calmer.

She might not be sure of her potential or talent as a wizard, she might not be sure about using the wand, she might not be sure she had any chance of winning this competition and finally gaining the skills to break free of her stepmother's spell, but she *was* sure about Ty. She was sure he was a boy who believed in her, who cared about her in a way no one else did—or ever had—who made her feel like she belonged. Looking into his eyes, feeling the warmth of his reassuring smile, and standing next to his tall, strong body, she felt as if she could accomplish anything she wanted.

"Hurry," said another wizard, robed in emerald green and not much older than her from the looks of him. He motioned to Cinderella. "You need to join the others."

"Good luck," Ty said. He smiled and bent down to gently place his lips against hers.

A spark of warmth and happiness shot straight from Cinderella's lips to her heart.

When he pulled back, she raised her fingers to touch her mouth, expecting it to be changed, or on fire.

The wizard in the green robe took her arm and pulled. "Come now," he urged her.

"Where will I find you?" Cinderella called to Ty, but he only touched the tattered cap he wore over his curls.

Now she was even more determined to win. The chance to see Ty more often—and maybe get another kiss—was an extra incentive for gaining her freedom.

The pumpkins were huge and Cinderella wondered if her stepsisters had possessed inside information, since they had been practicing all day on melons.

Another rush of relief that her stepsisters had decided to go for the beauty competition flowed through her. They, and her stepmother, were in the theater across the courtyard from the arena, no doubt primping and preening to pretty themselves for the pageant. Thank goodness they weren't in the stands—that was one less thing to stress over. And she wasn't short on stress, not by a long shot.

She leaned forward to peek down the row of competitors. A mixture of males and females, most looked to be in their late teens, but their ages appeared to range from as young as ten to about twenty.

A wizard in a shimmering black-and-purple-striped robe stood between the lines of contestants and pumpkins and raised his hands to silence everyone. "For their first event, the wand group must raise a pumpkin at least three inches off the surface of this bench. Each competitor must focus only on his or her own pumpkin. Interference will not be tolerated."

Cinderella rubbed the wand between her fingers. This task would be easy. She'd lifted objects *without* a wand. Lifting them *with* a wand should be a snap. Yet her belly kept doing backflips as she watched each contestant attempt to raise a pumpkin up to the level of the red bar painted on the board behind the bench.

After thirty-one attempts, only fourteen contestants had lifted their pumpkins high enough to pass, and there were no second chances. As soon as the pumpkin touched back down to the bench, that was it, game over, and it was on to the next contestant's turn. Each event in the competition yielded points from the judges, but if someone scored zero on any three tasks, he or she was out.

Watching the girl next to her raise her pumpkin, anxiety overtook Cinderella, stirring her insides and making her knees tremble. To combat the trembles, she thought about Ty, about the reassurance in his eyes. She thought about Max and how he'd been watching over her all these years, even though he'd been trapped inside the body of a cat. She thought about her father and how gentle and kind he'd been. How much he'd loved her. And she thought about how she'd suffered so many indignities and injuries at her stepmother's hand, and yet had survived.

Most of all, she thought about the mother she'd never met. Based on her father's stories, she'd been very talented, honest, and principled—known for never using magic for her own personal gain or to hurt others—and might one day have become the royal wizard, had she lived. Pride flooded through Cinderella, expanding her chest, as she thought about being the daughter of such a woman.

The girl beside her cheered her own success, pulling Cinderella out of her memories.

Her number was called and Cinderella pointed her wand toward the bright orange gourd. *Lift*, she thought. *Lift*. This shouldn't be that different than just using her mind. The wand was meant to enhance those abilities—provided she could control its power.

Her focus was intense, and all the sounds and smells and sights of the arena melted away until it was just her and the pumpkin, as if she were back in her garden.

She slowly raised the wand and the pumpkin rose, quickly reaching the required height. Not taking any chances, she gently set it back down. Why be a show-off? The judges hadn't awarded any extra points to the boy who'd lifted his six feet and made it spin.

The crowd applauded her success and she soon learned that those who'd been successful—fewer than half—were moving on to a bonus round, also involving the pumpkins. This time, it wasn't enough to simply lift the pumpkins. Each contestant had to lift his or her pumpkin from the bench, move it up and forward, and then set it down on the top of a six-foot pole with an impossibly small disk at its top. The pumpkins would barely fit on the disks, leaving no room for error.

There was no way she could she pull this off without the wand. She'd never moved anything so far, or placed it onto such a small target. She watched as the other contestants worked on their pumpkins. A tall girl, number 87 and dressed in a bright blue, loose-fitting jumpsuit, got hers right on the edge of the disk before it dropped.

Cinderella sucked in a sharp breath, her heart breaking for her competitor, but the girl thrust her wand forward, and the pumpkin stopped to hover a foot above the ground, intact.

The crowd roared its approval. Number 87 widened her stance, lifted her wand, and the pumpkin rose higher, until it was once again above the pedestal. She let it hover a few moments, sweat rising on her brow beneath her dark, tightly tied-back hair. Then 87 slowly lowered her wand, and the pumpkin came to rest on the disk.

The crowd went wild. Cinderella jumped up and down, clapping, and then realized she was the only other contestant doing so. Yes, she wanted to win, but she couldn't help but feel thrilled for this contestant. If Cinderella didn't win, she hoped that this girl did. If the prince was as tall and handsome as he was purported to be, they'd look fabulous dancing together.

A spark hit the ground at 87's feet and they both jumped.

Cinderella spun around, fearful that her stepmother had come into the arena and had been aiming for her. Hearing a commotion down the line of competitors, she looked toward it, and within seconds a rope appeared out of thin air in front of a tall boy with silver hair. The rope ensnared him, binding his arms to his body, then it led him off the arena floor, without any evidence of someone pulling. It must have been that boy who'd shot the spark at the girl who'd done well.

Number 87 fell back into the line of contestants as her score was updated on the huge sparkling board. Forty-eight points.

Cinderella had trouble keeping still as she awaited her turn. If she missed the first time as 87 had, there was no way she'd have the skill and concentration to catch such a huge, heavy object in midair and guide it back up. That seemed far beyond her capabilities.

"Number ninety-eight," the announcer called.

Calm down. Calm down. Calm down.

Her attempt at meditation wasn't helping and anxiety sent little spikes of fear up and down her arms, over her neck, and into her brain.

She gripped the wand and reminded herself how easily she'd lifted the pumpkin in the first round. Surely lifting it a little higher and moving it forward wouldn't be that different. Especially with help from her mother's wand. She could do this.

After bowing to the judges, she turned to the bright orange gourd and studied its off-kilter shape. It was a huge pumpkin, nearly three feet in diameter and likely so heavy she'd struggle to budge it with her body, let alone her mind. But the wand would give her a chance. If she hadn't found it, she wouldn't even be here and Max would still be a cat. She'd been meant to find it. Meant to use it, she was sure.

Using her ninja training, she drew five deep, long breaths, trying to force what felt like bouncing beans in her belly to obey. They slowed to hopping and, given the circumstances, she figured that was probably as calm as she'd get.

Aiming the wand, she reminded herself whose daughter she was and tried to mimic what 87 had done, but until 87 missed the disk the first time, she'd made it look easy. Several competitors had raised their pumpkins high enough to make the attempt, but only two had managed to land their gourd on the pedestal.

Energy from the wand coursed through her and she slowly raised it. The pumpkin rose, too.

Joy rushed through her and the pumpkin wavered. She sucked in a sharp breath, but let it out slowly, refusing to let panic creep in and ruin everything she had worked so hard for.

Focused on the pumpkin, she raised the wand again, and the instrument tingled in her fingers, almost as if it wanted to jump out and do this on its own, which made her hold on more tightly. Power surged along her arm, making it difficult to keep still as the pumpkin lifted higher and higher.

But she was doing it. With the wand's help—and her real mother's spirit—she was lifting the largest and heaviest object she'd ever tried to lift, doing as well as many of her competitors, and all of them had trained with wizards who'd guided them with more than meows and the occasional paw to the head.

About two feet away from the height of the pedestal, the pumpkin stalled. Just a bit more and she could slide it into place. Gripping the wand even more tightly, a powerful surge of energy flowed through her and she felt weightless.

The crowd roared, and yet the pumpkin was lowering, getting closer to the ground.

Wait—there was a reason she felt weightless. The pumpkin hadn't dropped lower; she'd actually lifted off the ground. Frowning, but concentrating, she focused back on the pumpkin and flicked her wand slightly, hoping to tame it to her will.

Her feet landed back on the ground.

The pumpkin exploded.

Everyone within twenty feet ducked as pumpkin flesh and seeds and chunks of rind flew everywhere. The crown of the pumpkin landed right on Cinderella's head. Standing with her mouth open, she picked a seed out before closing it.

"Thank you, competitor number ninety-eight," the announcer's voice boomed through the speakers. Then he turned and addressed the crowd. "Let's look to see what she scored for that very dynamic and creative attempt."

Cinderella lifted her head toward the scoreboard. Maybe she'd get some credit for lifting the pumpkin so high, for taking flight herself before it exploded? She twirled the wand in her fingers nervously.

The crowd gasped. So did she. Zero points. The judges had given her zero.

Even the contestants who'd barely lifted the pumpkin had scored a few points.

The announcer raised his hands to quiet the protesting crowd. "The judges tell me that destruction of the pumpkin means a default. That is too bad, as it was rather entertaining." The crowd shouted more dissent.

Cinderella's legs gave out and she slumped to the ground, burying her head in her hands. With zero points on this round, how would she ever win?

Before long, it was down to only twenty-three contestants in both the wand and no-wand groups combined. No one had a perfect record; each of the remaining wanna-be wizards would be out with even one more failure.

"Remaining wand contestants, step forward, please," the announcer's voice boomed, and the group of nine stepped onto the floor.

Ten wizards stood opposite them, arms crossed over their chests and all wearing different-colored robes. The crowd murmured as if they guessed what was coming, and Cinderella looked over to the faces of her fellow contestants to see if any of them could offer any clues. All she saw was abject fear.

She scanned the crowd for Ty. Seeing him right now might make her feel better, more confident, but he was nowhere to be found in the lower sections where she could make out some faces.

Higher in the stands, she saw that the prince was seated and had moved forward on his chair in anticipation. His purple velvet cape was lined with snow-white fur and his crown, sitting on tightly tied-back hair, glistened in the afternoon light.

Although she couldn't make out his features from this distance, she couldn't really understand why girls thought he was so special. Sitting on that fancy chair, his hair all tied back, his clothing so ornate, he really did look stiff and stuffy, despite what Ty had said about him.

The announcer waved his wand in a huge, sweeping gesture, and a second later, Cinderella saw her reflection. The announcer had used magic to build a clear wall a foot in front of the line of contestants. She and a few of the others tentatively reached forward to touch the barrier. Hard as rock but pulsating, it sent vibrations through her body, and she pulled her hand back.

From what did they need protection?

The first contestant, number 63, was called out from behind the screen. The largest of the entire group, he was close to six and a half feet tall, towering over the rest of them.

The announcer said something she couldn't hear from behind the clear barrier and 63 braced himself, raising his wand in front of his face in a defensive mode. He took a step forward, and that was when Cinderella noticed a red line about twenty feet ahead of the boy. It appeared all he had to do was cross that line. But it couldn't be that simple, could it?

He took another step, and a huge flame shot toward him.

Cinderella's head snapped toward the group of wizards across the arena floor, and she tried to guess from whose direction it had come, but was distracted as another wizard flicked her wand to send a huge swarm of bees toward the boy.

He ducked under the flame—it barely singed the cloth of his shirt—but he didn't move fast enough to avoid the bees. He waved his wand frantically, but it only seemed to increase the number of bees. Number 63 had barely regained his balance when a fireball hit him square in the chest. The boy was engulfed in flames and Cinderella gasped. Surely the wizards wouldn't let a competitor die!

The boy tossed his wand in the air—the signal of surrender and defeat. Immediately, the announcer flicked his wrist, and the flames disappeared. The crowd clapped politely, but it was clear from the expressions on the few faces Cinderella could make out in the crowd that they'd been shocked and disappointed by how badly 63, so far the favorite in the wand group, had fared.

Patiently yet eagerly waiting for her turn, Cinderella watched the other contestants, hoping to figure out some kind of strategy, but every new contestant was given different challenges. Where ducking the flame had worked for the first boy, the next flame shot had angled directly toward the contestant's feet, and jumping aside had been the only way to avoid being burnt to a crisp.

Cinderella kept thinking about the clear wall in front of them—built from thin air—and the swirling tornado she had recently created to fend off the wolves. Instead of dealing with each challenge one by one, she wondered if she could build a shield to protect herself from all of the magical weapons?

Two contestants had tried sprinting, only to be frozen in place or pushed back by winds, and the tall girl in the bright blue suit was the only one to have made it across the line so far. She'd done a dizzying display of acrobatics, leaping and flipping and twisting through the air, diving over fire, ducking under swarms of bats, and leaping over a river of molten lava.

Cinderella's acrobatic skills were good, but not that good, and she realized that her ninja warrior aspirations were still many years beyond her grasp.

Her number was called and, fighting to control her sudden shaking, she strode out from behind the shield to the starting line.

"You've seen the other competitors perform," the announcer said. "Any questions?"

She shook her head, unable to think of any except *How do I stop the horrible things they're going to throw at me?* And she knew he wouldn't answer that one.

"Are you ready?" the announcer asked, and she nodded in reply.

"Go!" he shouted.

Although a very big part of her wanted to sprint for the red line as fast as she could, she held up her wand, focused on a pole just past the finish line, and started to spin her body in circles. She kept her eyes focused on the pole, snapping her head around with each turn as a funnel of air formed around her. The air built and swirled, and she barely saw a flash of light when what must have been a fireball glinted off the side of her personal tornado and then shot toward the stands.

A roar rose, but she blocked it out. Concentration was crucial.

Still spinning, she moved forward, bringing her air funnel with her and continuing to spot like a dancer, keeping her eyes on the pole behind the finish line to avoid dizziness. Through the wall of swirling air, she now caught sight of a wall of water, a wave that had to be twelve feet high. It rushed toward her and she braced herself, concentrating as she pressed forward. The wave knocked both her and her tornado back a few steps and water drenched her from the funnel's top, but it held.

She could do this. She was almost there.

The pressure changed in her ears and the ground trembled. The line was right there. It was so close, but her limbs felt like lead, and pushing her tunnel of air forward became akin to pushing against a mountain.

Looking up, she saw what looked like a storm headed her way. Just a few steps to go, but no longer spotting the pole, she lost her balance and the wand wavered, moving erratically in her hand.

Her tornado forced her sideways. She was almost at the line. Enough with the funnel. Time to break it and run.

She raised her wand and flicked it, but must have done something wrong, because instead of disappearing, her wind tunnel turned to smoke. She choked as the acrid air filled her lungs and stung her eyes.

The next moment, she was slammed backward, her arms and legs flailing in all directions. A windstorm picked her up and she flew down the field to land on her back—the starting line was beneath her head. Refusing to give up, she rolled onto her belly and crawled backward toward the red line, but the force of the wind was too strong. Every muscle in her body strained; she turned and lifted her wand, hoping she could cast a spell to stop the wind.

Then a bolt of lightning struck her wand, and it flew from her hand.

The time horn sounded and the storm ended. She'd finished the event lying facedown on the dirt. Her wand, miraculously unharmed, was about four feet from her hand.

The announcer came over to offer her help, but she jumped to her feet and willed the wand to rise up from the ground and drift back into her hand.

The crowd roared its approval, but it didn't matter. She'd failed at the task. She hadn't been able to cross the line. This was her third failed event. For Cinderella, the competition was over, and her chance to win lessons with the royal wizard had died.

Her throat closed and she dragged herself over to the bench of eliminated competitors. Now she'd be trapped forever.

The courtyard outside the arena was filled with spectators hoping to congratulate the contestants, and Cinderella wished she were taller to improve her chances of finding Ty, if he were here. Sadness crept over her like a dark, heavy blanket. Not only had she lost, she'd lost her surest way to see Ty again.

Trying to think positively, she turned her face to the sun. It would likely be the last time she'd feel sunlight on her face for a while. Gauging by the sun's angle, she realized she had at least five hours before she needed to be home to save Max from a future as a rodent. This should be plenty of time to find Ty.

Her heart filled with excitement at this thought and she wondered whether she should risk telling him about her stepmother's entrapment spells. He seemed to know a few wizards, and one of them might be able to keep them from turning into stone when she spilled the beans. But the consequences of being wrong on that bet were too high, and she decided against it.

She couldn't take that chance, especially not with Ty.

Even if she never saw him again, even if she remained trapped for the rest of her life, she'd be happier knowing he was out in the world, happy and free. And Ty was both of those things. Ty's smile, his eyes, his posture—everything about him radiated joy and confidence.

She heard her stepmother's voice and her head snapped toward it out of habit. She ducked behind a group of people congratulating one of her fellow contestants.

"I'm telling you," her stepmother said, "if you don't immediately direct me to someone in charge, I'll turn you into a toad."

Cinderella shivered and ducked behind a large man. Maybe she didn't have five hours to get home, after all.

"Madam," one of the wizards who'd organized the event said, "I am certain your threat was merely a figure of speech. Threatening another wizard is an offense punishable by a minimum of three years in the castle dungeon."

Cinderella peeked out from behind the man shielding her.

"Well . . ." Her stepmother took a couple of steps back and her lips pursed. "Of course, of course. I apologize for my rudeness. But my daughters were robbed of their crowns in the beauty competition, and since a boy won the magic competition, I think it's only right that one of my lovely daughters gets the dance she surely would have won if she'd entered the magic competition instead." She glanced around and Cinderella ducked. "I'd also like to meet the young man who won. I'm always interested in young magic talent and I'd love to take the boy under my wing and—shall we say—mold his innate talents."

The wizard gestured behind him, a look of clear irritation on his face. "Feel free to look around, Madam. The contestants were invited here for a feast after the awards ceremony, but many have already gone on to the palace dressing rooms to prepare for the ball."

Cinderella reached behind her to remove the number from her back. Keeping her eyes on her stepmother, she dashed between groups of people so she could remain hidden from the evil wizard she'd lived with all these years.

A hand landed on her shoulder and Cinderella's heart froze. She'd been watching her stepmother, but had no idea where her stepsisters were. If one of them had found her, they'd reveal her location in an instant. She couldn't bare to look to see who it was.

"Excuse me," an unfamiliar female voice said. Cinderella slowly turned to find the most beautiful woman she'd ever seen directly in front of her. Gold and silver ringlets of hair danced around her fair skin, and her cheeks were tinged with roses. Her bright green eyes were like the grass after a rain. The woman's gown was spectacular too, intricately constructed with pleats and delicate overstitching and elegantly sewn from a pale blue fabric that reflected the sunlight as she extended a graceful hand toward Cinderella.

Hoping her stepmother was looking in the other direction, she curtsied to the woman.

"Oh, no need for such formalities," the woman said, and then laughed with a warmth that pushed aside Cinderella's fear and some of her awe. "I'm Jenna."

"Cinderella," she replied without thinking. Why would such an elegant woman even care what her name was?

"That's an unusual name," she said, taking Cinderella's hand.

"It's a nickname." Cinderella felt herself blush. "It's been my nickname for so long, I think I've forgotten what my father called me." Well, she remembered her father calling her Sweetie, Pumpkin, and My Tiny Love. But nothing else, and she'd been called Cinderella every day since he'd died. She couldn't imagine another name now.

"I think it's lovely." The woman's smile was so warm, so perfect, and her bright green eyes flashed something that could only be kindness. "You did very well out there today."

Cinderella shook her head and said, "No, I didn't." She tapped her wand, now tucked securely back in her pocket. "It was my first time using a wand, and I fear I'm not very talented."

"Nonsense," said Jenna.

Over Jenna's shoulder, Cinderella caught a glimpse of her stepmother walking in their direction, and her eyes widened in horror.

Jenna tipped her head slightly and, as if sensing something was wrong, pulled Cinderella to the side of the courtyard and turned so that Cinderella was hidden behind her. "I have a message for you," she said, and Cinderella's heart immediately lifted. From Ty? No, that was crazy. More likely that Ty would be delivering messages for this elegant woman than the other way around.

"I'm one of the queen's ladies-in-waiting," Jenna said. "Are you attending the ball this evening?"

Cinderella raised her fingers to her lips to stifle her gasp. "Oh, no," she answered, looking down over the pumpkin-splattered outfit Max had made her. "I would love to, but I'm afraid I don't have anything suitable to wear."

"Don't let that hold you back." Jenna reached her hand up and tucked a strand of hair behind Cinderella's ear. "The prince was impressed by your performance and would very much like the pleasure of a dance with you this evening."

"Oh, I couldn't. Not …." She gripped the fabric of her trousers, unsure what to say.

On second thought, maybe if she went to the ball, she'd have another chance to find Ty.

"Don't worry about your clothing," Jenna said. "It might take some hemming and a few nips and tucks, but I'm sure you'll be able to find something to your liking in either my dressing room or that of one of the other ladies-in-waiting."

"Really?" Her heart soared and then she stopped herself. "Oh, that's too kind of you, but I couldn't. I mean, what if I tore something? And I'd look silly in such fine garments."

"Nonsense," Jenna said. "I'm sure you're very pretty under those pumpkin seeds and the smudges of soot on your face." She rubbed Cinderella's cheek with her thumb. "Please say yes."

If you were Cinderella, what would you do?

OPTION A: Cinderella should take the lady-in-waiting up on her offer. She's got nearly five hours before Max turns into a mouse, and if she's really lucky, she might run into Ty at the ball. He said he'd be working there. If you think she should say yes, go to section 7: If the Shoe Fits (page 211).

OPTION B: Cinderella should tell the lady-in-waiting thanks, but no thanks. She's barely got five hours before Max turns into a mouse, and there's no way she's going to take any chances. It's much better to get through those woods before dark, anyway. She'd rather use what little time she has to find Ty and tell him how much she appreciated his help and support. If you think she should turn down the lady-in-waiting, go to section 8: Fall from Grace (page 245).

Section 6

baLancing act

6

C inderella drew a long breath of fresh air and turned her face to the sunshine. She truly loved being outside in the daytime.

Feeling free and alive, she almost forgot she was still on the grounds of the house and in a hurry. Watching Max use her mother's wand to alter the entrapment spells, make her a cool outfit to compete in, and get her outside the house had been amazing and reinforced her decision that she didn't have the skills or experience to wield that thing on her own.

She ran her small hands over the unfamiliar sleeves of the comfortable wraparound shirt that Max had made for her—like a real ninja's, but white—and looked down at the trousers that gave her much more range of motion than her skirt over pantaloons ever did. Plus, they were far sturdier and there would be much less of a chance her clothes would tear or fall apart during the competition—assuming she got there and was allowed to enter.

Who cared if the outfit would turn back into her rags at midnight?

"I'd better get going." She walked back to the front of the house, keeping her eyes on Max. "It's a couple of miles, and even running, I might not make it in time."

"Wait!" Max dashed into her vegetable patch, frantically pulled a few carrots and some radishes, and then dashed over to grab her metal watering can.

He'd gone mad! She was going to a magic competition, not a farmers' market. Too many years as a cat had turned his brains to catnip. "Um, Max. What are you doing?"

"Shh." He ran to the front of the house and set the watering can on the cobblestone path, then he ripped off the radish tops and placed the red vegetables at the base of the can—two on one side and two on the other. Next he put one carrot in front of the watering can, the other beside it.

He ran to the side of the path, selected four stones, and placed them neatly in two rows directly in front of the can, then laid the radish stalks along the stone's tops in such a way that they stretched back to the watering can.

Max really had gone insane, and although Cinderella worried about him, she stepped slowly toward the gate, hoping he'd thought to open it with his earlier spell. Whatever strange game he was playing, she couldn't waste any more time.

"Wait!" he yelled. "Don't you think it would be faster to get to the village in a horse-drawn carriage?"

She stopped, turned around, and put her hands on her hips. "Yes, it would. But I don't have one, so all I can do is run, and you playing with vegetables isn't gaining me any time."

"Patience, my dear. Patience." He turned back to his strange sculpture and raised the wand. Cinderella thought that maybe she should wait this out, after all. His magic thus far had been impressive and she realized she should probably trust him to do whatever he thought he was doing, even if she failed to see how a beat-up watering can, four stones, two carrots, four radishes, and some greens were going to help her get to the competition in time.

He circled the wand and sparks immediately swirled from its tip. Not pink sparks like the ones she'd seen inside. These were red and bright orange, and some of them were black, like the shiny mineral flecks she'd seen in some garden rocks. Max continued to circle the wand until he'd created a huge swirling mass of energy that Cinderella worried he wouldn't be able to control.

She stepped back and her stomach knotted. Max's behavior seemed both disturbing and pointless.

Bending his arm at the elbow, he drew the wand back, and then straightened his arm with incredible force. The mass of sparks and energy hurtled forward and engulfed his garden sculpture, circling, building, and expanding.

Now she felt sure she should run, but her feet were anchored to the ground. Her knees shook, and her muscles refused to make any other kind of move.

Under the mass of sparks, something began to take shape. The entire display elongated, and continued to expand. She heard a noise that sounded like a horse. She blinked several times to rid her mind of the bizarre image taking shape. No way, under all those sparks and smoke, were a carriage and horses forming. It didn't seem possible.

Max lifted his wand toward the sky and the sparks flew up to form a long trail before they headed back toward their creator.

"Look out!" Cinderella yelled. Max was going to be killed by his own spell. The very day she'd learned she had a godfather, she'd lose him—and her cat, too!

But the sparks remained under his control, and the wand seemed to devour them into its slender wooden tip.

She looked at the path and staggered back a few steps.

A carriage. Made of shiny metal, its bright red wheels had snowy-white spokes. She clapped her hands, realizing he'd transformed the radishes into wheels, and the watering can into the carriage cab. A tall man in an elegant orange jacket sat at the front of the carriage holding green reins that stretched forward to four beautiful strong horses, their coats the same shades as the rocks. Another carrot-coated man opened the gray door to the carriage, bowed, and a tiny amount of water trickled out and onto the path.

"Sorry about that," Max said. "I should've emptied the watering can first. I'm sure the seats will be dry."

Cinderella realized she'd been holding her breath and her chest heaved as she took in the marvelous sight. "Oh, Max! A carriage! How wonderful. Thank you." Now she had a chance to arrive not only in time, but in style. Imagine. She'd never ridden in a carriage before.

"My dear," Max said as he bowed toward her, and she noticed he was sweating everywhere, even on the top of his balding head.

She ran forward and he put his arms around her. Cinderella wasn't used to embraces; his hands felt so warm and safe that she considered forgoing the competition. But within a few seconds, Max pushed her back, leaving his hands on her arms.

"Are you sure I can't make you a ball gown?"

She considered it for a second, but there wasn't enough time. "I don't think I'll go to the ball. The competition's my priority."

"Okay," he said. He put his hand on her shoulder and looked her directly in the eyes, to make sure she understood. "Just remember the spell's limitations—it's not permanent, and unfortunately, this carriage won't last long, either. It's a one-way ride."

She nodded. "That's no problem. I understand. Thank you, Max." She hugged him around his neck.

"And remember, you must return here by midnight, when everything goes back the way it was."

"I promise." Getting back wouldn't be a problem. The competition was supposed to be over by dinnertime.

Cinderella leaped out of the carriage the second it stopped at the contestants' entrance to the arena. She spun toward the groom who'd opened her door. "Thank you."

He bowed, but said nothing. Apparently, carrots could bow, drive carriages, and open doors, but they couldn't speak. Good to know.

She grinned, and he bowed again.

"Thanks. Wish me luck," she said, and he tipped his green hat.

Cinderella ran to the door. "Where's the registration desk?" she asked the guard at the door, praying she wasn't too late.

The guard looked at the clock on the wall and raised his eyebrows. "You've just made it, lass. Through there." He tipped his head toward a desk near the entrance, behind which sat three wizards, dressed in multicolored robes.

The preparation room was filled with chatter that bounced off the stone walls, as did bright light, although Cinderella couldn't spot its source. From her quick glance through the crowd, she deduced that most of the contestants ranged in age from about ten to their late teens. A few looked to be in their twenties. As soon as she got her number pinned on, she was ushered along with the crowd through a long, dark tunnel.

Excitement built inside her. What would she be asked to do? Even if she performed terribly, she was sure she'd be glad to have come. She owed Ty a huge debt of gratitude for telling her about the competition.

Thinking of Ty, her stomach stirred in a different way. He'd said he watched the competition every year, and even if she didn't see him, she took comfort that he'd be somewhere in the stands.

The spectators' roar rolled toward them from the end of the tunnel, continuing to build, and then, one by one, sunlight struck the heads of the competitors ahead of her until she strode into the light. As soon as she entered the arena, she stopped in her tracks. A small girl she'd passed in the tunnel bumped into her from behind.

"Oh, excuse me." She glanced down at the girl's red curls and freckled face. And then both of them smiled, stood stock still, and turned their faces to take in their surroundings.

The circular arena was astounding. At least ten or twenty thousand people ringed the field in row upon row of seats rising into the bright blue sky. Colored banners fluttered in the breeze from dozens of poles at the top of the stands and suddenly the air filled with thousands of small white butterflies. Cinderella lifted her finger and one landed on it, batted its wings, and then took off again.

"Isn't it wonderful?" she said to the girl, and then realized she was standing alone. All the other contestants had gathered in the middle of the field. She ran to catch up.

"Welcome!" a huge voice bellowed. She peeked around the tall boy in front of her to see who had spoken. He stepped aside to let her stand in front.

"Thank you," she said, and he raised a finger to his lips.

She smiled her thanks, and then turned to the center of the field where a tall wizard was hovering about twelve feet off the ground.

It had to be the royal wizard himself.

His robes were flashing and glowing, transforming into flames, then water, then birds, then ice. She had never witnessed anything quite so remarkable.

Well, she caught herself and giggled. She *had* arrived in a watering can with radish wheels, stone horses, and carrots for grooms. It was just a remarkable kind of day, she supposed.

After nearly falling twice while competing in the tightrope event, Cinderella's entire body trembled in anticipation of the next test. The wand group was in the process of lifting pumpkins, something she could do in her sleep even without the advantage of a wand.

It seemed to her the wand group's tasks should be harder, not easier, than the non-wand group's, but even though she'd ignored Max's advice and brought the wand, it was too late to change to the other group now.

Shading her eyes from the sun, she looked up to the high pedestal from which the royal wizard watched the proceedings. Behind him was the row of judges, and then, high above that, the box reserved for the royal family.

Her stepsisters claimed Prince Tiberius was the most handsome man in the kingdom, but his chair was empty. It figured. All these girls battling for a chance to twirl around the dance floor in his arms, and he couldn't even be bothered to watch.

He was likely over at the beauty competition her stepsisters had entered. Ty could defend his employer and his family all he liked, but any boy planning to pick a bride at a ball without even knowing her had to be pretty shallow.

"Trying to catch a glimpse of your dance partner?" A hand landed softly on her shoulder, and Cinderella spun to see Ty, in his messenger uniform—although oddly, it seemed to be a different one, and it didn't fit.

Her heart swelled with joy.

"I saw you on the tightropes." His eyes lit up with a smile, and so did every nerve in her body. "You did very well."

"Thanks! I thought that last ball of fire was going to get me."

"Nah," he said. "Your jump cleared it by about two feet and you landed back down with barely a wobble."

A blush rose on her chest and face. It was true she'd managed the tightrope and fireball challenge with relative ease compared to many of the other contestants, and had somehow found herself among the top six on the leaderboard, but this next task would be different. Not just different. Impossible.

She looked down the field where the wizards and their helpers were busy installing dozens of hoops on long poles of varying heights.

"What's wrong?" Ty reached for her hand.

The contact sent a charge racing through her.

"I can't do this." She gestured behind her to the hoops course she was expected to complete blindfolded. "Maybe if I could use a wand." She nervously chewed on the inside of her lip to keep from telling him about finding her mother's wand hidden in the woods, or about her godfather, who also happened to be her cat. Sharing those secrets would lead to questions—questions she couldn't answer without turning Ty into stone. She bit her lip. "I really need to win this."

"Want a dance with the prince that badly, huh?"

She looked up, expecting to find him mocking her, but his face read as though he'd just received the best news of his life.

She laughed. "You know I don't care about that. I'm here for the magic lessons."

He dropped her hand and backed up a few inches. "Of course. Yes. Of course." As he dipped his head, sunlight glinted off the curls that had escaped his cap.

"What are you doing on the field?" she asked. "I thought only competitors and wizards were allowed out here."

She heard the crowd roar and glanced over her shoulder. One of the wand group had just landed a pumpkin on the top of a very high pole. She was no longer sure she would have won in that group.

"I know some people." He looked down and scraped the sole of his shoe along the dirt, and she noticed his heels were sticking out the ends of the too-small shoes.

"You're in uniform. Do you have messages to deliver today, to people in the crowd?"

His cheeks reddened and he looked up to the left before answering. "Not exactly, but I am working."

She stepped closer to him. "I hope the royal family appreciates you." But they likely didn't. Even if they didn't treat him as badly as her stepmother treated her, they couldn't even supply him with a properly fitted uniform.

"Since you're here"—he stepped forward—"can I assume you're also going to the ball?"

"In this?" She touched the hem of the shirt Max had made her. "This is all I've got to wear. Hardly the latest in formal wear."

"You'll attract attention, regardless of fashion," he said.

"Attention, yes," she said with a grin, "but the right kind? Everyone will stare at me if I show up like this."

He pushed his cap back. "You might have a point there, but I'm sure there's a solution. Someone will loan you a gown. In fact, I borrowed this uniform from someone." He looked at her, almost pleading. "Please don't let your attire get in the way of your chance to dance with . . . with the prince."

She tried to hide her smile. It seemed to her that he hoped for a dance himself, but was too shy to ask. "Who cares about a silly prince? If I do go to the ball, the only boy I want to dance with is you."

He beamed. "Do you really mean that?"

"Absolutely."

The side of his mouth cocked up, making a dimple in one cheek. "Well, just remember what I told you—the prince isn't such a bad guy."

"All evidence to the contrary." She crossed her arms over her chest.

"What do you mean?"

"You work for him, right?"

He nodded, but looked slightly awkward, as if he might be hiding something. She hoped she'd have time to get to the bottom of that.

"Then I think he should take better care of his employees." Cinderella gestured toward him. "Your pants are about five inches too short and your shoes don't fit."

"Oh." He ran his hand over the light blond stubble on his chin. "This isn't the prince's fault. He—I—had to borrow this and get changed in a hurry to come out here to see you."

"Do you mean you had to change out of your beggar disguise?"

He started. "Something like that."

She pushed some stray hairs behind her ear. Ty's clothing changes were perplexing.

"Hey." He reached into his pocket and pulled out a black satin ribbon. "Would you like me to tie your hair back so it won't get in the way for the next events?"

"Oh, yes, please."

She turned, lifted her hair, and wondered where he'd found such a fine ribbon, but the thought of asking vanished when his fingers brushed her neck, sending warm shivers through her.

He smoothed back her hair and tightly tied the ribbon as if he were quite practiced at the task. Finished, he let his hands fall to her shoulders for a moment.

Trumpets signaled that the wand group's pumpkin-lifting event had concluded, and Cinderella glanced up at the leaderboard. She was still on it, but had dropped to eleventh. She'd need a stellar performance in this next event, yet it still seemed impossible. She studied the hoops again and twisted her lips. Anxiety twisted her belly, too.

Ty's hand enveloped hers again, but not even his touch could calm her this time. Not when she was about to be a spectacular failure.

She studied the hoops, high up in the air and scattered over the field. The challenge was to throw tiny balls through those hoops but without using her eyes. It seemed impossible. However, she remembered a time when Max had climbed on her head and put his paws over her eyes while she was tossing chestnuts into a bucket one night. At the time, she'd thought he was doing it for attention, but now wondered if it had been a training technique.

Ty bent closer and put his lips close to her ear. "You can do this, Cinderella. It's just a matter of concentration and focus. Memorize where the hoops are, and then, once you're blindfolded, let your senses take control." He ran a hand lightly down her arm. "Just close your eyes and focus."

She did, but all her senses could focus on was Ty: the height of his lean, strong body next to hers, the caress of his hands, the warmth of his breath as he spoke softly.

"What are your senses telling you?" he asked.

Heat burned her cheeks. No way could she tell him the truth.

"Focus," he said. "What do you hear? Which way is the wind blowing? How far away are the stands?"

She took a deep breath and blocked out the shivery deliciousness of Ty's attention. The rest of the arena slowly came into focus in her mind's eye. The wind was light, blowing from east to west across the arena, almost perpendicular to the hoops. The nearest stands were twenty-two—no, twenty-three feet away, and the scent of a sausage hit her nostrils. A man in the front row burped.

Grinning, she opened her eyes and turned to Ty. "You're right. If I focus, I can feel things around me."

He gently squeezed her arm. "I knew it. I just knew it. There's strong magic inside you, Cinderella. Just let it guide you. Trust yourself. Believe in yourself."

"Thank you." She looked into his eyes and felt the strangest conflicting sensations. It was as if she were melting, yet becoming stronger at the same time. Stronger than she'd felt in her entire life. She could do this. She reached up to touch his face, then, realizing the boldness of her gesture, pulled away.

He caught her hand in his, held it, and bent to place a soft kiss on her cheek. "Good luck," he whispered. "I wish I could stay, but if I don't get back soon, I'll be missed."

Ty dropped her hand and stepped back, and she felt lost, as if something had been sucked from inside her, leaving a vacuum. "Can you come back before the next event?"

"I'm not sure." He looked down, then back up. "My duties."

"Of course." She'd been so silly. He was a servant of the royal family. He couldn't just drop everything because she needed him.

He bent down toward her, softly placed a kiss on her lips, and she felt as if her body had lifted from the ground. She rubbed one foot along the turf to be sure she was wrong.

"Come to the ball." He sent her a wickedly powerful and dimpled smile that shot straight into her heart.

"I'll try."

He nodded, then he turned to run back to the entrance of the arena.

"Who was that?" asked a tall girl in pigtails standing next to her.

"My friend." She had a friend. Her insides warmed at the words, but she couldn't think about Ty right now. It was time to focus on hoops, distances, and trajectories. She'd need to utilize a variety of tricks, depending on the weights of the balls and the wind speed as she made each throw.

"He's kind of cute," the girl said. "But you're nuts to let a servant boy kiss you." She wrinkled her nose. "I'm holding out for the prince."

Cinderella said nothing, but simply nodded at the girl and then excused herself to focus on the hoops course and the daunting task ahead of her. Nothing—even setting this girl straight—was more important than winning the competition.

Lost in the concentration of preparation, she jumped when someone nudged her. Her number had been called, and she stepped forward to let the wizard's assistant put a blindfold over her eyes. It didn't appear or feel thick, but the fabric was clearly enchanted; it quickly molded to her face, leaving her in complete and total darkness.

The assistant led her forward and then set her hand on the basket of balls. She suddenly realized she didn't even have any idea where the other competitors' scores lay, or how many points she'd need to do well; she'd been so distracted by Ty and then studying the course. Perhaps it was better not to know. Better to concentrate only on the hoops, the balls, and the task at hand.

A bell rang. It was her time to begin, and behind the darkness of her blindfold she pictured the heights and sizes of each hoop and their locations on the field. She picked up a ball, felt its weight and rubbery soft surface in her fingers, and then lobbed it, underhanded, toward the closest of the hoops.

A horn sounded. She'd missed.

Come on, Cinderella, she admonished and then quickly encouraged herself. *You can do this. Concentrate. Have confidence in your abilities. Believe in yourself.*

She picked up another ball, stood very still, focused, and then tossed it higher and farther, aiming for one of the mid-field hoops blocking the path to the ones at the back.

A cheer rang out from the crowd; it was so loud she almost didn't hear the bell signaling her success. She'd done it. If she had hit the hoop, she thought, she would have only scored four points, but that hoop would drop out of the way and clear her path to the ones yielding higher points downfield.

Four more chances and the time was ticking away. How much of it had passed? She wished she'd thought of some method to keep track of time. It wouldn't do for the clock to run out before she'd thrown all six of her balls.

She picked up another and concentrated on one of the rings at the far end of the field. It alone was worth twenty points and was one that no contestant thus far had attempted. But she could feel the ring's location, as if it were sending her vibrating messages. *Here I am. Here I am.*

Not confident she'd make the distance with an underhand throw, she wound up, stepped forward, and used her entire body's force to hurl the rubber ball at its target.

The crowd gasped, realizing which hoop she'd aimed for, and she instantly remembered the rule that contestants were immediately out of this round as soon as they missed two targets. If she missed, she was done with this event.

The collective gasp became a cheer and the bell sounded. She'd made it.

She pushed aside her joy and pride, ignored the roar and chanting of the crowd, and picked up another ball. She was going to aim for another of the hoops blocking the path to higher-scoring ones.

She lined up and threw. The crowd went wild and she could almost swear she'd heard two bells ringing. Yes, given the angle she'd thrown, it was possible the ball had sailed through two hoops. If she remembered the rules correctly, she'd score double for each. Pride swelled in her chest, but she couldn't rest on her laurels or get overconfident.

She threw the remaining balls, hitting her target each time, and then waited for someone to remove her blindfold. But it turned transparent and fell from her face on its own.

Blinking against the sunlight, she shielded her eyes and looked up to the scoreboard. Sixty-four points! Even some of her fellow contestants were clapping her on the back.

She scanned the sidelines for Ty, but couldn't find him. All she wanted was to see him again.

If she won the competition, she would have to share a dance with the prince, but she could suffer through that if it meant she would see Ty at the ball.

By the time a wizard led her non-wand group to their final event, Cinderella was in second place.

Her jaw gaped.

In front of them were dozens of rows of narrow beams, and they were not only impossibly—dangerously—high off the ground, they had gaps and other obstacles between them to make transferring between each beam treacherous.

One of the wizards shed his robe to reveal a loose-fitting black jumpsuit, and the announcer explained the wizard would demonstrate the event to prove passage was possible.

The wizard leaped into the air and landed on the lowest beam, nearly seven feet off the ground. Cinderella's stomach flipped over. She was an accomplished jumper, but to leap that high and land on the beam without losing her balance seemed impossible. She wondered whether it would be against the rules to land with her hands first.

She watched, amazed, as the wizard ran down beams with ease, jumped past swinging blades, and held his balance while the beams shook, spun, rose, and fell. He completed the entire course in two minutes and thirty-seven seconds—without even wobbling, never mind falling down. The contestants' time limit was ten minutes.

The crowd cheered as the wizard leaped from the final platform, nearly thirty feet from the ground, slowing himself to a hover before landing on one foot.

So graceful. So accomplished.

"Fabulous job, Anders, fabulous." The announcer turned toward them. "But the contestants should know that there's no requirement to complete the course exactly as Anders did. To have reached this far in the competition, all of you have demonstrated some innate magic abilities as well as physical agility and strong powers of logic and concentration. This difficult event will require extremely high levels of those same skills."

He stepped back and addressed the crowd. "The event ends if the contestant falls or if any part of his or her body other than the feet or hands touches the beam. Competitors will be judged based on the number of beams traversed in the least amount of time, and extra points will be assigned for style and danger."

The crowd murmured their approval. Cinderella's belly voiced its dissent. Points for danger? She didn't like the sound of that. Her magic skills weren't strong enough to pull this off. But there was a bright side: because of her *Way of the Warrior* book, her body and mind were well prepared to do their parts.

"Spotters will be provided on request." The announcer gestured toward a group of wizards in robes of various colors who bowed toward them slightly. "The spotters will prevent any contestant who falls from hitting the ground."

Cinderella heaved a sigh of relief, as did several others around her.

"However," the announcer continued, "any contestant who forgoes the spotters will automatically score ten bonus points simply by landing successfully on the first beam, and another ten points for landing on each successive beam to the end of the course."

Wow. She could feel the tension in her fellow competitors. If they completed even half of the seven-beam course without spotters, they'd score an automatic thirty or forty points. But the second they fell, unless they could roll through their landing, or possessed the skills to stop themselves midair, they'd end up smashed to pieces. Hard to believe even the best magic healer could fix that kind of damage.

"And now, we begin." The announcer pulled a number from an upturned hat that appeared out of thin air, and one by one, the competitors took their turns, all opting for spotters, until number 22 was called. The tall, strong boy was ahead of Cinderella on the leaderboard.

Dressed in leather breeches and a shirt, 22 strode up to the starting line and flipped over the black panel hanging from the pole to indicate he was opting for no spotter. The audience hushed, electricity filled the air, and for a moment Cinderella couldn't breathe. She'd been hoping no one would opt for the no-spotter route to make her choice easier.

She braced herself and bit her lip as the boy ran forward, leaped into the air, and waved his arms before landing on the first beam with a thud.

In spite of his heavy first landing, he nearly floated as he ran down the ten-foot length of the beam and leaped up to swing on the bar that, if he were lucky and had timed it correctly, would catapult him up to the level of the next beam. He made it.

She watched, impressed, as he continued along the course. Even if he looked somewhat awkward, bending his legs in the air and flapping his arms to maintain balance, she figured she was watching her main competition. She hoped. What if someone else was even better? She forced that thought out of her mind. No sense in imagining challenges. Reality was challenging enough.

When 22 reached the third beam, it started to shake. He was the first contestant to reach that height, more than twenty-five feet from the ground, and he'd done so without the comfort of spotters.

The next beam had been rising and falling, sometimes as much as ten feet above the third beam and sometimes as many feet below it. Number 22 raced down the shaking beam and leaped for the fourth. Risky move. If he didn't time it right, he'd have problems. He aimed high. The crowd gasped as the beam plunged while he was in the air.

The boy's arms windmilled frantically as he tried to regain control, but it was no use. Cinderella put her hands over her eyes and peeked through her fingers as he landed on the next beam—not on his feet but on his backside.

She gasped. Even if that was allowed—which it wasn't—it had to have hurt.

A horn sounded. Two ropes appeared and wrapped around his body under his outstretched arms. The ropes lifted him off the beam and slowly lowered him to the ground, where a wizard rushed to his side. The boy limped forward, clearly in a lot of pain, but waved to the crowd, which went bananas.

No matter what his score was, he was clearly now the crowd favorite. Bravery obviously counted for something with this group. Either that or they were out for blood.

Instead of watching the next few contestants perform, Cinderella kept her eyes on the fourth beam—the one 22 had crashed onto—and tried to discern its pattern of movement. At first it all seemed random, but she soon figured out a sequence of thirteen positions, with a varying number of seconds between lurches up or down.

She was so focused on verifying that the pattern was in fact a pattern, she jumped when her number was called.

Walking to the starting line, she gathered every ounce of bravery inside her and flipped the card to show she'd decided against spotters.

The noise from the crowd swelled in response. Behind her, she heard a few snickers. Clearly, many didn't think the tiny blonde girl was up to the task, but if she wanted to win, she didn't have any choice after that boy had scored sixty-two points.

"Are you ready?" the announcer asked. Cinderella nodded, but knew by now that it was a rhetorical question. Several contestants had been left standing stunned when the horn sounded as they were busy answering no.

It was on. The horn sounded loud in her ear, but all she focused on was the image of landing on that first beam. Because she was so much shorter, she'd need a little magic right from the start. She had to believe she could do it. She ran forward, did a round-off and three back handsprings to gain speed, and then launched off the ground, her back high and arching. It was the highest she'd ever jumped. She watched her hands as they flew up and back, envisioning the beam between them until it appeared just six inches below her.

She clasped the beam as her body was upside down, and she easily stepped out of her backflip, legs solidly planted in a lunge.

A roar rose in her ears, but she forced out the sound. All she could think about was her task, keeping safe, living through this event so she could win the competition.

She turned to face the end of the beam and gripped it with her toes. The sharp edges dug into the soles of her feet, but she welcomed the pain as a clear signal of where the boundary of her safety zone lay. She inhaled deeply using her diaphragm, and then slowly exhaled, forcing all the air out.

After inhaling again, she ran along the beam and jumped up to grasp the bar at the end, arching her body to maximize the momentum she'd get as she swung forward. Not feeling confident she'd achieved the proper reach, she swung back again and heard the crowd groan. Clearly they'd assumed she'd given up, but the few extra seconds to execute another swing would be worth it if it assured a clean landing on the next beam, nearly six feet away and five feet higher.

On her second swing, she let go and somersaulted before landing on her feet on the second beam.

The crowd roared. She'd been the first to do a flip between the two beams, but she hadn't just done it for style points. As she'd suspected, the extra propulsion from the flip had made it much easier to get that second beam.

The beam, starting at twelve feet from the ground, would rise an additional ten feet as she traversed it, but it would do so slowly, so she considered performing some other kind of trick while crossing, but that would be showing off. Even if it might earn her a few points, she didn't want to be cocky. Confidence was one thing, overconfidence another, and she'd barely started this event.

Besides, this beam's main challenge wasn't its increasing height—reaching over twenty feet by the end—but the hoop at its end, which she'd have to jump through. A hoop that had just burst into flames. Although she knew the hottest part—the section that would cause her clothing or hair or skin to ignite—was only at the hoop's edges, the action of diving straight through what amounted to a disk of flames would take all the courage, concentration, and careful calculation that she could summon.

Most competitors had stopped before reaching the flaming hoop. The few who'd dived through but failed had mistimed straightening their bodies for landing on the next beam, and had hit the top edge of the hoop with their backs or legs.

She had a different technique in mind.

After tightening the hair ribbon Ty had loaned her, she took a deep breath and ran, focusing on her flaming hoop target.

She dove through the hoop, her body straight as an arrow, not even trying to adjust to a vertical position for landing. Instead, after clearing the flames, she placed her hands on the next beam, pressed down to lift her body and control her momentum, and then swung her legs forward in a V shape, pointing her toes. Nothing but her hands had touched the beam, and hands were allowed.

Swinging her legs back, she pushed up to a handstand. The beam started to vibrate.

Don't look down. Don't look down.

She looked down.

How could she not look down? Her face was pointed to the ground, now twenty-two feet below her and impossibly far away. Taking the no-spotter option had been a huge mistake. Not only wouldn't she win, she was going to die.

She wobbled, but split her legs in the handstand to regain her balance, and stepped down, fighting to keep the beam's vibrations from stealing her balance. She had to keep her mind focused.

From the reading she'd done on ninja mind exercises, she figured the key was to be one with the beam—not to fight the vibrations, but to allow them to flow through her. Essentially, to give up control and vibrate, too, so that walking down the shaking beam would be as natural as walking along the floor in her cellar room.

Letting her body vibrate, she crossed the beam quickly, focusing instead on the swinging blade between this beam and the next.

And the sharp blade wasn't the worst of it. Not only would she have to time her leap forward so the blade wouldn't slice off any body parts, she also had to take into consideration that the next beam—the one 22 had failed to land on—kept dropping and rising. She only hoped she'd properly figured out the pattern from field level.

Remembering the thirteen-step pattern, she waited for the perfect time to transfer: that precise moment when the beam's height would be up only two feet from this one, just before it shot up four more and then plunged.

Cinderella focused back on the blade. To avoid it and time the pattern correctly, she'd have to leap just a second before the beam shot up.

She strode forward and jumped, making sure she didn't leave a foot dragging behind. The breeze from the passing blade licked her back, but she easily landed on the next beam. It shot up four feet, but she held her balance and paused in relief.

The noise of the crowd flooded in. They were going insane, acknowledging that by landing on this beam, she'd gotten farther than 22, who'd scored the most points so far. And the only contestants still to complete this task had scores way below the leaders.

Now she had to wait until the plank leading to the next beam would be level with this one. Since it was wide, she could leap down to it, but she was still puzzled by the fact that the demonstrating wizard had waited to step onto it, and had crossed the plank more slowly than he'd crossed any of the narrow beams. She decided to use his example and proceed with caution.

Each time her current beam was still for a few seconds, she stepped forward quickly and bent her knees to brace for the next jolting shift up or down. On the ten-foot drop, her stomach rose to her throat, but she didn't falter. Instead, she took advantage of the five-second pause at the bottom to move to the end of the beam. From there, she could brace herself through the remaining shifts, up and down, until she was ready to step onto the plank.

Knees bent, torso tight, she endured a rise, a plunge, another plunge, and then saw why the wizard had moved so slowly on the comparatively wide surface of the plank leading to the next beam.

It was covered with broken glass. Hundreds, if not thousands, of glass shards and bits glinted in the sunlight, and Cinderella couldn't imagine walking across the beam without numerous cuts and scrapes. Fear gripped her, and as the beam rose three feet, she wobbled, almost losing her balance.

She could not give up now. If she died, she might never see Ty again, and just thinking of his face, his encouragement, his soft kiss, she felt calm enough to fight her fear.

Broken glass. No problem.

She'd never tried walking over anything sharp or hot, but had read about techniques to do so in her book. The tricks were to stay calm, carry her weight evenly, walk flat-footed, let the glass settle as she took each step, and ensure no single part of her sole took all her weight at one time.

Mind over matter. Gathering her center and building her courage, she stepped onto the plank with one foot. The edges of the glass dug in, but didn't cut, and she drew a deep breath.

Do not panic. Do not tremble. Do not allow the glass to win.

She focused on the end of the plank and, rather than looking down, she carefully stepped forward, imagining she was walking over the grass in her garden. Step after step, she moved forward until the glass underfoot felt almost soft against her skin.

Before stepping onto the next beam, which was quickly rotating, she focused on its far end. Timing it perfectly, she stepped onto the beam and it rotated away from the end of the plank. She took two careful steps and a block of wood shot up from the beam to a height of six inches, not far from her right foot.

Her heart shuddered and her breath caught in her chest. Apparently, the course held more than one secret not visible from the arena floor, now nearly thirty feet below. She slid her focus from the end of the beam toward the place from which the block had risen.

There had to be some kind of clue as to where and when the blocks would shoot up. If one rose beneath her foot, or worse, part of her foot, she'd be tossed off in an instant. And since she was now spinning on this rotating beam, she'd not only fall thirty feet, she'd be flung to the side, and who knew where she'd land.

She searched for clues on the beam to indicate where the other blocks might rise, but couldn't see a thing—not a line or a seam, not a break in the grain of the wood.

Careful not to let her focus drift from the beam to the swirling scene below, she returned her gaze to the end of the beam and then lifted her foot to step over the block.

Midair, she had another thought: what if the next block was placed to shoot up right ahead of the first? Instead of stepping over the first one, she placed her foot directly onto it, and it glided down into place until her foot was level with the beam again. Simultaneously, another block shot up about three feet further along. *Please let that be the next one.* She stepped forward, feeling the beam for clues or seams, until she reached the next block. Once again, she stepped directly onto it. Again it lowered under her weight and another block, this time a mere four inches ahead, was revealed.

Her heart soared. She'd figured it out.

But Cinderella couldn't celebrate yet, not this far from the ground. She forced herself to concentrate, to keep her focus on the beam to avoid getting dizzy as it spun. The next beam, the one she couldn't look ahead to now, was like a seesaw, tipping back and forth and changing angles as well—at times slowly, at times abruptly—and she wished she'd had time to memorize its pattern, too.

Truth was, she hadn't considered that she might get this far. But no sense worrying about crossing that beam until she reached it. She'd have to believe her magic would help.

One by one, she stepped onto each block that arose until she reached the end of the beam. She realized the speed of the beam's rotations had slowed, and she closed her eyes for an instant. When she opened them, she searched for the tipping beam.

All she saw at first was a blurry flash of color and light from the multicolored clothes of the crowd. Nausea started to build, but she kept her eyes open and searched until the beam came into view. Keeping her eyes on it, she went through several more rotations, snapping her head around like a dancer to spot herself each time.

The wizards had made the next transition easier than she'd expected. With every second rotation of whichever beam she was on, the level of her current beam very nearly matched the height of the next. She counted a few more rotations to be sure. No sense in getting overeager now and falling.

When she was sure, she stepped onto the tipping beam, then leaned back to alter her center of gravity as the angle grew steeper. She pressed her toes down into the wood to keep from sliding forward. But as soon as the end of the beam reached its highest height, it dropped and Cinderella skittered forward, adjusting her body to the changing slope. Reaching the fulcrum before the tipping was reversed, she looked down while she had the chance. Nothing but the ground, thirty feet below.

Her throat tightened, but she forbade fear to invade. Not now. The next beam was the highest, and from the ground it had looked as if its only challenge was a set of six man-sized bags swinging across it. All she'd have to do was reach that final beam and cross it without being knocked off.

With one foot on each side of the middle point, she balanced while the beam tipped back and forth three more times, calculating the timing to make sure she'd get to the end of the beam at just the right moment. This had looked so much easier from down on the ground.

Her muscles tensed as she braced for the right moment, and then she started up the beam as it started to tip down. When it leveled out, she sprang forward as fast as she could run, knowing if she waited too long she wouldn't reach the end of the beam before it dipped below the level of the next.

She leaped and landed squarely on the next beam, but a huge stuffed leather bag—at least twice her height and girth—swung quickly toward her. She jumped out of the way just in time, watched for the next oncoming bag, and then the next, carefully making her way down without getting hit.

Panting, heart pounding, she reached the end of the beam and braced herself for the next danger, but then joy surged through her. There were none. Unless you counted the fact that she was thirty-five feet above the ground, standing on a four-inch-wide piece of wood with nothing to hold on to. She was done.

The roar of the crowd was deafening. Ropes appeared out of thin air, held by nothing she could see, and she raised her arms as they wrapped snugly around her, then lifted her off the end of the beam and lowered her slowly to the ground.

The announcer put his arm over her shoulders, pulled her forward, and the other contestants gathered around, offering congratulations. "Well done," the announcer said. "No one expected an inexperienced wizard to complete that course."

"I'm not a wizard," Cinderella corrected him.

"Yes you are, my dear. Yes, you are."

The announcer pointed up to the leaderboard where her points for the event flashed. They had been added to her overall score. She was in first. Ahead of everyone else. Way ahead. The announcer bent down to whisper into her ear. "Brace yourself, dear." He straightened and a hush fell over the crowd. "The judges have reached their final decision. No remaining competitor has a chance to pass number forty-eight. She is the winner!" He bent down. "What's your name, dear?"

Cinderella opened her mouth to speak, but suddenly froze. If the beauty competition had ended early, her stepmother might be in the crowd. The longer she could keep her escape a secret, the longer this adventure would last and the greater the chance she'd be able to speak to the royal wizard and find out the details of her lessons.

"Cat's got her tongue," the announcer said, and the crowd laughed. The announcer raised Cinderella's arm high, and the crowd cheered so loudly they seemed to have forgotten they didn't know her name.

Out of curiosity, Cinderella looked up to the box where the royal family had been watching, and a young man she assumed to be the prince bowed toward her. He was too far away to make out his features, but he was dressed in shiny satin with a fur-lined velvet cape and a simple gold crown that at this distance disguised even the color of his hair.

None of this really mattered to her. Even though she was supposed to dance with him tonight, she couldn't go to the ball without a gown, and none of that mattered as much as finding out when and where her lessons would start and making sure she got home in time to save Max from a mousy fate.

A tall wizard in a deep brown robe handed her a bundle of flowers, then so did a female wizard in dark gray. Others added to the pile and soon she could barely see.

"Do you need some assistance?"

She turned her face out of the flowers to see a group of the six most beautiful women she'd ever seen. The one who'd spoken smiled and started to take a few bouquets off the top, handing them to the others.

"Congratulations," she said.

"Thank you." Cinderella curtsied. It seemed the thing to do. Given their fine clothing, these women had to be members of the royal court.

"Oh, no need to be formal." The woman set a soft hand on Cinderella's forearm. "I'm Jenna, one of Queen Eleanor's ladies-in-waiting."

"Oh, my." Cinderella curtsied again.

But shaking her head and smiling, Jenna guided her up. "After that performance today, we should be curtsying to you." A friendly smile bloomed on her face.

"Curtsying to me?" Cinderella was sure that Jenna was joking. "I'm nobody."

"Nonsense," Jenna said. "The royal wizard is looking forward to teaching you." She winked. "As for the more important prize . . ." The ladies all giggled. "Let's find you something to wear to the ball."

If you were Cinderella, what would you do?

OPTION A: Cinderella should accept the lady-in-waiting's offer. She has nearly five hours before Max turns into a mouse, and if she's really lucky, she might run into Ty at the ball. If you think she should say "yes," go to section 7: If the Shoe Fits (page 211).

OPTION B
Cinderella should tell the lady-in-waiting thanks, but no thanks. She barely has five hours before Max turns into a mouse, and there's no way she's going to take any chances. Much better to get through those woods before dark, anyway. She'd rather use what little time she has to find Ty and tell him how much she appreciated his help and support. If you think she should turn down the lady-in-waiting, go to section 8: Fall from Grace (page 245).

Section 7

if the shoe fits

Fresh from a glorious warm bath, Cinderella gazed in the mirror at the four hairdressers who worked in perfect unison to pile her hair in soft tendrils. They'd adorned her locks with hundreds of tiny diamonds. The gems had to be enchanted, as she couldn't see any visible clasps, and when she turned her head under the lights, the diamonds shot reflections of pure light all over the room.

Her whole life, she'd envied her stepsisters their freedom and their mother's love and approval so much more than their beauty and fine things. But seeing herself like this, her skin so fresh and flushed, her hair shimmering as if it were gold and bedecked with diamonds, she was filled with joy. She'd never felt quite so beautiful, so special.

The hairdressers guided her back to the ladies-in-waiting and Cinderella gasped as she walked into Jenna's dressing room, full of beautiful things. The colors and textures were like spring flowers blooming around her.

"My clothes will be too long for you," Jenna said as she pulled out a periwinkle blue silk gown and held it up to Cinderella. Jenna shook her head and put it back. "But that's all right. The palace has several seamstresses on call."

"Oh," Cinderella said, "I can sew. No need to bother anyone, and I'll be very careful to ensure my alterations can be reversed." She couldn't bear the thought of ruining her gown.

"Don't be silly." Jenna pulled out a gown of such pale coral, it barely had a hint of color. "This one might work. Let's try it on."

After Jenna and her two dressing maids helped Cinderella into the gown, Jenna clapped her hands in glee. "His Highness will come running when he sees you."

Cinderella's skin crawled at the thought of some man she didn't know racing toward her—especially if it were for no reason other than her clothing—but she planned to stay away from the ballroom and concentrate on locating Ty.

The fine taffeta gown, trimmed at the bust with rows of tiny pearls, matched her skin tone perfectly. And underneath the skirt were multiple layers of luxurious tulle. She turned and the skirt caught a beam of light. It was as if the fabric itself had been woven from crystals. Cinderella blinked back tears of happiness.

"Now all we need are slippers." Jenna pulled a pair of delicate pink slippers from the shelf and held them up to the dress but shook her head and said, "No, these are too dark." She put them back and selected a silver pair encrusted with tiny crystals, then tipped her head to the side. "Not perfect, but I suppose they'll have to do."

"They're wonderful." Cinderella reached for the shoes, but Jenna crouched down to hold out a slipper for her to slip into.

Jenna stood and stepped back, pursing her lips. "Those will never do." She turned to the dressing maids. "Her feet are so tiny, even if we stuffed the toes she won't be able to walk in any of my slippers, never mind dance." Jenna shook her head. "No cobbler can make slippers in time."

"I can go barefoot," Cinderella said. The layers of tulle and taffeta would cover her feet.

"Oh, no." Jenna shook her head. "We can't have you go to the ball without slippers."

Cinderella's heart sank. She wasn't going to the ball after all. Just as she was getting used to the idea, it had been snatched from her grasp yet again . . . by something so small as a pair of shoes.

"The royal wizard?" Cinderella gasped. Her nerves had hit their limit, but before she could even consider why Jenna had summoned him, the wizard appeared, dressed in a robe of silver, his black and gray hair flowing all around him, as if he were surrounded by a wind that no one else felt.

"Well, young lady, we finally meet. You did very well today, and I've heard so much about you."

Cinderella started. Who could have been talking about her to the royal wizard? The other wizards on the arena floor hadn't seen any more of her than he had. It could only be Ty.

"You show great promise as a wizard," he said. "By the time you'd completed two events, I'd decided I wanted to offer you a position as one of my pupils, regardless of the outcome."

Cinderella's heart swelled, but then fell quickly. She still had to cross the huge hurdle of gaining permission from her stepmother or she'd never be able to attend classes. Now that the lessons were within her grasp, Cinderella realized she'd probably been fooling herself thinking her stepmother would just let her go.

It was possible that the royal wizard would have a solution for releasing her entrapment, but with Jenna and her maids present, Cinderella couldn't tell the royal wizard about the dark spells cast against her. Even if the wizard could counteract the black magic, she could not be responsible for turning her new friend into stone. Perhaps she'd find a way to have a quick private word with the wizard later.

Cinderella realized that while she'd been lost in her own fear, Jenna and the wizard had been talking, staring at her, and she still had no idea why he'd been summoned.

"I know just the thing." The royal wizard stepped back and lifted his wand, his silver robe shimmering in the light. "Raise your skirt a few inches, young lady."

Cinderella's hands trembled as she did as he'd asked, and the wizard shot a ball of light and sparks at her ankles. She sucked in a sharp breath, expecting pain.

But instead, the sparks tickled as they swirled and danced in circles around her feet. Her heels rose, support arrived under her arches, and her feet felt hugged, as if they'd been wrapped in soft, warm cloth. Still, she couldn't see anything. She pulled the skirt up farther and the light glinted off her feet as if they'd been coated in something shiny.

The wizard stepped back and crossed his arms over his chest. "There. I'm not much with women's fashion, but I think those are lovely."

Jenna and the maids clapped enthusiastically. "Oh, how wonderful!" Jenna remarked, hugging the wizard. "Don't you think so, Cinderella?" She gestured toward one of the full-length mirrors and Cinderella wondered if she could move.

She lifted one foot and was relieved to find it was neither detached from her leg nor anchored to the floor. She stepped over to the mirror, and, gasping, twisted in the light. "What are they made of?" She turned to the wizard, who was looking pretty pleased with himself.

"Glass," he said, spreading his arms out with a flourish. "Ta-da!"

"Glass slippers?" Her mouth fell open. "Won't they break?"

"Not these." His expression fell with his arms. "You don't like them?" He turned to Jenna. "I told you I'm not good with this kind of thing." He raised his wand again, but Cinderella shook her head.

"No, no. Don't change them. They're beautiful. And so light and comfortable. I've never seen anything so extraordinary." She twisted her foot in the mirror, marveling at how her feet looked bare, yet were supported up on a heel and protected. They were so much better than anything she could have imagined, and went perfectly with the pale, shimmering gown.

"Well then, what are we waiting for? Let's get you ladies to the ball." The wizard pivoted, his robe swirling along with him, and strode from the room.

Even from where she stood in the shadows of a side entrance, the ballroom was more spectacular than Cinderella could have ever imagined. Crystal chandeliers filled with thousands of tall tapers hung from the ceiling and the candles' light bounced off the dozens of gold-edged mirrors scattered about the room. The mirrors also reflected the many fabulous and wonderful colors of the ladies' gowns. She'd thought she'd blend into the background with her pale dress, but as hard as she'd tried to stay in the shadows and edges of the room, heads had turned her way as soon as she entered.

Cinderella saw Jenna approach, and slipped back out of the ballroom. She didn't want to be rude, but she needed the time she had to find Ty.

Moving into one of the many rooms between the palace entrance and the ballroom, Cinderella looked up to the ornately carved vaulted ceiling as the sounds of the orchestra drifted toward her.

She'd looked everywhere. She'd circled the ballroom five times, keeping to the edges and studying every male server she spotted. She'd wandered through every corridor she could find, and had asked countless maids and butlers if they knew a messenger named Ty. The palace staff had to be vast, she concluded—not a single one of them had heard of him.

A server with a tray of empty glasses went into a dark corridor she'd not spotted before, so she headed toward it, but turned as she heard the clack of high-heeled shoes behind her.

Her breath caught in her chest. Her stepmother was crossing the mosaic-tiled floor.

Heart sprinting and rising to her throat, Cinderella knew she should run, but her feet wouldn't move. If only she could melt into the floor, or disappear into the gilded walls to avoid notice.

She braced herself for a tirade, but instead her stepmother curtsied. "Excuse me, miss, could you direct me to the dining hall? I'm seeking my disobedient daughters and if I find them stuffing their faces with food . . ." Her voice trailed off, realizing she'd shared more than she'd meant to, and she smiled in a manner that looked almost polite.

Cinderella decided not to question her good fortune. Perhaps the festivities had put her stepmother into a good mood. "The dining room is just down this corridor." She gestured in the direction her stepmother should follow. "But I was just there and didn't see Agatha or Gwendolyn."

Her stepmother started and her face lit up. "You're acquainted with my daughters?"

"Of course." Cinderella looked at her stepmother quizzically. This had to be some kind of cruel trick, the setup for a crushing blow.

"I'm not surprised." Her stepmother touched Cinderella's arm with a gloved hand. "Possessing great beauty like your own, I have no idea how the prince will choose between them."

"Whom am I meant to choose between?" a male voice asked, and Cinderella's heart nearly stopped.

The voice had come from behind Cinderella, and her stepmother fell into a deeper curtsy, lowering her head, so Cinderella followed suit. This had to be the prince, but his voice sounded oddly familiar.

A pair of simple but finely made black leather shoes came into view and Cinderella tipped her head from her curtsy to let her eyes drift up black trousers to the deep purple velvet waistcoat of a man with a very fine shape. A fine shape, indeed. It was Ty.

"Stand, ladies, please," he said.

She snapped up. "You. Wha—" She wanted to question Ty, but couldn't give him away to her stepmother. She knew by now how much he liked disguises, but certainly he'd be in deep trouble if he was caught impersonating the prince. Especially tonight.

"I'm so glad I finally found you," Ty said with a soft smile on his face as he looked into her eyes. "Have you been avoiding me, Cinderella?"

She sucked in a sharp breath. Ty. Tiberius? No, it wasn't possible. Just a coincidence. It couldn't be.

Diverting her gaze from Ty to Cinderella, her stepmother's respectful expression transformed into one of surprise, then hatred. But just as quickly, she donned her mask of graciousness and turned back to Ty.

"Your Highness, I am so honored to meet . . ." Her tight voice trailed off midsentence as anger strangled her clipped words.

"This is my stepmother, Your Highness," Cinderella said. She disliked using the formal greeting for Ty, but if he'd fooled her stepmother into believing he was the prince, she might as well keep up with the charade.

"I feel sure we've met before," Ty said as he bowed slightly toward her stepmother. "In any case, I'm delighted to meet Cinderella's family." He sent Cinderella the briefest of mischievous glances before turning back to her stepmother and continuing. "She's quite enchanting, if hard to track down. I've been hoping for a dance with her all evening."

"I didn't realize you were acquainted," her stepmother said through gritted teeth.

Cinderella felt sure that at any moment fire might fly from her stepmother's eyes.

"Cinderella," her stepmother said, her voice dripping with icicles, "you are a selfish girl. You really must introduce your sisters to the prince."

"Yes, of course." Cinderella looked at Ty, starting to think he really might be the prince.

Ty turned to her stepmother and said, "Madam, if your other daughters are half as charming as Cinderella, I should very much like to meet them. Might you locate them for me right now?"

"Oh, yes, of course." Her stepmother bowed and curtsied as she backed away, but still managed to sneer at Cinderella.

It was no matter. The happiness surrounding Cinderella formed a shield. Whether Ty was a messenger or a hunter or a prince didn't matter; she'd found him.

As soon as her stepmother had gone, she turned to Ty. "Are you *really* the prince?" She looked up at what had to be a genuine royal crown ringing his tied-back blond curls, then backed up a step. He was the prince—and he'd lied. "You tricked me."

"Not on purpose. But I am sorry. Can you forgive me?" He reached for her hand.

She resisted the temptation to pull her hand away, and her fingers felt small and warm as he held them.

"I'm so sorry I deceived you," he said. "I can't see the kingdom, not really, unless I go out in disguise. It's amazing how no one recognizes me when I've got my hair down and I'm not wearing all this finery." He ran his hand down the front of his velvet jacket. "Dressed as a servant, or beggar, or hunter, most people dismiss me, and don't bother to notice my resemblance to, well, myself." He grinned. "Helps that I borrow clothes from different people all the time, too."

Cinderella couldn't imagine ever seeing Ty's eyes, his kind smile, and the sharp, strong angle of his jaw without instantly recognizing him. She winced as she remembered how incredibly rude her stepmother had been to Ty over the past few days. She marveled at how polite he'd been to her now.

Speaking of her stepmother . . . "I understand what you mean about some people not seeing past clothing or circumstance or what job you hold. It just happened to me."

"What do you mean?" He rubbed his thumb over her knuckles, sending a spark of joy through her that warmed her cheeks.

"My own stepmother has seen me every day since I was five years old, yet she didn't recognize me tonight, dressed like this. Not until you said my name."

A look of shock flashed over Ty's face and he pulled her closer. Her skirt brushed against his clothing.

Ty looked into her eyes, and Cinderella felt as if more than their hands were touching. Her heart thumped, her breaths quickened, and her chest rose and fell. The air had suddenly turned thicker and sweeter this close to Ty.

"Your stepmother must be as blind as she is rude." His voice was low and deep. "Your beauty shines through, no matter what clothes you are wearing."

"My stepmother's never seen me in anything but rags."

"Really?"

Cinderella nodded and bit down on her tongue. If she slipped and told him about the entrapment spells, they'd both be turned to stone, and there was no assurance any wizard could break her stepmother's black magic.

Taking her hand, Ty led her into another room, farther from the ballroom. "I don't want us to be interrupted if your stepmother finds your stepsisters. You're the only member of your family I want to talk to tonight."

She couldn't stop smiling. "Are you really the prince?" She mostly believed it, but wanted to be sure . . . and change the subject. There was no way she would let her family taint her thoughts.

"Disappointed?" His brow wrinkled.

"Why would I be disappointed?"

"Well, I heard from a reliable source that the prince is stuck up, not to mention a jerk who expects any girl he meets to immediately fall at his feet." He gave her a dimpled grin.

Her cheeks grew hotter and she averted her gaze for a moment. "I'm sorry. I was wrong to make assumptions. Can you forgive me?"

He cupped her cheek. "I might forgive you if you grant me a kiss."

Her breath hitched and the world seemed to spin around her as if she were lost in space and time, floating, caught up in magic, although she felt sure no spell had been cast.

His lips brushed over hers, soft as a butterfly landing, and her body instantly arched to close the distance between them. His hand shifted to her lower back, rested there, and their lips pressed together more firmly. Being in Ty's arms felt more wonderful than anything she'd felt in her life. Exciting yet safe, powerful yet gentle, foreign yet home.

"Excuse me, Your Highness," a voice said, breaking though the heavenly haze. Ty's lips lifted from hers.

Nerves suddenly overtaking her, she stepped back and ran her hands over the bodice of her gown, hoping to quiet her pounding heart, which surely everyone could hear. The man who'd interrupted was dressed in a uniform like the one Ty had been wearing when they first met.

"What is it, John?" Ty asked the intruder, while his intense gaze, so deep she felt it inside her, never left Cinderella.

"The king and queen have requested your presence in the ballroom," the messenger said.

Ty stepped closer to Cinderella, and regret came through his smile to his eyes. "I must step away for a moment, but I expect a dance from you later—several, in fact. Alas, for now, duty calls. Will you please excuse me?" He kissed her hand.

"Of course." If anyone understood obligations, Cinderella did.

"On second thought," he said, "come with me. It took so long to find you, I'm not letting you out of my sight again." He took her hand.

Suddenly, she glanced up to the grandfather clock at the side of the room and gasped. "I have to get home."

Sadness crept into his eyes. "But we haven't even danced."

Although she couldn't dance, although she hated the idea of all those eyes in the ballroom upon her at once, she couldn't imagine anything sweeter than being back in Ty's arms and twirling around the dance floor. But she had less than thirty minutes to get home.

"I really must leave," she said.

"Don't be silly. It's not even midnight." Ty grabbed her and spun her around so quickly she burst out laughing. "Besides, you need to be here when I announce my choice of bride."

Her cheeks burned, the back of her throat caught, and her heart galloped wildly. Surely he didn't mean he'd pick her, but if not, mentioning it like this would be cruel—and Ty was not cruel.

She looked into his eyes. "I'd stay if I could, but it's crucial I arrive home by midnight."

"More important than this?" He leaned forward, his face close to hers. She thought he might kiss her again, right in front of the messenger, but Ty only winked.

"Do you really have to leave now?" he asked.

"If I don't get home by midnight . . . it's a life-or-death situation." *Life or mouse, anyway.* "But I can't explain."

"Does this have to do with your stepmother, perchance?"

Cinderella looked down and clutched the fabric of her dress.

He pulled her hands from the dress and held them. "I know you'd stay if you could." He turned to the messenger. "Tell my parents I'll join them shortly." He leaned in close to whisper into Cinderella's ear. "But not until I arrange for someone to escort you safely home." He signaled to a footman, who nodded and darted off.

"Thank you." Her heart swelled. In one of his carriages, she'd arrive home in time to save Max.

"And with your permission"—he shot her a nervous grin as they walked hand in hand toward the front entrance—"I have something important I'd very much like to discuss with you. Something related to the announcement I'm supposed to make."

As they stepped outside, her heart nearly burst with joy, but she tried not to raise her expectations too high. The idea flashing through her mind—that Ty might actually chose her to be his bride—seemed outrageous, given her standing in society, or rather, her lack thereof. But if she was right and became engaged to the prince, there was no way her stepmother could keep her enslaved. She'd be free.

She tried not to let herself get carried away. Better to enjoy the fantasy while it lasted.

They paused at the top of the stairs heading down from the castle to the drive.

"The carriage will be here in a moment." He brought her hands to his lips and gently kissed them, spreading warmth inside her.

"This has been the most marvelous day," she said. "I had no idea. I never imagined . . ."

"I take it the prince wasn't as bad as you expected?"

"Hardly." She squeezed his hand. "I'm so glad I managed to suffer through meeting him."

He leaned down toward her, and she closed her eyes in anticipation of another kiss.

When his lips failed to land, she opened her eyes to find him frozen in place, inches from her, lips puckered.

"You ungrateful brat!" her stepmother shrieked, and Cinderella spun around to see the evil woman striding toward them, her wand raised and ready to strike again.

Her stepmother had used black magic at the ball after all. At any moment, one of the guards or the carriage could arrive. Her stepmother was taking huge risks considering that she could be easily detected, but at this point, it seemed she'd do anything to kill Cinderella's happiness and punish her.

She glanced down the drive, and her heart sank. The carriage, about ten feet away from the base of the steps, had stopped, too. She looked up to see one of the guards looking down from a balustrade, a grin on his face, clearly hoping to get a peek at the kiss. Her stepmother had frozen them all. Had she frozen time, too?

"Unfreeze him," Cinderella said, bracing her shoulders. "He's the prince! What are you doing?"

"Yes, he's the prince, and you're unworthy of him, not to mention a conniving, disobedient liar who broke my spell and sneaked out of my house!" Her stepmother circled Cinderella and the frozen prince, eyeing him as if he were one of her glass statues that she might break with the flick of a wrist. "I wonder which you care about more—your life, or his." She poked Ty's frozen arm and he wobbled.

"Stop that!" Cinderella's chest tightened with anger, defiance, and fear. "What have you done?" She strode toward her stepmother and grabbed her arm. She needed to leave to save Max, but couldn't bear to leave Ty frozen this way.

Cinderella looked up at the clock tower. "Unfreeze him. Now, please. I'll do anything you ask of me."

Her stepmother grinned and tapped her wand against her palm. "Anything, hmm? I'm feeling generous. Perhaps we can strike some sort of a bargain."

Cinderella gritted her teeth.

"If you promise never to disobey me again, never to leave the house, and, most importantly, to forget today ever happened . . ." Her grin widened, but her eyes narrowed before she continued, ". . . then I promise not to turn your prince into dust."

Cinderella cringed as she was smacked by the full impact of her stepmother's boundless cruelty. Her thirst for power over others seemed insatiable, and if it were left unchecked, she wouldn't stop until she ruled the kingdom. No matter what happened here tonight, Cinderella vowed to spend the rest of her days finding a way to expose her stepmother's evil ambitions.

Cinderella looked at Ty, such a strong young man, yet rendered helpless by her stepmother's spell. A breeze blew her skirt to the side and Cinderella shivered—not from the cold, but from terror. Even if she never saw him again, even if she remained trapped by her stepmother for the rest of her life, even if she never knew another day of freedom, she couldn't live knowing Ty had been turned to dust.

And there was Max to think about, too.

She looked at the clock tower. The minute hand ticked forward. Apparently time hadn't frozen, just the people in it, and in twenty minutes Max would be transformed into a mouse.

"Yes, fine. You have a deal," Cinderella said, her heart twisting.

Her stepmother grinned, flicked her wand, and Ty staggered forward where Cinderella had been standing before the spell. The carriage pulled to a stop in front of the steps. Ty turned to Cinderella, confusion covering his face, and her stepmother flicked her wand at him again.

He staggered back a few steps, then took off his crown and ran his hand over his hair. "What happened? Where am I?" He turned to Cinderella with a confused expression.

Cinderella ran forward. "Are you all right, Ty?"

He started and looked at her, confused. "I'm sorry, have we met?" He rubbed his eyes. "I can't focus. Just give me a moment." He turned away.

Cinderella gasped. He didn't recognize her. Not at all. She charged toward her stepmother. "We had a deal."

"And I kept it. Do you see any dust?" Her stepmother laughed.

"What did you do?"

"Cleaned up your mess, that's what. Now the prince won't have the burden of remembering you. In fact, it will be as if he's never ever seen you, never even heard your name."

Rage rose in Cinderella's chest. "How could you be so cruel?" She turned to Ty. "It's me. Cinderella. You know me. Look at me. Please."

He lifted his head, but quickly looked away again, as if he could focus anywhere but on her.

"Time's a-ticking, Cinderella." Her stepmother gestured toward the carriage. "And don't think anyone else here tonight will remember meeting you, either."

Cinderella felt as if someone had punched her in the stomach. "Ty, I have to leave."

"Good night," he said, and waved without even looking toward her. Every fiber of Cinderella's being wanted to run to him, to force him to see her, to force him to remember who she was, but she looked up at the clock.

"Are you coming, Miss?" the groom asked from the carriage door. "Because if you're not, we've got other places to go." He waved to the driver, who cracked the reins and the carriage started.

"Wait!" Cinderella cried out and ran down the stairs. Halfway down, she turned back to see Ty, still still dazed, still not recognizing her.

Down on the drive, the carriage had slowed but hadn't stopped. As she ran down the stairs, one of her glass slippers fell off. She didn't break stride; there was no time to retrieve it.

Anyway, what use did she have for glass slippers now that she'd be trapped for eternity?

"Oh, Max." Cinderella flung herself into her godfather's arms in the middle of telling him about the evening.

"Now, now," he said as he led her to the stool to sit down. "It couldn't have been that bad. For one thing, your gown is very pretty." He looked down. "Too bad it will change back into your rags in a few moments. And your—one shoe? Is that made of glass?" He tried to smile, but his cheeks quivered as he sat down on the edge of the table. "Now why don't you sit and finish telling me what happened? Quickly." He glanced at his pocket watch.

As he helped her take all the tiny diamonds out of her hair, she started at the beginning and told him about the competition and how the wizard wanted to teach her and how it turned out she'd known the prince all along, but then she stopped and bit down on her lip as pain stabbed her chest and throat. Now it was her smile that quivered.

"From what you've said, the prince will come for you," Max said softly. He took the diamonds and put them in her pewter goblet.

"No, Max, you're wrong." Tears welled up in her eyes and she got up and walked to the side of the room. "He won't come for me."

"You don't know that, Cinderella." He followed her and set a hand on her shoulder.

She turned and grabbed his hands. "She took his memories. He didn't even recognize me and couldn't see me as I fled. And it wasn't just Ty. She tampered with everyone's memories. Even the royal wizard won't remember he granted me lessons, and Jenna will have no idea why her dress is missing."

"Oh, dear." Max pulled her head into his chest and patted her shoulder for a few moments, then snapped back. "I must dash. I need to be outside by midnight or I'll be stuck down here."

"Why? Please don't leave me." She couldn't take any more. "You won't turn into a mouse, will you? I got home in time." If that happened, after all she'd been through . . .

"Not a mouse, no. But remember when I said there would be a cost for temporarily suspending your stepmother's spells?"

She gasped. "You mean you'll be a cat again? That was the cost?" Her heart nearly broke. "That's not fair."

"Don't worry about me." He patted the sheath where he'd hidden her mother's wand. "I'll figure some way to cast a spell in cat form and be human again. But it won't be possible if I stay on her property."

"Let me help you. After midnight, I can help change you back again." After today's events, Cinderella had more confidence in her skills.

"It won't be so easy this time. Plus, your stepmother will be home soon. We can't take that risk." He kissed her forehead and then ran for the door to the garden.

She followed and stood at the door. He took out the wand, placed it in his mouth, and ran across the lawn.

At the stroke of midnight, her beautiful dress turned back into her rags and she looked down. The gown—was it gone forever, or would it magically reappear in Jenna's closet?

She looked up for Max, but he'd disappeared. "Max!" she called out, running through the garden, searching for him. She saw a cat run behind the potting shed.

"Max! Max!" She ran after him, but could no longer see him. "Watch out for the wolves! Oh, Max." She would never have let him break the entrapment spell if she had known the cost was that he'd turn back into a simple cat.

Her day out hadn't been worth the cost. She'd lost Ty, lost the lessons, lost her chance to escape, and now Max had lost his human form. Defeated, she returned to the cellar.

"Cinderella!" Her stepmother's piercing voice rang out, shaking the floorboards.

Remembering the diamonds, Cinderella dumped them from the goblet into her apron pocket. Best to keep them well hidden. The next time the gong at the front door sounded, she might be able to use the diamonds to get help. Although she wasn't quite sure how.

The door to the cellar banged open, and her stepmother towered in the entrance, anger shooting from her eyes like fire. "How dare you defy me and sneak out of this house? I should have killed you back at the palace, but I didn't want to deal with the mess."

Her stepmother spotted the glass slipper Cinderella had foolishly left on the table. It flew through the air to smash on the stairs, shattering into hundreds of pieces. Cinderella gasped, but then her jaw dropped and hung open as she watched the broken glass re-form itself into her shoe. The royal wizard's magic was powerful.

Backing away, Cinderella widened her stance and raised her chin. She said to her stepmother, "You can't hold me here forever. I've met people now. People who care about me. People who will do whatever it takes to get me out of here." Except they'd forgotten who she was. But she wasn't going to show any fear.

"You are such a fool!" Her stepmother strode around the room, her anger spreading like the stench of rotten eggs. "If you think anyone cares about you, or even remembers meeting you, you're wrong. And as for the prince"—she tossed back her head and laughed—"even if he spoke to you tonight out of charity, even if his carriage brought you home, believe me, darling, that's over. He doesn't even know you exist."

Cinderella sucked in sharp breaths through her nose, trying to control her emotions. Where was her inner ninja when she needed it?

Gathering her courage, she lunged at her stepmother, but a force shot her back and sent her flying into the stone wall. She crumpled to the floor, fighting to get her breath back.

"Insolent girl," sneered her stepmother, her eyes glowering. "I see you've learned nothing from today's events." She heaved a dramatic sigh. "It will be a great sacrifice on my part—I suppose I shall have to hire more help—but from this day forward, you will never again leave this room. Not ever—not even to clean." She circled her wand and black sparks descended over both doors.

Her stepmother laughed as she climbed the stairs, leaving Cinderella on the cold floor of the cellar.

As the full weight of her new reality sank in, Cinderella's chest clenched and her stomach imploded. Pain snaked through her body, tightened her throat, and squeezed her temples. It was a pain far worse than any she'd suffered as the result of a physical injury. Ty didn't know her, didn't know she existed. If she couldn't leave this room, he would never get a chance to know her, either. And she was even more trapped than before.

When they'd talked, not an hour ago, she'd allowed herself to believe that Ty might actually love her, might actually ask her to be his bride, but she couldn't have been right. If she'd been right, if he had actually loved her, then love had proved to be disappointing.

She'd imagined love to be the most powerful kind of magic, but thinking about her life to this point, she wondered why she'd ever thought that. Everyone who'd ever loved her had vanished—her mother, her father, Max—and now Ty.

Love wasn't magic. In fact, love was so weak it could be wiped away with the flick of a wand.

"Did you hear?" Gwendolyn raced down then stood at the bottom of the stairs that led from the cellar into the house—stairs that Cinderella could no longer climb.

"Hear what?" Cinderella crossed her arms over her chest.

"The prince is visiting every house in the kingdom, looking for his true love." Gwen held one arm behind her back.

Cinderella's heart accelerated, but she fought her excitement. Why should her heart race at the idea of Ty? He no longer knew who she was. She replied calmly, "So?"

Gwendolyn leaned against the wall and grinned. "Too bad you've chosen to stay down in your room and wallow in self-pity."

She strode toward Gwen, who backed up a couple of stairs, but when Cinderella reached the opened door at the bottom of the stairs, it was as if she'd run into a brick wall. She shook her head to recover. "You know full well I'm not down here by choice."

It was just as well that she'd been stopped. Slapping Gwen wouldn't do her any good, even if she weren't trapped down in the cellar. "Someday your mother's black magic will be discovered and you'll all be punished."

"Whatever." Gwen flipped her dark hair. "Just thought you might want to know the prince found your stupid glass slipper. And get this. He thinks his true love lost it." Gwen's fake smile wavered.

Cinderella straightened her back, allowing a little hope to enter into her chest.

"But"—Gwen's smirk solidified—"the poor boy can't remember the name of the girl who owned it, or even what she looked like. So now every girl in the kingdom has a shot at convincing the prince it's her shoe. I plan to prove that it's mine."

"How will you possibly do that?" Cinderella asked. "It won't fit you. Your feet are huge."

Gwen wrinkled her nose. "There's no need to be mean."

"*I'm* being mean?" Cinderella replied, her head feeling as if it were about to explode.

"I forgive you." Gwendolyn offered a huge fake smile. "Especially since I have a secret weapon." She pulled the second slipper from behind her back.

Cinderella stepped forward. "That slipper's mine. It was made especially for me. You'll never get it on." Cinderella was nearly hyperventilating. Clearly, the royal wizard had crafted the slippers so that their form couldn't be altered. Her stepmother would likely have tried to make it bigger to fit Gwen.

Gwen shrugged. "I won't need to try it on. Haven't you heard that possession is nine-tenths of the law?" She snickered. "Having the shoe will be proof enough." She dangled the slipper from the end of her finger. "What do you think the prince and I should name our first baby? I'm thinking Gwendolyn if it's a girl, and Tiberius if it's a boy."

Cinderella's fists clenched. "He'll never love you." But did she know that for sure? Love had so far proven to possess a disappointing lack of potency, and anyway, if her stepmother could use black magic to make Ty forget her, then perhaps she could also use her magic to make Ty fall in love with Gwen.

She didn't want to believe that. Plus, knowing Ty was out there looking for her—or at least looking for the girl who'd lost the glass shoe—made her wonder if love had poked some holes in her stepmother's memory spell. Maybe if Ty saw her, now that he'd had a chance to recuperate from the freezing spell, he'd remember.

Gwen turned as the gong sounded. "Oh!" she said excitedly. "The prince—I should say, my future husband—is here. I must dash." She wiggled her fingers at Cinderella in a mocking wave and skittered up the stairs.

Cinderella pulled her stool to the window, stepped up on the precarious perch, and pounded her fists on the glass, but it was so thick, there was no way she'd attract any attention, even if someone were out back to hear. She wondered if Max had been able to use her mother's wand to turn himself into a human being yet. She tried using her mind to break the glass, but it was no use, as the panes were too thick.

Stomping and thinking, she paced the room. There had to be something she could do. She shoved her hands in her pockets and cried, "Ouch!" She pulled her hand out and sucked on the tiny cut where one of the diamonds from her hair last night had jabbed into her finger.

Diamonds . . . diamonds could cut glass.

She stepped down from the stool and stared at the jewels in her hand. Her stepmother might have trapped her down here, but she hadn't taken away her natural talent for magic. It was a talent so strong, even the royal wizard had commented on it.

Concentrating on raising the diamonds, she held her palm out, and the gems drifted up a few inches. Feeling the magic flow through her, she caused the hard stones to swirl in a circle, building up their speed and force.

She could do this. She had to believe in herself. Her powers had grown during the competition, and so had her confidence. Never had she felt so totally and completely in control. Inhaling to prepare, she raised her eyes to the window's thick glass, and then shot the diamonds toward it with all the force she could muster.

With a screeching sound, they pierced the glass with a hundred tiny holes. She smiled. The glass hadn't broken, but her limited magic power might be enough to finish the job.

She concentrated on breaking the glass, and a few of the holes formed cracks. But no matter how much she believed she could do it, her magic lacked the strength and power required to break such thick glass.

If magic wouldn't work, perhaps brute force would. She looked around for something to slam against the cracked glass. The stool was the hardest thing in her room, but the window was so high, she needed to use the stool to reach the glass.

She turned to the fire and saw the cast-iron grate. She pulled it out from under the ash, and then climbed back onto her stool. Holding the grate in both hands, she raised it high above her head and brought it forward into the glass with such force that she felt the reverberations right down to her toes.

The glass cracked, and hundreds of tiny lines flowed out like a spiderweb from the holes where each diamond was embedded. But still it didn't break.

She lifted the grate again, drew in a deep breath, and shouted loudly as she mustered every ounce of energy she could find—from her legs, from her back, from her shoulders, from her lungs—and transferred it into her arms to slam the grate into the glass.

Her heart sank. The glass appeared to be intact. But then she heard a crackling noise. A noise like the one she heard when she tapped the film of ice that formed on her water buckets if she left them filled overnight during the winter.

A shard of glass fell, then another, and after a few more shards dropped to the floor, the entire window crumbled apart, sending tiny pieces of glass clattering everywhere.

Her heart lifted. Now all she'd have to do was get through the small space without shredding herself.

She paused for a moment to regain her composure and then raised both hands, palms forward, toward the window. The broken glass flew out into the yard, clearing her path. From her perch on the stool, she jumped up and grabbed the outer frame of the window, which was made of sharp stone.

Her fingers and forearms were outside the house. There was no magical barrier anymore. She'd done it.

Straining, Cinderella pulled herself out until her arms could bend no farther, then pushed down and lurched forward, her hands scrambling onto the gravel, her body still half inside. She searched for something to hold on to, and slipping back, panic shot through her, but she fought back, pushing down into the gravel with her arms and wiggling her body until her weight transferred onto her hips inside the frame of the small window. She twisted from side to side, working her way through the window frame, and finally felt a release of pressure. She'd made it through, and was lying on the gravel at the edge of the building.

She leaped up and ran to the front of the house. No way was she letting Ty get off this property without speaking to him. Even though his feelings had proven too weak to withstand her stepmother's magic, her feelings hadn't diminished, much as she'd tried to set them aside. In fact, the thought that Ty was lost to her forever had only intensified and clarified her emotions.

She loved him. And as much as she'd tried, she couldn't shake the ache in her heart, the flutter in her stomach, the tingly feeling in her entire body at the thought of seeing him again, even if he didn't recognize her.

The front door opened, and her heart plummeted to the soles of her feet. Ty was holding Gwendolyn's hand, and she was beaming. Ty didn't seem quite as enthusiastic, but Cinderella still felt as if her heart had been trampled into a million pieces.

This was wrong, so wrong. She couldn't let Ty think Gwen was the girl he was searching for, the girl he'd loved but forgotten. She couldn't let him believe Gwendolyn's lies.

Cinderella stepped forward.

"Hello there," Ty said. "Do you live here, too?" He continued down the steps with Gwendolyn in tow. "Look—I found the girl who I was searching for."

"Are you sure?" Cinderella's heart hammered against her ribs. "Did she try on the slipper?"

"Better. She had the other one." He turned to Gwendolyn, who held up a velvet bag, presumably containing Cinderella's glass slippers.

"What if she's tricking you?" Cinderella could barely hear herself over the pounding of her heart. "Maybe using magic?"

"That's not possible," Ty said as he descended a few steps. "The royal wizard, suspicious of my memory loss, cast a spell to protect me from mind control today."

Cinderella wished the royal wizard had come with Ty. Surely he'd sense the black magic hanging over the property. Surely he could take down her stepmother in person. But he must not have realized a spell had been cast on *him* last night, too.

Even without the royal wizard's help, she couldn't let her stepmother win. If she couldn't make Ty remember her, she would have to use logical reasoning.

"What if Gwen *found* the slipper?" Cinderella asked, resisting the temptation to use the word "stole," even though that was the truth. "What if the girl you're looking for lost *both* of her slippers?"

"That seems unlikely," Ty said with a frown, but he appeared to be thinking it over. "The slippers are unique and Gwendolyn remembered exactly where she lost the one I found." Ty turned to Gwen again and wrinkled his brow as if questioning her story, or perhaps searching for memories. He shook his head. "I wish I could remember more about the ball."

"We had a fabulous time," Gwendolyn said, gripping his arm.

Ty shook his head. "I woke this morning with the most curious mixture of happiness and loss in my heart. I knew I'd found love, I knew I'd found the girl I wanted to marry, but the odd thing was I couldn't remember her face, her name, how we met, or even why I'd fallen in love. But my only real clue was waking with Gwendolyn's glass slipper in my hand."

"How sweet that you slept with my shoe." Gwendolyn reached out to touch his face, but he stiffened under her touch.

Rage pounded up from deep inside Cinderella and she blurted, "It's *my* shoe."

"What?" The prince turned toward her. He dropped Gwendolyn's hand and strode down the rest of the stairs. Gwen skittered down behind him and reached for him again, but he pulled away.

Ty met Cinderella's gaze and their eyes locked. She didn't see recognition there. Not with certainty. Yet, she could see his confusion, how he knew in his heart that Gwen wasn't the one, in spite of the "evidence."

Cinderella stepped forward and spoke softly. "The glass slippers are mine, Ty."

He started at her bold use of his nickname, but then nodded curtly and said, "Continue."

"The slippers were custom-made for me by the royal wizard so I could go to the ball." She stepped forward again. "We've met a few times. We were friends before I knew you were the prince. You encouraged me to enter the magic competition—"

"Stop this nonsense right now," her stepmother called out as she thundered down the stairs. "Get away from the prince, you worthless servant girl, or I'll turn you into a rat."

Ty's head snapped toward her stepmother, who dropped her raised hand and said, "Just a figure of speech."

Narrowing his eyes, Ty turned back to Gwendolyn. "May I have the slippers, please?"

"Why?" She moved them behind her back.

"If you've told me the truth, the slippers will fit you. However, if *she's* telling the truth"—he bowed his head toward Cinderella—"they'll fit her. One way or the other, it should be easy to settle this dispute."

Gwendolyn turned toward her mother, panic stretching and tightening her forehead and mouth, and her mother gestured with her head, jerking it from Gwen toward the cobblestone path.

Cinderella gasped. If Gwen threw the slippers, they'd smash into a million pieces, and there was no way to know for sure that they'd re-form again. The magic might be wearing off. If she couldn't try on the slippers, she had no way to prove they were hers. Gwen swung her arm and the bag flew up in a huge arc.

Cinderella used her ninja training to banish fear and panic from her mind so that she could instead focus all her energy on the bag.

She lifted her arm toward it. *Stop.*

The bag stopped six inches above the cobblestones—six inches from destruction.

"Great job!" Ty exclaimed as he stepped across the drive. "Did you say you entered the magic competition?" He bent down and snatched the bag from midair. "I'm not surprised. I'll bet you did well."

Cinderella stepped toward him, nerves crawling through her like spiders. "I'm still learning."

"You're very good." The prince held the velvet bag close to his chest to ensure it wouldn't fall again. "I've been training with the royal wizard since I was young, but I can't imagine pulling off what you just did— especially without a wand. We should train together."

Cinderella smiled softly, daring to hope. "I'd like that. Very much."

Their eyes remained locked and she saw the same expression of admiration and affection she'd seen in his eyes when they first met, but it wasn't the look he'd had in his eyes at the ball. It wasn't even the same way he'd looked at her the second time they'd met, or the third. But his interest and admiration gave her hope that, given a chance, they'd be able to start over.

Ty stepped off the path and onto the grass. "Seems safer over here," he said. He removed the slippers from the bag, knelt down on one knee, and held up a slipper for Cinderella. She blushed, and her heart swelled at her love for this boy. A prince, and yet so humble and kind.

She stepped out of her worn, dirty shoe and lifted her foot. Never breaking eye contact with her, Ty lightly touched her calf and her skin tingled under his fingers as her foot glided easily into the slipper.

Ty's eyes widened, and he quickly reached for the second shoe and slipped it onto her other foot. The instant both were on, lights swirled around the slippers, as they had when they were first created, and the glass molded to hug her toes and support her feet like a second skin.

"Cinderella?" The prince looked up from her shining shoes to her face. "Cinderella. That's your name, isn't it?"

She nodded, but the back of her throat caught and stole her ability to make words.

He rose and took her hands in his. "I remember. I remember everything, my love." He bent to kiss her, and excitement spread through Cinderella's body like wind skipping through the night forest.

"No!" her stepmother yelled, and they broke their kiss. "No!"

Cinderella scrambled to remove the glass slippers; with Ty's help, she put them back in the bag. There was no way she'd lose them again.

A bolt of lightning shot toward them and scorched the ground at their feet, sending sparks flying all around them.

Will Cinderella and Ty escape
her stepmother's black magic?

To find out, turn to section 9: And So it Ends (page 279).

Section 8

————— ⋙❁⋘ —————

faLL
from
grace

inderella kept to the edge of the village square, enjoying the delicious food that had been set out after the competition. The other competitors reveled in the attention, but she felt self-conscious. Worse, the risk of attention from the wrong people was too high. Her stepmother and stepsisters might be lurking anywhere.

The beauty pageant crowd had also spilled into the courtyard, but from the few conversations she'd overheard, most of those girls had forgone eating and headed straight for the palace to get bathed and dressed for the ball.

She still hadn't spotted Ty. He must have gone to the palace already, probably to help set up.

"Cinderella, I finally found you."

She cringed at hearing her name, but looked up to see none other than the royal wizard headed toward her. She glanced around nervously, worried that his arrival might draw unwanted attention.

"I can't wait to train you," he said.

She shifted so that his dark gray robe shielded her from the rest of the crowd. "Really?" She had to admit she felt proud. Even though she'd done well, all she could remember right now were her mistakes.

"Not two events in," the royal wizard continued, "I decided I wanted to train you, regardless of the outcome of the competition. Your innate magic abilities are very strong. Who has been guiding your training?"

"No one, Sir."

"Well, that's even more impressive." He put his hands on his hips and a wind swirled around him, picking up some dust that sparkled in the sunshine. "You are a very special young lady."

Special? Her? She blushed and wondered if she dared mention the entrapment spells now. His powers were vast, but so were her stepmother's. Imagine if the royal wizard turned to stone, right here, because of her.

"I need to ask you something," she said. As dangerous as it was, if she didn't ask, if she didn't find some way past the entrapment spells, she couldn't take the lessons. She realized she'd been silly to think her stepmother would let her go out of fear that someone would find out about her black magic. That woman feared nothing.

"Certainly," the royal wizard said.

"Hal!" a woman's voice rang out. "I'm ready to go. You might not need time to prepare for the ball, but I do."

The royal wizard leaned forward, a conspiratorial grin on his lips. "My wife," he said, raising his eyebrows. "She won't let me use magic to get her ready, but demands that I snap to her schedule."

He rested his hands on Cinderella's shoulders. "Why don't we save your question until our first lesson?" Then he spun away so quickly that she lost the chance.

Her heart sank. Unless the royal wizard could break her stepmother's entrapment spells, she wouldn't get the opportunity to take his lessons.

Cinderella let herself get lost in the crowd of contestants and spectators heading from the square to the palace, and scanned the group as best she could for Ty on the off chance he hadn't already gone to the palace. Although she tried not to stand out, every couple of minutes someone congratulated her on her performance in the competition—even her spectacular failures.

Nearing the gates to the castle, disappointed she still hadn't found Ty, she jumped onto the wall lining the path to get a better look at the crowd. Even if he had to work during the ball, he might have time to chat on the walk over.

She shielded her eyes with her hand, but instead of spotting Ty she spotted her stepsisters, not ten feet away on the opposite side of the cobblestone road.

Worse, Agatha spotted her, a questioning look and shock in her eyes. Cinderella dipped her head and crouched down, wishing she could disappear, but when she peeked back up, Agatha had turned away and was pulling Gwendolyn down the path.

Her heart pounding, Cinderella waited for an opening in the flow of pedestrians below her so she could jump back down and once again stay hidden among the crowd.

Keeping her head down, she passed through the gates into the castle's entry hall. She lifted her gaze up to the high-vaulted ceilings and spun with wonder at the glass skylights capturing the spring sunshine. Stone carvings that looked like vines wound their way around the ceiling, encircling each skylight. Portraits of the royal family's ancestors, all dressed in fine furs and rich velvets, were hung throughout the room.

Cinderella froze. One of the portraits—which, based on the style of the subject's clothing, seemed to have been painted at least a century ago—looked very much like Ty. What an interesting coincidence.

"The ballroom is through these large doors to your right," a man in a dark gray and burgundy uniform said from the top of a high staircase above her. "And the dressing rooms are through the smaller doors to the left and right of those doors. Left for the men, right for the women."

The crowd tittered in excitement and the man continued, "If you sent it ahead, each of you will find your gowns and suits inside and a dresser to help you freshen up." He bowed slightly. "If you have questions, any one of the castle staff will be most happy to assist you."

But where was the rest of the castle staff? If Ty were working as a dresser, helping the men press their suits and shine their shoes, she might not see him until the ball started. Her best bet was to hope he was on ballroom setup duty, or perhaps preparing refreshments.

As the rest of the girls skipped and ran into the dressing room, Cinderella opened the huge door to the ballroom and slipped inside. Her breath caught in her chest. "Wow!" she said, and quickly raised her hand to her lips, embarrassed she'd spoken aloud.

But no one seemed to notice. Servants buzzed about the room draping silk covers over chairs and lighting hundreds of candles in huge crystal chandeliers. A team was hoisting an already-lit chandelier up to the ceiling, using thick ropes and pulleys. Another group was adjusting and placing huge arrangements of white, pink, and red flowers on tables covered in splendid damask cloths.

Cinderella pulled her eyes from the splendor to concentrate on her search for Ty. On a high balcony at the far end of the room, a man leaned onto the stone railing. At this distance, she couldn't make out much detail, but his clothes seemed especially fine and his hair was tied back from his face. Could it be the prince?

She shielded her eyes against an illuminated chandelier as it passed between them, but before the man came into focus, he stepped away from the railing and into the shadows.

Oh well. She wasn't here on a prince-spotting mission anyway.

"Where's your uniform?" asked a woman dressed neatly in a servant's uniform. She had silvery-gray hair, pink cheeks, and a warm smile. "Go get into it, girl." The woman nodded toward the wall of the ballroom, where one of the panels between the mirrors turned to let a line of servants holding fresh candles enter the room.

Cinderella made a beeline toward the panel, and it nearly hit her as it swung into the room.

"Watch it!" A maid in a blue-and-silver-striped apron nearly crashed into her. "It's a one-way entrance. Weren't you here for the briefing?"

"Sorry." Cinderella nodded and then saw a waiter in a black tunic with white gloves exiting the ballroom through another panel. Realizing some were for entering and some for exiting, she followed the waiter and pressed the panel open.

Behind it lay an arched corridor lit by gas lamps, constructed entirely of blocks of stone. At intervals, paths led off to the right, while smaller arches along the left marked the entrances in and out of the ballroom. From this side, they were clearly marked "In" and "Out."

Cinderella stepped out of the path of a waiter carrying a huge tray of crystal goblets and decided to head forward, keeping her eyes on everyone she passed, hoping to find Ty.

"Excuse me." She pressed herself against the stone wall to avoid four large men carrying an ice sculpture of a swan. Then, as soon as she moved again, an even larger block of ice, carved to look like a fountain and being rolled on wheels, came barreling toward her. She glanced over her shoulder. Everyone had vanished. Was she supposed to outrun it?

She turned and ran, but someone grabbed her arm from the side and pulled her into a tunnel.

The ice rumbled by.

"That was close. Thanks." She smiled at the slight woman who'd saved her, but the woman only scowled.

"Didn't you hear the signal?" she asked.

"I'm sorry," Cinderella said instead of answering the woman's question. She *had* heard a bell ring, but hadn't thought much of it since the corridors were so filled with sound.

"I've not seen you before." The woman put her hands on her slim hips. "Who did your training sessions?"

"I didn't hear the bell," Cinderella said, hoping that had, in fact, been the signal. "I was distracted. I'll be more careful."

The woman shook her head. "Where is your uniform?"

"I was just headed to get changed right now." She hated to lie, but she also didn't want to get kicked out of the palace before she found Ty.

"Well, off you go then." The woman took her by the shoulders, pointed her down the same side tunnel she'd pulled her into, and gave her a tiny push. "Spit-spot. No time to waste. The first guests will be arriving in the ballroom any moment."

Cinderella turned to give a short curtsy and then continued down the narrow, dark hallway. She had to assume the corridor led to where the servant uniforms were stored. Perhaps she'd find something to put on that would help her blend in. Maybe she'd even help out. It wasn't as if she lacked experience in serving.

She crossed under a gaslight into a dim section of the tunnel and focused on the dark floor, blinking, hoping to coax her eyes into adjusting to the darkness more quickly.

"Hello there."

She stopped short at the male voice and looked up. "Ty!" Reaching up, she threw her arms around his neck.

He laughed and one of his hands brushed her waist.

Suddenly embarrassed, she backed away.

He adjusted the buttons on his waiter's uniform, as if he'd just finished dressing. "Where are you headed?" he asked.

"I was looking for you."

"That's quite a coincidence." His bright smile caught the glow from a gaslight. "Because I was looking for you."

"You were?" Her grin spread down to her toes. "You must be busy. I don't want to bother you, but I wanted to thank you for your all your help and . . ." She paused, then continued, ". . . I wanted to see you again." Her cheeks burned and she was thankful for the dim lighting.

"I wanted to see you, too." He brushed a hair back from her face. "I have a message for you from the royal wizard."

"You know the royal wizard?" Ty did get around.

"I heard him tell the prince he was impressed with your performance today, and wants to train you."

"Oh, I saw him back at the courtyard."

Ty ran a hand through his curls. "Fabulous. I knew you'd do well."

She tried to keep her feet on the ground, but they wanted to leap and skip and dance. As for her arms, they wanted to throw themselves around Ty again, so she pressed them into her sides. "I'd give anything to take his lessons."

"Cinderella, you don't need to give anything. You just need to show up. He wants you—on full scholarship."

She looked down and brushed one of her shoes along the stone floor. She couldn't tell him about the huge obstacle still standing between her and the royal wizard's lessons.

He put his hand softly on her arm, just below her elbow. "You're in. What's the problem?"

She lifted her head. "My stepmother. She's very strict. I'm not sure she'll let me."

His hand slid lightly down her arm until he was holding her hand, and her entire body tingled. Even if her stepmother turned her to stone tonight, she'd die happy.

No, she told herself. She didn't want to die. Not if it meant never feeling this way again. It was greedy, but now that she'd had a taste of whatever was buzzing inside her, all she wanted was more.

"I'm sure she'll let you go." The calm, reassuring sound of Ty's soft, deep voice made it easy to believe him, so she decided not to argue. She couldn't explain why he was wrong without endangering his life.

"Once you're a trained wizard," he said, "what will you do? What are your dreams for your life?"

"Dreams?" She hadn't allowed herself the luxury.

"Close your eyes," Ty said softly and moved closer toward her. So close she could feel his heartbeat. "Imagine yourself doing anything you want. What would make you most happy?"

Cinderella tried to slow down her galloping heart to allow herself to think clearly, but his thumb rubbed her hand softly, and the tiny gesture gave her a rush of adrenaline. Banishing the tension and fear perpetually stored in her shoulders, she took a moment and dreamed.

Eyes closed and with the comforting warmth from Ty, she exhaled a long, slow breath. "First, I'd like to sleep in one day, just to see what it feels like." She smiled. "And I'd like to travel around the kingdom, see faraway places." She'd been so sheltered to this point, the freedom of travel was beyond appealing. Happiness trickled up inside her. "And I'd like to be a great wizard and use my magic to help others and be a real ninja warrior so I could save people from thieves and make sure no one in the kingdom ever practices black magic or is forced into doing anything they don't want to do." She had to stop to catch her breath.

He laughed. "Those are great dreams."

She opened her eyes and laughed, too. "I know it's a lot. I'm not really so greedy."

"Not greedy at all." He tipped her chin up with his finger and kissed her. His kiss was gentle and soft, but she felt it right down to her toes, and her knees turned to jelly. He caught her waist. "You are a remarkable girl, Cinderella."

"Remarkable? No. There's no one more ordinary than me. I've lived my entire life—" She stopped herself. "I've been sheltered, a servant. Before I met you I'd barely left the house where I work. But what am I saying?" She shook her head. "You're a servant, too. You know how it feels not to have choices."

"No choices?"

Feeling bold, she reached up to his face and closed her eyes at the feel of his strong, warm jaw under her palm, his cheek under her thumb. "I know what I most want to do once I'm a trained wizard."

He bent his lips close to her ear. "What will you do?"

"I'll find a way to earn enough money so that neither of us will have to work as servants. I'll come to find you."

Leaning down toward her, he said, "You'll take me away from all this?" His words felt hot against her ear, but his tone was slightly teasing.

She leaned back. "You don't believe me. You don't think I can do it."

He shook his head. "I believe you. I believe you can do anything you set your mind to."

She raised her hand to touch the locket under her dress, and then tugged on the thin chain to pull it out.

"What's that?" he asked.

"It was my mother's. She died when I was born."

"I'm so sorry." He touched her cheek. "It's lovely. Almost as beautiful as you are."

She blushed all over, feeling as if a hundred tiny lamps had been lit inside her. Running her thumbnail along the thin crack of the heart-shaped locket, she concentrated on her feelings for Ty and the locket snapped open.

"What's inside?" he asked.

She tipped the locket into his hand to show him.

"It's a heart." He studied the small enameled heart as if it were a ruby. "How precious."

He reached to put it back in the locket, but Cinderella shook her head. "Keep it, so you'll never forget me."

"I could never forget you, Cinderella."

She felt something stir in her belly and heart. Was it love? She wasn't sure, but it was certainly potent and seemingly magic. "It might be a while before I can see you again."

"That would break my heart," he said. "I'm sure we'll see each other soon, but I will promise to keep this until then." He wrapped his hand around the small heart, and then bent to kiss her.

Cinderella wondered if it would ever be possible to be happier than she felt this moment.

A loud gong sounded, and they pulled apart.

"I have to go," Ty said. "The guests are coming into the ballroom. Please promise you'll dance with me later."

"You're going to dance at the ball? Aren't you working as a waiter?"

"Trust me," Ty said. "I have a surprise. I don't have time to explain now, but find me and we'll dance."

"I can't go in there like this." She ran her hands over the clothes Max had made for her, still dirty from the dust of the arena.

"It doesn't matter what you're wearing, you'll be the most beautiful girl in the room."

"Ty!" She slapped his arm lightly in jest to punish him for the tease, but it was the nicest thing anyone had ever said to her.

"If you're really worried about your clothes"—he headed back toward the main hall, his hand in hers—"then stay up in the balcony. You can access it through a staircase that's eleven more alcoves farther down the main corridor."

"Eleven."

"Yes. Wait for me up there. I'll find you and we can dance in the shadows above the party. It'll be better up there, anyway. More private."

Cinderella's body hummed with excitement. "I'll wait for you there."

They reached the main corridor and he ran off in the other direction, blowing her a kiss.

Cinderella felt lighter than ever and skipped down the tunnel, avoiding collisions with servants and counting the alcoves. She was going to dance at the ball after all, even if no one would see her. Certainly not the prince.

She nodded to a waiter carrying two trays laden with fruit and strong-smelling cheeses, but she'd have time to eat later. She wanted to get up those stairs to the balcony and wait for Ty. Nothing had ever felt more important.

Cinderella leaned over the stone railing. The party was in full swing and the sweet sounds of the orchestra filled the air. The colors in the ballroom were breathtaking and time passed quickly as she admired the fabulous gowns and hairstyles of the dancing guests. So much time had passed that she started to wish she'd mentioned her curfew to Ty. If he didn't come up here soon, she'd have to leave to get home to save Max.

Remembering the heat of his hand on her waist and his kisses, she shuddered at the thought of never experiencing that feeling again. It was time to take matters into her own hands and find him.

There were only two parts of the ballroom she had trouble seeing: the area directly below her, and the area where the prince was dancing with his female suitors. The girls were so tightly packed in a small circle around him, she'd barely caught a few glimpses of his crown.

How insulting to her gender that the girls were practically begging for a turn. Her life was pretty horrible as horrible went, but she couldn't imagine sinking so low. Did these girls have no pride? And they were increasingly restless. Even from up on the balcony, the sound of rustling taffeta and tulle was deafening.

Suddenly the tight ring around the prince parted, and a collective sigh of disappointment fell over the girls. Either the prince had picked his bride, or he was taking a break.

In spite of herself, Cinderella watched as the end of the circle burst, and the crowd continued to shift to form a kind of funnel for the prince to walk through.

She saw the prince. Dressed in rich, dark purples, his blond hair was pulled back and tightly tied with a black bow low on his neck and held down on top by a crown—a simple ring of gold encrusted with small jewels. He reached the edge of the dance floor and looked up.

It was Ty. Her breath caught in her chest. What was he doing?

He smiled up at her and waved, and she looked back at him with questioning eyes. If he was impersonating the prince, he'd be caught and jailed when the real prince showed up.

Except . . . she raised her hand to her mouth. How could he impersonate the prince at the royal ball? Could he actually *be* the prince? All the horrible assumptions she'd made about the prince and the royal family raced through her mind. When she'd said those things, he hadn't seemed offended, but that mischievous look he'd sported . . .

His eyes still on her, he blew her a kiss, and a collective gasp rose from the crowd. He couldn't possibly have fooled all these people. He had to be the prince.

Every eye in the room looked up toward her, and she blushed. She wasn't used to being under anyone's scrutiny except her stepmother's, and that scrutiny always held more coldness than curiosity.

Her stepmother. Panicked, she let her eyes drift from Ty to search the crowd, but then she looked back to Ty and calmed down. She was silly to be so scared. Even her stepmother wouldn't use black magic at the ball, not in front of all of these people.

Ty gestured for her to come down, but she shook her head and pinched the shoulder of her ninja outfit to remind him of her attire.

He nodded and continued forward, the crowd parting for him until he'd moved nearly under the balcony. She hoped he was headed for the stairs, and leaned forward over the railing so she could watch him as long as possible, still not convinced her eyes weren't playing tricks on her. Her Ty was Prince Tiberius? The thought had never crossed her mind.

Ty disappeared from sight and she was about to step back down when someone grabbed her leg from behind and tipped her forward.

Headed straight for the ballroom floor many feet below, she grabbed for the pillars under the railing, but the stone stung her hands.

In shock, she let go and saw her stepmother backing away, the most evil grin she'd ever sported dressing her face.

Below her, everyone shrieked, and Cinderella tried to tap into her magic to slow herself down. But it was no use.

She landed in Ty's arms.

"Now, that's an entrance," he said. "Are you hurt?"

She'd lost her wind, but shook her head as the crowd pressed in around them.

His thumb caressed her back as he held her. "You must have slowed yourself. You landed as light as a feather."

"Oh, I doubt that." But she felt so safe and warm in his arms, she didn't want to let go. Her hands laced together behind his neck, near where his curls were constrained by the black ribbon.

"What happened up there?" he asked.

She bit her lip. "Why didn't you tell me you were the prince?"

"Are you angry?" His eyebrows rose.

"Not angry, just surprised." He'd misled her, but she realized that if he'd been honest from the start, they'd never have had a chance to get to know one another.

"That's good." His face softened in relief. "Because I have something very important to ask."

"What do we have here?"

Cinderella stiffened at the sound of her stepmother's voice.

Ty tightened his hold on her, but she pushed against him and he let her feet slip to the ground, keeping her close by his side.

"Your Highness." Her stepmother curtsied. "I am so sorry that you've been bothered by this lowly servant girl."

"Madam, I am not bothered by Cinderella in the least." Ty laced his fingers through Cinderella's. "In fact, I'm enchanted." He raised her fingers to his lips, pressed the lightest kiss onto her knuckles, and Cinderella nearly burst with joy.

"You are too kind," her stepmother said, glaring at Cinderella. "For surely this servant girl nearly killed you with her clumsy fall." She grabbed for Cinderella's other hand. "Allow me to escort her from the ballroom. Certainly she took a wrong turn to arrive here."

"Madam, I assure you there is no need." Ty tightened his grip on Cinderella's hand.

"Then at least let me find her a suitable gown." Her stepmother's fingernails dug into Cinderella's flesh as the woman tugged on her arm. The crowds pushed in, eager to see the scene.

"Wait," Cinderella said. "You will tear me in two."

"I wouldn't want that." Ty dropped her hand.

With that, her stepmother yanked her away, and Cinderella looked over her shoulder toward Ty, but the crowd had already filled in.

"What is the prince thinking, wasting time with a servant?" Her stepmother threw her voice, so the words sounded as though they were coming from several feet away.

"Yes, why dance with *her*, when *our* daughters have yet to meet him?" This time, her stepmother threw her voice in the opposite direction. "Scandalous! Where did that urchin come from? How did she get in here?" Her stepmother continued to throw her voice, creating the illusion that many women shared the idea that Cinderella should be thrown from the room.

Soon, other mothers joined in with cries of dismay and forced their daughters toward Ty, making it impossible for him to break through the crowd without physically knocking some of the young women and their mothers aside. Soon, Cinderella couldn't even locate him among the huge pack of taffeta, tulle, and tenacity.

Her stepmother continued to drag her out of the room. "You stupid, presumptuous girl." She glared so hard that Cinderella feared she might burst into flames from the hatred. "How did you break my spell to get here?" She lunged forward and took Cinderella's chin in her hand, squeezing hard. "You inherited your mother's magic, didn't you? I knew I should have killed you years ago. But no, I had to be kind, had to let myself worry what my real daughters might think."

Cinderella pulled out of her grip and resisted the urge to rub her jaw where her stepmother had gripped her. "Oh, please. You just kept me alive hoping I knew where my mother's wand was."

"Where is it?" her stepmother demanded.

"I'll never tell you. And yes, I do have magic skills. In fact, the royal wizard wants to train me, and he'll find out about your black magic and—" Panting, she realized she'd shown too much of her hand.

"You ungrateful, horrible child." Her stepmother spun Cinderella and threw her up against the wall just outside the entrance to the ballroom.

Shards of terror crept up and down Cinderella's spine.

"You need to be punished for ingratitude and disobedience. Let's see . . ." Her stepmother pressed the end of her wand into her cheek. "Oh, I have a good idea." She flicked her wand back through the open doors to the ballroom and a blanket of gray sparks spread over the room and fell onto the crowd.

Cinderella didn't see anything happen. "What have you done?" She'd been sure her stepmother wouldn't risk black magic in front of so many people, but she appeared to have been wrong.

"Just cleaning up your mess." Her stepmother stepped forward, pressing Cinderella into the stone wall behind her. "No one. Not one person. Not even the royal wizard will remember meeting you today. Not one of them will even remember you exist. And I put in a little extra for the prince."

Cinderella crumpled under the weight of her stepmother's words.

When she'd woken this morning, all she'd cared about was winning the lessons so she could escape, but now the thought that Ty might forget her was too much to bear. She pushed off the wall past her stepmother and ran into the crowd, looking for Ty, surprised her stepmother didn't stop her.

"How rude," a woman dressed in emerald said as she brushed by.

"Who let you in?" a man said in disgust, grabbing her shoulder.

She struggled in the man's grasp as she called, "Ty! Over here!" Heads turned toward her, and the crowd parted to reveal Ty at its center, another girl in his arms.

He stepped forward, wondering who'd called him.

She smiled, but he looked straight through her. It was as if he didn't see her, couldn't see her. She froze in her tracks, trying to process what was happening.

The man pushed her toward the edge of the room, where her stepmother was standing, her arms folded over her chest.

"Thank you, Sir," she said to the man. "I'll take her from here."

"No, you won't." Cinderella broke free from the man. All she needed was some time to talk to Ty. Even if he didn't remember their past conversations, she'd start from the beginning. He liked her—the *real* her. He might even love her, and no matter what kind of forgetfulness spell her stepmother had cast, it hadn't changed who he was, who she was. She just needed some time.

She looked up at the huge clock at the end of the ballroom and her heart sank. It was eleven thirty. If she stayed, even if she could fight off all the other girls and their mothers seeking Ty's attention, it would mean the end of Max. Staying and trying to win back Ty's affections would be selfish. She had no choice.

Her stepmother laughed, and rage bubbled up inside Cinderella, but this was a battle she didn't have time to fight. Not if she was going to get home in time to save Max. She turned from her stepmother and started along the side of the room toward the door.

Her stepmother landed in front of her. "Do you plan to walk home? We can't have that."

Cinderella stepped around her, but her stepmother kept in stride beside her. "It's very dangerous out there. Especially at night. If you go into those woods, the wolves will surely eat you."

Cinderella kept her jaw firm. Getting through the forest at night was not without dangers, that was true, but she'd proved today she could withstand more than she'd ever imagined. Right now, facing her stepmother seemed more dangerous than encountering any wolf or thief in the woods.

"I've done my best to protect you, Cinderella."

She was only twenty feet from the front entrance. Once through, she'd break into a run, and surely her stepmother would let her go. Surely her stepmother would be happy if she were eaten by wolves.

"But clearly," her stepmother continued, "I won't have done my motherly duty if I let you out tonight into that dangerous forest." She tapped her wand against her palm. "I must get you safely home."

Cinderella stepped out the doorway and turned to her stepmother. "You've done enough. I can outrun the wolves and thieves and whatever other dangers are in those woods tonight. Please. Just let me go."

"Not a chance I'll risk it. You're too valuable. You need some transportation." Cinderella realized her stepmother was worried she wouldn't go home. Her stepmother had no idea she needed to be back by midnight, and thought she planned to escape for good.

"I'll not only send you home," her stepmother added. "To keep you safe, I'll make sure you never risk this sort of escapade again."

Cinderella tried to run, but her feet wouldn't move. Someone . . . some spell . . . had nailed them to the floor. She tugged on her limbs, but her efforts were useless.

Max. If she didn't get away soon, she wouldn't get home in time.

"I have an idea," her stepmother said. "One that will keep you out of trouble. From now on, whenever you are outside our home, your tongue will be tied."

Cinderella opened her mouth to object, but it felt as if it had been stuffed full of cotton. Then a huge flash of light blinded her and she was lifted off the ground. Air rushed around her as if she were being pulled through a long, windy tunnel. She tumbled, spun around, and flailed against her will.

She landed on her bottom with a thud, on something hard. The light around her cleared and her eyesight returned.

"Cinderella? Are you okay?" a male voice said, and then a careful hand fell onto her shoulder.

The world came back into focus—she was in her cellar room—and she stood up slowly. When she turned around and saw Max, she let out a cry of joy and threw herself into his arms.

Over the next five minutes, Cinderella told Max everything that had happened. When she got to the tongue-tying part, a look of fear rose in Max's normally reassuring eyes. "Quickly," Max said as he took her hand and pulled her toward the cellar door. "Let's get outside before midnight, and I need your mother's wand."

"What will happen at midnight?" She held back.

Max stared down at the floor. "Just come with me, before it's too late for us to talk." He flung the door open and she raced to keep up with him as he dashed outside and then turned toward her. "Try to talk to me," Max said, nodding his encouragement.

Cinderella opened her mouth to talk but nothing came out. Her tongue felt like lead. All she could do was make strange, unintelligible noises. She put her hand in her mouth and, though it didn't seem possible, her tongue was actually tied in a knot.

She looked up at Max, fear coursing through her body like a flame through kindling.

He held out his hand and said, "Give me the wand." He cast a spell, but Cinderella's tongue remained tied. This time her stepmother's magic was too strong for Max to undo.

"Go back inside," Max said, "before she gets home." He checked his pocket watch. "I'll stay out here."

She grabbed his arm and shook her head.

"Cinderella," he said softly, "at midnight I'll turn back into a cat. That was the cost."

No! She tried to yell, but only a garbled sound came out. Max was turning back into a cat? That didn't seem fair. Nothing that had happened in the past hour seemed fair. Just as she'd thought all her problems were solved, they'd all landed back on her in a huge, messy heap.

In the distance, Cinderella heard the tower clock at the palace begin to strike midnight. Worse, she heard her stepmother's carriage coming down the path.

"Go inside—now!" Max put the wand in his mouth and ran across the garden. At the final stroke of midnight, Max leaped into the forest, his human form changing to a cat in midair. He landed behind a tree on his soft paws, making not even the slightest noise, and disappeared from view.

Her knees crumpled and she dropped to the ground. The cost had been too high. Max had sacrificed his human form for nothing. She hadn't won her freedom, and she'd lost Ty.

At least Max had the wand. She hoped he could find a way to use it on his own and turn himself back into a man.

"Who was she?" Gwendolyn slowly and methodically stirred her porridge as Cinderella slumped against the back of a dining-room chair, patiently waiting for her sisters to finish so she might eat a few bites of their leftovers.

"Who was who?" Agatha asked.

"The girl." Gwendolyn threw her spoon, splattering spots of porridge and cream across the table before it clattered onto the wooden floor. "The little peasant girl the prince saved. They say she cast some sort of a spell on him."

"I feel certain I saw her," Agatha said. "But I can't remember what she looked like."

Cinderella gripped the seat of her chair.

"Well?" Gwendolyn said. "Well? Well?"

Cinderella jumped, realizing that Gwen was addressing her. "You're asking me? Why would you think I know anything about her?"

"Fool." Gwen pursed her lips and shook her head. "The spoon. Are you going to pick up that spoon?"

Cinderella picked up the spoon and slowly handed it to her stepsister, who threw it back at her. It bounced off of her chest and clattered onto the floor.

"Get me a new one, you imbecile. I'm not about to eat with a spoon that's been on the floor. I'm not a little piggy like you. Some of us have manners." Gwen snickered and looked to Agatha for a reaction, but her younger sister kept her eyes on her porridge.

"Why are you so mean?" Cinderella said softly.

"I beg your pardon?" Gwen raised her clean white linen napkin to her lips.

"What have I ever done to you? I don't understand why you hate me so much."

"Nonsense." Gwen turned to her sister for a moment, then back to Cinderella. "I don't *hate* you. How can one hate a gnat?" She giggled and turned to Agatha again, but Agatha remained silent, spots of bright, rosy color rising in her cheeks.

Cinderella reached out her hand and retrieved a spoon from the sideboard using magic.

Gwendolyn's eyes opened wide. "Big mistake, Cinderella. Big mistake. Our mother will be very interested to hear you're using magic inside this house. Very interested." She turned back to Agatha. "You never answered. Did you see her?"

"Who?" Agatha's voice was small and soft, as if she were scared.

"The piece of trash who enchanted the prince. They say it's her fault he didn't announce his choice for bride last night."

Cinderella's insides woke up, as if they'd been asleep for days. Ty hadn't chosen his bride at the ball? She clasped her hands in front of her apron.

"He did act strangely for the rest of the evening, that is true." Agatha pushed her barely touched bowl of porridge forward. "I only wish I'd had a chance to dance with him."

"Don't be silly, Agatha. He was never going to choose you. Did you see the way he looked at me when we danced? I feel sure that if that little mouse hadn't caused such a commotion, Prince Tiberius and I would be engaged right now."

The door to the dining room burst open and her stepmother entered. Cinderella resisted the urge to back up into the corner and hide, but instead kept her feet planted solidly on the floor.

"Fabulous news, girls! Fabulous!" Dressed in a deep brown gown embellished with ivory ribbon trim, her stepmother strode to the end of the long table.

"What is it, Mother?" Gwen bounced up to her feet and her hand came down on the spoon handle sticking out of her bowl. Sticky porridge flew everywhere.

If Gwen had cleaned up even once in her life, thought Cinderella, she wouldn't be so careless.

"The prince is coming to visit." Her stepmother ran her hands down the bodice of her dress, and if Cinderella didn't know the woman better, didn't know she was incapable of real human emotion, she'd almost swear her stepmother was excited.

"He chose me, didn't he?" Gwen threw herself toward her mother, who patted her awkwardly on the back.

Her stepmother brushed a stray tendril of dark hair off her daughter's face and then held Gwen at arm's length, studying her. "Don't get ahead of yourself, my dear."

Agatha jumped up. "It's me?"

"His choice hasn't been announced." She shook her head. "It sounds as if the poor lad is confused." She chuckled. "According to the announcement sent to all the households in the kingdom this morning, he's convinced that a girl he met last night"—she paused to pull a scroll of paper out of her pocket and unroll it—" 'has a place for his heart.' " She shook her head. "The poor boy is daft, but we can work with daft as long as he's rich and powerful."

Gwendolyn giggled, but Agatha just looked confused.

"Come, girls. Let's make sure each of you can show him a spectacular place for his heart."

The stepsisters dashed toward the door, but before her stepmother left, she spun back toward Cinderella. "And don't you get any ideas about talking to the prince." Her eyes narrowed as her smile widened. "Since it's such a special day, I think I'll allow you outside in the sunshine. We can't have you inside the house when the prince comes. Can't have you talking his ear off now, can we?"

Cinderella's heart sank. She hadn't thought it possible for it to sink any lower. In the house she could talk, but outside she couldn't. At least she'd be free from the cellar, and she could make sure Ty saw her. Perhaps that would spark his memories.

"And clean up this disgusting mess." Her stepmother gestured toward the porridge-spattered table. "Really, after all I've done for you. You are such a lazy girl."

Cinderella pulled against the chains clamped to her ankles. This went beyond cruel and vicious, even for her stepmother. Not only had she cast a spell so she couldn't speak, but as an extra precaution, she'd tied her up in the back garden like an animal. Cinderella couldn't move more than five feet in any direction, and out here behind the house, she'd be completely invisible to Ty when he arrived.

She heard a commotion in the distance. Galloping horses.

She pulled against the chains, but the shackles dug painfully into her ankles, so she stopped. As badly as she wanted to see Ty, to make him remember her, or even to set her eyes upon him one final time, she wasn't about to hurt herself to do it.

Think. Think. Her confidence in her magic had grown since meeting Ty and entering the competition, but she'd certainly never done anything like break a chain.

Concentrating, she stared at a couple of links about two feet from the shackle, and soon they glowed red, but heat rose in the metal around her ankle, too. Clearly, she wouldn't be able to use magic to break the chain—not without burning herself.

The horses pulled to a stop in front of the house. Voices drifted back on the wind, but she couldn't make out a single word.

She dragged the excess chain back to the steel peg and the ring to which it was attached. Squatting down, she wrapped the chains around her arms a few times and then used every muscle in her back, legs, arms, and shoulders to pull and pull. She collapsed. It hadn't budged. Whatever black magic her stepmother had used to drive the peg into the ground was powerful.

Gathering every bit of strength inside her, she tried again, yelling the way the martial arts masters recommended. Although her effort was the greatest she could muster, the sound that came from her throat was muted by her stepmother's tongue-tying spell.

Seeing no movement in the stake or the chain, she slumped back to the ground. A flock of sparrows, disturbed by her attempted shouting, settled back onto the raspberry bushes at the edge of the garden.

Noise—where magic and brute strength had failed, perhaps noise would succeed. If Ty was already in the house, he might not hear, but it was worth a try.

She shook the links, then swung the excess chain, over and over, into the spike that held it. The noise vibrated through her, numbing her hands, numbing her ankles, numbing her entire body. And of course her ears protested the deluge, but they could rest later.

As deafening as the clanging seemed to her, no one came out of the house. She stopped for a moment, thinking she saw some movement in the shed, and wondered if Max was hiding there—and if he'd been able to turn himself back into a human with her wand yet. Encouraged, she clanged again, and this time the back curtains of the house swayed. Agatha waved through the window and brought a finger to her lips.

Not likely, thought Cinderella. Thrilled that someone in the house had heard, she continued to swing the chain.

Just when the muscles in her arms were past the point of fatigue and screaming in protest, just when every swing of the chain felt as if it carried a thousand pounds, she saw movement at the side of the house.

Ty rounded the building from the side yard, followed closely by her stepmother and stepsisters.

She stopped banging, waved her hands, and then ran as far as the chain allowed.

"See?" her stepmother said. "It's just one of the servants who's gone mad. Sad, really. But nothing with which Your Highness should be concerned. Now, if you'll take another look at the lovely velvet-lined box my daughter Gwendolyn showed you. Surely it's the place you seek for your heart."

Ty ignored her stepmother and strode forward, and Cinderella realized what might bring back Ty's memory. Her locket. Could his cryptic message about a place for his heart really mean what she hoped?

Even though his expression showed no recognition, he smiled as he approached, and she pulled the locket out from under her dress, holding it tightly in her hand until he was close. If her stepmother saw it before Ty did—well, that was a risk too high to take.

He approached until he was just out of her reach. "Are you hurt?"

She shook her head.

"Don't get too close, Your Highness," her stepmother said. "She can be violent." Her stepmother loomed behind Ty.

He cocked his head to the side as if weighing her warning or—Cinderella hoped—deciding if he recognized her. "She doesn't look mad or violent." He looked into her eyes. "Have we met before?"

Cinderella's heart skipped and she nodded.

"Don't be ridiculous," her stepmother said. "Where would you have met a mad servant girl? Come, Your Highness, you really must look more closely at the place my daughter Gwendolyn has for your heart."

Ty turned away and Cinderella tried to cry out, forgetting she had no use of her voice.

He turned back and stepped toward her, but her stepmother intercepted. "Poor thing is mute."

Cinderella held out the locket. She'd have no chance to show it to him privately and would have to just hope for the best.

"What's that?" the prince asked.

"Careful." Her stepmother grabbed his arm to stop him from moving forward, and then dropped her hand, as if she realized she'd overstepped her bounds. She curtsied. "I'm only concerned for your safety."

"Madam, I assure you that I am perfectly safe. She's so delicate, and her eyes seem kind. I'm sure she's harmless. Release her immediately." Ty's voice was stern.

Cinderella's love for Ty surged at the fierce look on his face—and then so too did her fear for his life. Angering her stepmother never paid off, and she wondered what type of spell the evil woman might cast.

Her heart racing, she appealed to Ty with her eyes as she held out the locket to him.

"Unchain her at once," he demanded.

Her stepmother turned to Agatha. "Please fetch the key from the pantry, dear."

"What key? From where?" Agatha asked, but her mother shot her such a harsh glare that Agatha quickly ran toward the side door of the house even though Cinderella knew the poor girl had no idea what her mother was talking about.

Ty crouched and tugged on the chain and then slowly turned toward her stepmother. "If I learn that any part these bindings are based on black magic . . ."

"Oh, wait," her stepmother said as she stepped forward, a false smile on her lips. "Look, I have the key right here." She held a key she'd pulled from her pocket, most likely conjured an instant before.

Ty held out his hand. "Give it to me."

"Oh, Your Highness. There's no need for you—"

"Give it to me!" He took the key, unlocked the shackles, and gently ran his fingers over the welts that had risen on Cinderella's ankles. "Forgive me for being forward, Miss, but these must hurt."

She smiled, hoping to show him she didn't mind his touch at all. It sent the most marvelous shivers through her.

He rose and stood so close, Cinderella could feel the magnetic pull of his body, but still he showed no indication he recognized her.

"Did you want to show me that?" He bent to look at the locket.

Filled with love for Ty, she opened the locket with ease, and watched his eyes open wide. He lifted his gaze to her eyes, looking more confused than anything else, but then reached into the leather pouch tied to his belt and pulled out the small metal heart.

He slipped it inside the locket. "What is your name?" His voice was soft and breathy, as if he couldn't quite get his lungs to function properly.

Cinderella shook her head, knowing she still couldn't talk.

He looked deeply into her eyes and she tried to convey all she felt in her heart. She recalled her father telling her that love was the greatest magic of all, and Max saying that two wizards joined by love became stronger. If that were true, then surely love could break her stepmother's spell and let Ty remember.

"Cinderella," he whispered, and she nodded, joy rushing through her.

He pulled her into his arms, and she felt as if all the magic in the world had hit both of them at once. If it didn't feel so wonderful, she might have thought her stepmother had cast another spell.

Ty moved his lips close to her ear. "It's you, my love."

At his words, Cinderella felt her tongue untie. "Ty, you remember me." His mention of love had broken the spell on her tongue. Love *was* strong magic.

He pressed a soft kiss into her forehead and then turned to her stepmother. "You knew this was the girl I sought, yet you intentionally hid her from me." He turned to Cinderella. "Let's get you out of here."

Holding hands, they ran to the front of the house, where a groom was holding the reins of two horses. They'd been fast on foot, but her stepmother had flown around the other side and was already on the front steps of the house when the couple arrived on the lawn beside the path. Agatha tentatively stepped out of the house holding a large ring of keys, and Gwendolyn, who had followed Cinderella and Ty, moved toward her mother and sister.

Her stepmother pulled out her black wand and a fierce color rose in her pale cheeks. "This . . . this . . ." her stepmother sputtered and screamed, ". . . this is unacceptable!"

She raised the wand and shot a bolt of lightning that exploded into the ground in front of Cinderella and Ty.

Will Cinderella and Ty escape
her stepmother's black magic?

To find out, turn to section 9: And So It Ends (page 279).

Section 9

and
so it
ends

Struggling against an unseen force, Cinderella and Ty clung to each other as acrid smoke rose from the ground.

"Mother!" Gwendolyn yelled, "Kill Cinderella, but not Prince Tiberius! Think of what you're doing!"

Her stepmother shot a bolt of energy toward Gwendolyn and knocked her back a few feet. "Silence, you stupid girl! If you'd done your job and charmed him, this wouldn't be necessary."

Gwendolyn fell onto the stone steps of the house, her eyes wide, her body trembling, and Agatha ran down to help her. Cinderella wished she could feel sorry for her stepsisters. But she couldn't. Not even Agatha.

"Madam." Ty's voice was bold and strong. "Stop this right now." He tried to move toward her, but couldn't. He looked down.

Ty's legs were buried in the lawn up to his ankles. Cinderella bent down to try to dig him out.

"You stupid, worthless boy." Her stepmother spat at Ty. "You think you're fit to rule this kingdom one day? Ha! You're weak. Your parents are weak. That bumbling idiot your father installed as royal wizard is weak." Anger leaped from her face. "It should have been me. If I'd had the right wand, it would have been me."

Unable to release Ty's feet, Cinderella looked up. "Stepmother, please. Let him go and I won't disobey you again." She didn't mean it. Not in the least. But she had to keep her stepmother from hurting Ty.

"Shut up." She stalked forward. "Your idiot parents share blame in this, too. That wand. Your mother's powers. They should have been mine."

The evil wizard raised her arms, a dark cloud appeared, and a storm pelted Cinderella and Ty with freezing rain and sleet.

Cinderella leaned into the strong wind and rain. "Stepmother!" she shouted, but her words were blown back by the wind. "Let the prince go—do what you will to me, but let him go!"

Behind her stepmother, Cinderella spotted Max—again a human, not a cat—entering the grounds and holding her mother's wand. Sparks flew from the magic wand and struck her stepmother, knocking her clear off her feet.

"Max, you did it! When did you become human again?"

"Just now," he said. "It was trickier this time."

The pelting wind and rain stopped, and Cinderella clung to Ty. But her stepmother wasn't down for long. Soon she and Max were engaged in battle.

Cinderella and Ty struggled to dig his feet out of the dirt, but it seemed the more they dug, the deeper his feet sank into the ground.

"Stop!" Ty grasped her hands. "It's no use digging. It's a spell."

She nodded and looked up. Her stepmother flew through the air, spinning so quickly, all Cinderella could see was a dark brown blur. "Go, Max!" she shouted, but the blur shot a terrifying bolt of red energy at him.

Max tumbled back, end over end across the garden, until he was almost in the forest.

Her stepmother shot a bolt of lightning from her wand, and the tree behind Max cracked in half and fell on top of him, burying him in branches and leaves.

Cinderella gasped.

Max shot out from the fallen tree's branches and flew into the air. He mounted a counterattack and shot an enormous ball of red, orange, and blue fire at her stepmother.

But his spell was stopped midway by another spell. The mixture of sparks and fire and energy shot up toward the sky, twisting and spinning, as if the spells themselves were at war.

Her stepmother's spell won, and the mass headed back to Max, lifted him into the air, and left him spinning.

"We have to help him," Cinderella said to Ty.

Her stepmother dropped her arm and Max slammed into the ground near the house in a lifeless heap. Cinderella lurched forward, but Ty held her back. "It's important we work together, and believe in ourselves." Ty's body felt warm and strong against hers, and in spite of everything, he didn't look scared. "I believe in you," he said.

"I believe in you, too." The strength in Ty's posture fueled enough courage inside Cinderella to combat her terror.

A powerful force ripped Cinderella away, spun her in the air, and slammed her onto the ground. When she opened her eyes, she discovered she was about twenty feet from Max, who still lay motionless.

A sob rose in her chest, but her determination rose faster. Adrenaline raced through her and she scrambled along the gravel toward her godfather. Max was still breathing, but unconscious, and still had the wand. Her stepmother must not have recognized it yet. Cinderella retrieved the wand from Max's limp hand and turned back toward Ty.

Her stepmother had encircled the prince in black sparks.

"Gwendolyn is the one you love," she said to Ty in a calm, convincing voice. "Cinderella practices black magic and must be reported and put to death." She repeated the words over and over, chanting.

"No." Cinderella ran forward, aiming her mother's wand at her stepmother. Silver sparks flowed from the wand, struck the evil wizard, and sent her tumbling to the ground, away from Ty.

Ty looked dazed as Cinderella ran toward him. Had her stepmother made him forget her again? Not from the look in his eyes. The royal wizard's protective spell against more mind control had held, even against her stepmother's black magic. Just before she reached Ty, she ran into an invisible wall and bounced back.

Her stepmother landed in front of her. "You horrible, lying child. You've had the wand all along."

Cinderella scrambled back, trying to regain her breath after the slam to her face and chest.

"That wand is mine, you little troll! Give it to me!"

"No!" Cinderella hid it behind her back. "It's not yours. It was my mother's and now it's mine."

Her stepmother seemed to grow in height. "After everything I did to get that wand, don't think I'll let a tiny obstacle like you keep it from me. You're weak. You're pathetic. You can't do anything to keep it out of my hands."

Cinderella fought against the power of her stepmother's words, remembering what Ty had said. She needed to believe in herself. She gripped the wand, feeling its energy connect with hers. Concentrating, she shot a bolt of energy toward her stepmother, who staggered back a few steps.

the kingdom with terror. But Cinderella couldn't sacrifice Ty. Not even to save the kingdom.

Her stepmother shrugged and then flames shot from her wand to encircle Ty. The flames crept closer to him as he struggled to release his trapped feet.

Gwendolyn ran down the steps. "Mother, stop it!" she yelled. "What are you doing? Surely if Cinderella marries the prince, it will benefit us all."

Not even looking behind her, her stepmother swung her wand and Gwendolyn flew through the air to land on the roof of the house. She slipped, but then grabbed onto the crow-shaped weather vane.

The flames rose higher, and Ty alternated between shielding his face from the heat and frantically brushing sparks and flames from his clothing. Cinderella's heart pounded. She had no choice. She threw the wand at her stepmother, who snatched it nimbly out of midair.

The flames died down and the evil wizard turned the wand over in her hands, her eyes wide with malicious delight. "Fool! With this wand, I can rule the entire kingdom!" She waved it once, and every leaf on every tree surrounding the garden died and fluttered to the ground.

Cinderella had no time to second-guess what she'd done. She ran toward Ty. The grass around him was scorched, the fabric of his trousers singed. She threw herself into his arms. "I love you," she said.

Ty held her tight and said, "I love you, too."

Cinderella felt a surge of energy flow through their joined bodies as if they were gathering light from all around them. The ground softened beneath them and Ty was released. Clearly, declaring their love had increased their powers.

"We need to stop her," he said.

"I don't have a wand." As soon as the words were out of her mouth, Cinderella realized she didn't need one. The magic already inside her had been magnified and sharpened by Ty's declaration of love.

She looked up at Ty and found a reassuring determination on his face. He lifted his wand, and together they shot a bolt of energy toward her stepmother. The force of it sent her crashing to the ground, still clutching the treasured wand.

Cinderella and Ty continued forward, but moved apart to approach her stepmother from either side, so she'd have to divide her attention to attack them both.

Her stepmother rose from her feet and chose Cinderella as her first target, shooting foul-smelling black sparks toward her.

Tapping into her ninja training and feeling more in control and powerful than she ever had in her life, Cinderella cartwheeled to the side, and then leaped and flipped above the next flash of sparks.

Staying airborne longer than she thought she could, she stared down at the scene below her, feeling as if everything was moving in slow motion. Her stepmother dodged a rope from Ty's attempt at a binding spell, and before Ty could regroup, her stepmother shot another spell at him.

Cinderella shouted to warn him, but it was too late. A powerful force slammed into Ty's chest, threw him back, and he fell to the ground, unconscious.

"No!" Cinderella landed, then sprang forward and planted a powerful kick directly into her stepmother's chest, sending her into the ground on her back.

Her mother's wand fell from her stepmother's hand. Cinderella dove and grabbed it, but her stepmother grabbed it too, and they struggled on the ground for control of it.

"It's mine!" Cinderella shouted through gritted teeth as she flipped her stepmother onto her back, her every muscle burning with effort. "Not yours!"

Her stepmother's eyes glowed red. Momentarily blinded, Cinderella turned away. Her stepmother took advantage of the opportunity and rolled Cinderella onto her back. No longer focused on the wand, her stepmother wrapped her hands around Cinderella's throat.

Cinderella gasped for air, dropped the wand, and clutched at her stepmother's hands, trying to draw on Ty's love, but with him unconscious, she couldn't. There was no way she was strong enough to battle her stepmother alone.

Her lungs burned, lights flashed behind her eyes, and a fog invaded her mind. Drifting out of consciousness, she remembered her father telling her she was going to have a new mother and two sisters. She'd thrown her arms around her father's neck because she'd thought a new wife would make him happy. Now that she understood true love, she knew how childish she'd been to assume love could be replaced so easily. He'd only married this horrible witch in order to give his daughter a family. If only he'd known.

Struggling to stay in the present, Cinderella fought to keep her eyes open and assumed she was hallucinating when she saw Ty appear and wrap the crook of his elbow around her stepmother's neck. He pulled her back.

The vise grip around Cinderella's neck released and she gasped for air.

Her stepmother leaped up, ready to lunge for Ty, but Cinderella felt a surge of enchanted power inside her. She threw her hands forward and froze her stepmother in midair.

Her stepmother's rigid body dropped to the ground.

The next thing Cinderella knew, Ty was holding her in his arms. A rush of warmth and safety overtook her before she snapped back into focus. "My freezing spell won't last."

They turned to her stepmother, but she—along with her real mother's wand—had disappeared.

Cinderella spun, searching for the evil wizard, but it was no use.

"She's gone," Ty said. "You're safe for the moment." He tightened his embrace and Cinderella's breaths came out hard but shallow.

Had her stepmother given up? That was highly unlikely. Even if she didn't come back right away, she had her mother's wand and would have to be stopped.

"Max!" she cried, breaking away from Ty and running to where her godfather had lain in a heap since her stepmother's attack. Cinderella fell to her knees at his side. His chest rose and fell, but his forehead was gashed, his eyes remained closed, and his normally flushed skin was nearly gray.

Her eyes filled with tears. "Max, I'm so sorry. This is all my fault."

A warm hand fell onto her shoulder and she looked up to see the royal wizard dressed in a scarlet robe of fine silk. Ty stood beside him.

"How? Why?" She looked up into the royal wizard's eyes. "When did you get here? How did you know to come?"

"The prince's groom rode to alert me. I'm sorry I didn't arrive before the wizard who attacked the prince fled. Who are you?"

Cinderella gasped. Still under the effects of her stepmother's spell, the royal wizard didn't remember he'd seen her before. She turned to Ty and said, "My stepmother cast a spell last night. He doesn't remember me, just as you didn't at first."

Ty stepped up beside the wizard and said, "This is Cinderella, the girl I was seeking." He reached down to touch Cinderella's face. "You were planning to train her."

The royal wizard scratched his head. "I was?" He frowned.

Cinderella stepped forward. "My stepmother made everyone at the ball forget they'd ever met me, even Ty—I mean, Prince Tiberius." She looked into his eyes.

Ty pressed a kiss into her hair. "Our love brought my memory back."

The royal wizard's jaw hardened and a wind swirled around him. "It takes a powerful wizard to cast a spell over me without my detection. I will find this wizard and break her black magic spells forever. Her actions will not go unpunished."

Cinderella grabbed the royal wizard's arm. "My godfather was hurt trying to help us. Please, is there anything you can do?"

"Let me take a look." The royal wizard crouched down and then, keeping his hands about two inches above Max's motionless body, he ran his open palms down his torso and legs, then back up again, as if trying to sense where and how badly he'd been hurt. As he scanned his hands back and forth, tiny sparkles of light bounced over Max's body, intensifying near his head.

Ty took Cinderella by the shoulders, helped her up, and held her tightly. "Give him room. There's nothing we can do but let the wizard work his magic."

She turned to press her cheek into Ty's warm, broad chest and inhaled the leather scent of his vest. "Max helped me so much. I wouldn't have even made it to the competition or the ball if it hadn't been for him."

The royal wizard put his hands above Max's face. Light spread from the royal wizard's fingers. It encircled Max's head and Cinderella fought back her tears. In spite of all that had happened, this should be the happiest day of her life, but if she lost Max . . . she shuddered at the thought. The royal wizard held his hands just above Max's face.

Her godfather's eyes opened, and Cinderella lurched out of Ty's arms. "Max!" She fell to her knees in the grass beside him.

Max blinked several times, as if trying to focus on the royal wizard's face. "Hal?"

The royal wizard started, then nodded. "Fred? Is it really you?"

"What's with the fancy robe, old friend?" Max's voice was weak and he rubbed his eyes.

"I was appointed royal wizard ten years ago." He ran his hands above Max again.

"Impressive." Max nodded and then winced and raised his hand to his head.

"Where have you been, Fred?" the royal wizard asked. "You disappeared—it must have been at least twelve years ago. Have you been living here?"

Max sat up. "I've been doing my best to protect Isabel's daughter. Quite a challenge, since I was transformed into a cat."

Cinderella gasped. Isabel. Her mother's name and her own name at birth. Although now she couldn't imagine herself being called anything but Cinderella.

The royal wizard turned toward her, his brow furrowed. "You're Isabel's daughter?"

She nodded.

"No wonder you have such amazing powers." He turned back to Max.

Max sat up quickly. "Where is Helena?"

"Helena's behind this?" The royal wizard stood and looked around the grounds.

Max stood up, aided by the royal wizard. "She tricked Isabel's widower into marrying her, hoping to get her hands on her wand. She killed him and kept Isabel's daughter trapped and enslaved."

Cinderella slowly absorbed what the two wizards were saying. Helena must be her stepmother's name. She'd lived with the woman for so long without knowing. "She got away," she told them. "And she has my mother's wand." She crouched down beside Max. "I'm so glad you're okay. How did you turn yourself back into a man?"

"It was harder this time because my feline form was the cost for suspending her other spells, but because I was farther away from your stepmother's influence, I was able to make it permanent. I hope." He ran a hand through his hair. "After I got the magic into the wand, I had to figure out a way to balance it on some twigs so I could pass under it." He shook his head. "I'm glad to be rid of that cat body for good. I only managed to break the spell moments before I got back here."

"You saved me, Max." She reached out and squeezed his hand.

"Glad I could help, but you saved yourself."

"Fred," the royal wizard interrupted, "why is this young woman calling you Max?"

A chuckle burst up from Cinderella's chest. "Max was my cat for thirteen years. He failed to mention his name was Fred, so I picked one for him."

The royal wizard tossed his head back and laughed. "You know, I think Max suits him."

"I thought so, too," Cinderella said. She heard a voice calling out, and remembered Gwendolyn.

She backed up to see Gwendolyn still clinging to the weather vane on the roof.

"Who is that?" the royal wizard asked.

"My stepsister. Can you get her down?"

The royal wizard raised his wand and a rope appeared out of thin air. Gwen struggled against it at first, then allowed it to wrap snugly under her arms. The royal wizard lowered his arms and the rope gently brought Gwendolyn off the roof and back to the ground.

The shrubs rustled a few feet away and Agatha pushed her way out, pulling a leaf from her hair.

"Thank goodness. We're saved." Gwendolyn ran toward Cinderella with her arms wide, as if she planned to hug her.

Not so fast, thought Cinderella. She backed up and Gwen got the hint and went to Agatha instead.

"And who was in the bushes?" The royal wizard came up to stand beside Cinderella.

"My other stepsister, Agatha."

"Were you hiding from your mother?" the royal wizard asked.

"Yes," Gwendolyn said quickly, and Agatha bit her lip and nodded.

The royal wizard turned to Cinderella. "Anything I should know about here?"

Cinderella drew in a deep breath and let it out while considering how to answer. "They're harmless enough—just misguided." She resisted the urge to say more.

Several dazed-looking servants emerged from the house and stood on the steps, scratching their heads and rubbing their eyes. A stout older woman wiped flour onto her apron, and two men in grooms' uniforms, one with a pipe in his mouth, staggered down a few steps and sat.

"These people are clearly recovering from an enchantment." The royal wizard shook his head. "Casting magic to control the behavior of servants . . ." He turned toward Cinderella. "Your stepmother, once apprehended, will be tried in court, and based on what I've seen here, she'll be locked up for a very long time."

Cinderella imagined her stepmother locked in a dungeon and thought of what a fitting punishment it would be, after everything the evil woman had put her through.

"Now, young lady," the royal wizard said, "before I search for Helena, someone's got to explain what's been going on here."

Cinderella drew a deep breath and wondered if she could safely tell the royal wizard about her entrapment spell. He'd already deduced that her stepmother had been practicing black magic, and Max had mentioned she'd been held captive, and no one had turned into stone, at least not yet. Still, *she* hadn't said it.

"Can I ask you a question in confidence?" she asked the royal wizard, and he nodded.

Cinderella looked over to Ty for reassurance and he blew her a kiss as she and the royal wizard walked to the side of the house.

"What is it?" he asked.

She considered her words carefully. "Hypothetically, let's say my stepmother cast a spell, and part of that spell was that if I told anyone about it, both that person and I would be turned into stone." Cinderella paused, making sure she hadn't been turned into a statue. "Well, I guess what I'm wondering is, could a spell like that be broken?"

The royal wizard scratched his head with his wand. His long black and gray hair flared back. "Don't you worry, I can break any spell once I know it's there."

Cinderella smiled, then froze in fear.

Her body tingled and stung all over. She knew this feeling all too well. She rubbed her arms and looked up toward the royal wizard, then over to Ty, but it was too late. A force lifted her and she flew through the air.

Wind rushing and screaming past her ears, Cinderella tumbled end over end. She covered her face as tree branches and twigs scraped at her arms and legs and tore at her clothes. The air had pressed out of her lungs and she felt them burn as her dizziness intensified. She smashed into one tree branch, then another, and sailed through the leaves to land hard on the ground.

Her stepmother was surely the one behind her impromptu flight. At least she wasn't stone and she hoped beyond hope that the royal wizard wasn't a statue. Gasping for air, she curled into a ball on her side, hoping to protect herself.

"Coward," her stepmother said, but Cinderella didn't move from her fetal position. What chance did she have against an experienced wizard with two wands? Especially when one was her mother's? Especially without Ty at her side?

If it made her a coward to protect herself from whatever horrible torture her stepmother planned, then so be it. No way could she battle her stepmother on her own. Her best bet was to hope everyone would head down the path looking for her. For now, it was best to stall.

Her stepmother kicked dirt toward her and it settled over her still body.

"I knew the wand would be wasted on you," she cackled. "After all, you're one half your useless father."

"He wasn't useless," she whispered into the dirt.

"Useless, dishonest, and a coward."

Rage built up inside Cinderella and she sprang to her feet. "That's not true!" Her father had been a sad man, a single parent whose wife had died, but—

Cinderella drew deep breaths to keep from flying forward in a flurry of kicks and punches. Her stepmother was purposefully baiting her, hoping she'd attack, and she would not make it easy for her stepmother to kill her. Even ninjas knew when to hold back.

"My father was good and kind and generous." She spoke as calmly as she could. "The only mistake he ever made was marrying a murderous villain like you. If my father knew how cruel you've been—"

"What would he have done? Tell me." Her stepmother paced in a tight circle around Cinderella, hate wafting off her like the smoke from burned hair. "He wasn't even a wizard."

"Why are you so horrible?" Cinderella glared at her stepmother. "What did I ever do to you?"

Her stepmother held up the wand in answer.

"I didn't even know where that was until two days ago." Cinderella fought to stay calm. "I was only five when you locked me down in the cellar, and terrified. If I'd known where it was I'd have told you. Any child that age would have caved. You knew that. Why did you keep me trapped, anyway?" Cinderella tried to calm herself, but it was getting harder to control her pounding heart, her rage, and her fists and legs that wanted to punch and kick. And harder still to control the magic she knew was no match for her stepmother's. Especially alone.

Her stepmother put a long-nailed hand on her hip. "I couldn't let you go blabbing my secrets around the kingdom now, could I?"

Cinderella stepped forward. "Then why didn't you just kill me?" Even if she was baiting her stepmother to kill her now, she needed to know.

"Because, darling, you were such fun to torment." Her stepmother flashed an evil grin.

Cinderella felt as if she'd been punched in the gut. "Fun?"

Her stepmother shrugged dismissively. "And good practice, I suppose. Now that I have this wand, it won't be long before I have control of the entire kingdom."

"Never." Cinderella felt magic energy build up inside her. If her mother had been as powerful as everyone said, then maybe the power inside her was stronger than she thought. She had to believe in herself, believe in her powers. Anything was better than standing here waiting for death.

Cinderella raised her hand and shot a bolt of energy at her stepmother. Before the wizard could react, Cinderella leaped to deliver a twisting side kick straight into her stepmother's stomach. Caught by surprise, the evil wizard staggered, but then used her black wand to shoot a flame toward her stepdaughter.

Twisting as she dove, Cinderella dodged the flame, jumped up to an overhanging branch, and then swung out to land another blow to her stepmother's arm. She knocked one of the wands away, but it was the black wand, not her mother's. Better than nothing, she thought.

After landing on the dirt lane, Cinderella concentrated on her stepmother's wand that had dropped to the ground, and imagined it going up in flames—and it did, sending charred fragments flying in every direction.

But from behind, a huge force slammed into her and lifted her high up in the air. Cinderella started to spin so fast she couldn't see and could barely breathe. Using every muscle in her body, she forced her limbs to move in the opposite direction to the spin, hoping to slow or stop the crushing rotation.

The blur of trees came into focus. She'd slowed down.

Her stepmother, on the dirt road below, looked shocked as Cinderella hovered in the air. Cinderella felt a surge of confidence flow through her, and she pushed her hands toward her stepmother. The wizard staggered back. Then her stepmother swirled her mother's wand in the air. Hundreds of sparks built up, taking form and growing, until they formed the shape of a dragon.

How could she battle a dragon?

Losing confidence, Cinderella dropped, plunging toward the ground, but caught herself just in time and landed in a ninja crouch. The dragon, nearly twenty feet tall, rose up and roared. Fire shot from its mouth and burned the leaves in the overhanging canopy to a crisp.

Cinderella scrambled back a few steps as her stepmother laughed.

Wait. She squared her stance. "How dare you use my mother's wand against me?" Cinderella's voice was strong and clear. "If that wand was tuned to my mother and I've inherited her powers, you can't use it against me."

She had no idea if this was true, but figured it should be.

"Stupid girl." Her stepmother flicked the wand.

The dragon shot fire toward Cinderella but missed, hitting the road about five feet away.

"See?" Cinderella shouted. "That dragon is mine, not yours." She lifted her arms toward the magical monster.

It turned and raised its head to the sky and shot a flame upward. If nothing else, all this fire would pinpoint their location and the royal wizard might arrive in time to help . . . if he hadn't already been turned into a statue.

Concentrating on the dragon, Cinderella stepped to the side and raised one arm, and the dragon mimicked her movements. She *could* control it. Confidence coursed through her, pushing aside her fear.

She made the dragon rear up in front of her stepmother and shoot fire toward her feet. The hem of her stepmother's gown caught on fire, and when she bent to stomp it out, she dropped the wand.

Cinderella reached forward and the wand flew through the air and into her hand.

Her stepmother, a stricken look on her face, turned and ran down the road.

Cinderella concentrated, thrust the wand forward, and her stepmother slammed into an invisible wall that sprang up in her path.

Her stepmother staggered toward the forest, clearly stunned by the impact. Cinderella created invisible walls all around her stepmother, trapping her.

Her stepmother threw herself against one side, then another, slamming her fists against the invisible walls.

Panting, Cinderella staggered back a few steps. She'd done it. She'd really done it. Simply by believing in her own powers, she'd defeated her stepmother. Cinderella's heart filled with joy, but her body trembled with exhaustion.

She collapsed in a heap on the dirt road, only now registering the stinging pain from her many scrapes and scratches, and the aches of the bruises she'd received from her crashing flight through the forest.

Horses approached from down the forest path, and she soon found herself being lifted from the ground and into Ty's arms. She wrapped her arms so tightly around his neck that she worried he might break, but the feel of his strong muscles beneath her hands and against her body dashed away that fear—and every other fear in her heart.

Looking up, she saw that the royal wizard was patting his hands against the invisible container she'd built for her stepmother and nodding in approval. He stepped back, raised his wand, and shot a huge stream of sparks toward the evil wizard that swirled up and over the walls of air and down around her stepmother to bind her tightly in ropes.

"That should contain her," he said. "Even better, all her previous spells have been broken." He turned toward them and then looked as if he'd been jolted.

Cinderella tensed. Had her stepmother somehow cast another spell, after all? But then the royal wizard flashed a broad, genuine smile and approached her.

"Cinderella. Of course. I can't believe I forgot you." He put one hand on her shoulder and another on Ty's. "I am so happy you've found each other and tapped into your true powers. Cinderella, I knew your mother well and am not surprised by your abilities." He winked. "Perhaps you won't be needing my lessons after all, my dear."

"Oh no," she said. "I need your lessons now more than ever."

A smile spread on his face and he backed away a few steps. "And you have just proven how much you deserve and will benefit from training. Both of you had natural talents on your own, and now that your powers have fused together and been strengthened with love, they'll only continue to grow. But recognizing that you still require training shows that you will use your powers wisely." He bowed to them, which made

Cinderella extremely uncomfortable, and when he came out of his bow, he spun to check that her stepmother remained secure.

The next thing Cinderella knew, her stepmother's carriage appeared in the road. Gwendolyn, Agatha, and Max spilled out of it. Gwendolyn ran forward while Max went with the royal wizard to make sure her stepmother's bindings remained secure. Agatha hung back and stayed by the carriage.

"My dearest sister," Gwen said to Cinderella. "I'm so glad you're safe and sound."

"Thank you." Cinderella pushed her lips tightly together to keep from snapping at Gwen. Her stepsister might not have any real magic powers, but her cruelty was as vast as the oceans.

"Consider me your humble servant." Gwendolyn curtsied. "If you ever need me, say as a lady-in-waiting, I'm at your service."

"Not now, Gwen, please." Cinderella's cheeks burned, embarrassed at the assumptions Gwendolyn was making about her and Ty, and furious that her stepsister would think she'd want her anywhere near her. "Leave me alone."

"Certainly, certainly." Gwendolyn backed away, nodding.

Finally, Cinderella was left alone with Ty.

Still holding her, he looked into her eyes and the world fell away. The warmth and love that came from Ty's eyes was the best and most overpowering sensation she'd ever experienced. Joy and love spread through her as fast as fire through straw.

Not only had she found the magic inside her, not only had she gained the confidence to defeat her stepmother, she'd found love. Love of a magnitude she had never imagined possible. And Ty wasn't just any boy. He was the prince and would one day be king.

Her heart pounded in her ears. Her, a princess? A wife? A queen one day? She wasn't at all prepared for any of those roles.

And there'd be a trial. She'd have to tell people how she'd been treated, how her father had been murdered. She'd have to relive her past. And her stepsisters—what would happen to them? They hadn't broken any laws, unless it was against the law to be mean.

She looked back at Agatha, whose head hung in shame. Always the follower, maybe Agatha could stand on her own two feet if she weren't constantly under the influence of her mother and Gwendolyn. Maybe, with some work, they could actually be sisters to each other someday.

"You look sad, my love." Ty ran his hand down her cheek. "Tell me what's wrong."

"I'm just thinking about what will happen to my family."

A soft, dimpled smile spread on his handsome face. Ty shook his head and then pressed a kiss into her forehead. "Imagine you thinking of them, after all they've done." He kissed her lips in a way Cinderella felt in every part of her body. "Will do you me a favor?" he asked when their lips parted.

"Anything," she said, and she meant it.

"Let's not give black magic or trials another thought today. We've got so much to celebrate, and I can't wait for you to meet my parents."

Sitting in the palace library, books spread around her, Cinderella felt as if she'd become someone else, or had been living in a dream this past week. She pinched her arm to make sure. Nope, the only things affecting her now were happiness and love.

Even thoughts of her stepmother had barely invaded. The evil wizard's trial for practicing black magic and murdering Cinderella's father would be held in two weeks and Cinderella, Ty, and Max would be witnesses. Agatha had also agreed to testify.

Not wanting to ever go back to her house, Cinderella had given it to Max, and he'd hired Agatha and Gwendolyn as maids—to teach them a lesson, he said. She'd asked him to go easier on Agatha.

The past week had gone by in a whirlwind of happiness. But between parties and dress fittings and training sessions with the royal wizard, Cinderella had barely found time to see Ty, and they'd had no time alone. They were constantly chaperoned, and his duties kept him busy. She'd only seen him at meals with his parents, and during magic training sessions with the royal wizard.

Ty hadn't mentioned a word about love or marriage since they'd defeated her stepmother, but she hoped it was only because they hadn't had time alone. The way he looked at her hadn't changed.

She grinned as warmth spread inside her. Not only was she living in a palace, she had access to this glorious room of books. She glanced around at the dizzying array displayed on the shelves that lined the walls from the floor to the ceiling, and then back to the twenty books she'd selected. If only she could read more quickly. If she had a thousand years, she'd never run out of books to read in this room. There were reference books on every topic imaginable, and almost better, she'd discovered a whole wall of books containing nothing but stories meant to entertain. Who knew such enjoyable books existed?

"Excuse me, Miss." One of the maids entered the library.

Cinderella rose and started to tidy up the books from the plush rug. "I'm sorry about the mess."

"Oh, it's no worry at all, Miss," the maid said. "I can straighten those up for you if you like, or perhaps take them up to your room to read there? Or if you prefer, you may leave them as they are now and return to them whenever you get the chance. No one will be bothered."

"Really?" She exhaled, remembering her stepmother's rules weren't in effect here. Weren't in effect *anywhere* anymore. "Thank you."

The maid curtsied. "The prince asked me to find you, Miss."

Cinderella's heart rate increased and she rushed forward a few steps, hopping over an open book. "He did?"

"Yes, Miss." The maid averted her eyes coyly and a blush rose in her cheeks. "He's asked me to bring you to him, out on the terrace, so he can have a private word."

Could this be it? Was Ty finally going to ask her to marry him? If he didn't, she'd take matters into her own hands and ask him. At that thought, nerves scrambled inside her and twisted her belly. Could she really be bold enough to do that?

But wait . . . what if he had bad news? He loved her, but what if his parents disapproved and were forcing him to marry one of the many young girls more educated in the ways of society and better able to represent the royal family? After all, they had forced him into that pick-a-bride-at-the-ball fiasco.

As she walked down the long hallway toward the terrace, her belly buzzed and flipped and twirled. She brushed her hands down the pale pink bodice of the simple but beautiful dress she'd chosen to wear this evening. It was the color of the apple blossoms in the royal orchard. Days ago, Ty had promised to take her for a walk there, but had been called into an important meeting, so she'd gone on her own. Strolling among those trees, she'd felt so happy and free.

"Impressive," her stepmother sneered. "Now hand it over."

"Never." Gathering all her focus, Cinderella used the wand to shoot a flame at her stepmother. It struck her arm, and she dropped her wand, but after looking startled for an instant, she recovered quickly and the wand flew back into her hand.

"Look here, you ungrateful brat." She strode forward, her face filled with hatred. "The only reason I married your father was to get my hands on that wand. It's not my fault he was too stubborn to hand it over, even on the threat of death."

Cinderella fought to control her emotions. "What do you mean?"

Her stepmother's smile turned even uglier than usual. "Your father wouldn't hand over the wand, so I tossed him off the roof, you idiot."

Cinderella felt her throat close in grief. Her father's fall had been no accident. Of course it hadn't. The evil wizard had killed her husband just days after their marriage.

Rage burst through her grief. "Murderer!" she cried as she shot white sparks from the wand, but this time her stepmother was ready and deflected them. The sparks struck Ty instead and Cinderella ran toward him, but a force pulled her away and flipped her over onto her back on the ground.

Her stepmother towered above her, eyes searing with hatred. "I'm a fair person, so I'll give you a choice."

Cinderella scrambled to her feet. "I've seen enough of your so-called deals and choices to know not to trust you."

"I'll make this simple." Her stepmother stretched her hand out, her fingers like the talons of an eagle. "Wand . . . or prince?"

Cinderella gasped and backed away. She was more sure than ever that if her stepmother had her real mother's wand, she'd be able to rule

She started to skip. Ty loved her. She loved him. And with everything they'd gone through to be together, surely their union was meant to be. Whatever happened, even if they couldn't get married, she had to count her many blessings. She'd spent most of her life enslaved by an evil wizard and now she was free and would be trained by the royal wizard. She had so many things for which to be grateful.

She stepped out onto the terrace, and the cool night air feathered through her hair and brushed over her skin. She raised a hand to her chest. She wasn't used to dresses cut below her collarbone, and the air on her exposed skin made her feel slightly vulnerable. She inhaled deeply and the night air carried the scent of pine forests and, closer by, night jasmine that grew in pots arranged around the perimeter of the terrace. The fresh scents soothed her nerves.

Ty stepped out from a shadow, and her heart bounced and bounded. He held out his hands and she stepped forward to take them.

"Thank you for meeting me here," he said. His eyes brightened and his smile lit up the night. He was so handsome. His curls were loose under his crown.

"Of course, Your Highness," she said as she curtsied, but then she shot him a mischievous smile. She expected Ty to laugh at her formal tone and demeanor, but he didn't. Instead, he looked down at his feet. His hands started to feel damp in hers, and his lips twitched as if he wasn't sure what to say. He was nervous.

Even though she'd been thinking he might deliver bad news, she still found it hard to believe that would transpire. But why would he be nervous if his news was good? He knew she loved him; she'd already told him and had fought so hard to be with him. He couldn't possibly question that.

No, the news was bad. It was the only explanation she could think of for his nerves. Her heart squeezed, but she refused to show her pain. She needed to make this easier for him. "Ty," she said softly, "no matter what, I'll always love you. I'll always be your friend."

"My friend?" He looked into her eyes with an expression of pain and fear. "You only want to be my friend?"

She wanted to leap into his arms, to wipe away his apprehension while calming her own nerves. But she couldn't; she had to stay strong—for both of them.

"Cinderella"—he cleared his throat—"I have something very serious and important to discuss with you."

At his formal words and tone, her belly tightened, but she used her ninja calming techniques to hide her distress.

"I know I deceived you when we first met." He dropped one of her hands and ran his fingers over his hair. "I know I hid who I was."

"I understand why. No need to apologize."

He lifted his head. "Apologize?"

She started. "Oh." What was going on? The butterflies in her stomach came back. So much for her ninja emotion-control techniques.

He dropped her other hand and rubbed his on the velvet of his trousers, then looked down at her sheepishly. Color had risen in his cheeks, but it only made him more handsome. "I'm not sorry about the deception," he said. "Not really, because if I hadn't done it, we'd never have met."

She forced herself to smile. "Yes, I understand. We don't exactly run in the same circles, it seems." Until recently, the only circle she'd run in had been her cat's.

"What I'm trying to say is"—Ty chewed on his lower lip—"as a member of the royal family, I have certain obligations."

Here it came. "I understand."

"You've seen this past week how busy my duties sometimes keep me, and that will increase in the future, when I become king."

She nodded, still confused about where this was going. Surely he hadn't decided never to marry at all.

"My wife will have duties, too. Some will be rewarding." He smiled, but his nerves shook his lips. "But other duties will be horribly tedious. Balls, teas, ceremonies, learning traditions and protocols, and teaching these traditions to any princes and princesses who might be born." His flush grew deeper.

"Yes, I know." She took his hand and rubbed her finger on his palm. "Where are you going with all this?" If he was going to dump her, she wanted it over with.

Ty cleared his throat and sucked in his cheeks. "Well, you've made your feelings about formal events pretty clear. You'd hate royal life."

She stepped back and pulled her hand from his. "I'm getting used to it."

He took off his crown, tossed it onto a padded settee, and ran his fingers through his hair again, releasing some of his curls. "But I want your life to be wonderful, everything you've ever wanted or imagined. I don't want your life to be something you have to get *used* to."

She looked down to the irregular stone pattern of the terrace floor. "No life is perfect. Everyone has to get used to some things." Annoyance had started to rise up in her chest. She looked up at him. "So you plan to make this decision for me?" Was he refusing to ask her to marry him because he thought she didn't want to be a queen one day? "It's true I never imagined life as a royal, not for a moment."

"Sometimes I hate that I'm a prince."

"It's not your fault you were born into this family, Ty." No more than it was her fault her mother had died and her father had made a poor choice with his second wife.

Ty looked as though his heart was breaking. So was hers. And she no longer felt like asking him to marry her. If making her decisions, making assumptions about how she'd feel without asking was his way, then perhaps she'd be better off without him.

Her throat tightened and she could barely breathe. It was over—over before it had even begun.

He went down on one knee and reached for her hand again. It was a very strange way for him to bid her good-bye.

"Get up," she said. Her fingers trembled under his touch and her heart slammed against her ribs. In this gown with its scooped neck, she felt sure he could see her heart beating.

But he didn't get up. Instead, he cleared his throat and looked up into her eyes. "I love you, Cinderella. I love you with all my heart, all my soul, all my being."

"I love you, too." Her words drifted out on a soft breath.

"Then I hope—I mean, it is my greatest wish that you will change your mind." He was breathing heavily, almost gasping for words.

"Change my mind?" She looked at him quizzically.

He bent to kiss her fingers. "Please, Cinderella, I don't know how I'll survive if you won't be my wife."

The air trapped in her lungs and she gasped for breath. "Your wife?"

He lowered his head for a moment, and then looked up into her eyes. "It won't be as bad as you think. It won't always be so busy. Well, there is the little matter of my governing the kingdom after I become king, but my father is still young and healthy and I'm sure he'll live a very long time, and I promise we'll still be able to train as wizards and do whatever else you've always dreamed of doing." He paused to catch his breath. "If you will do me the great honor of being my bride, I promise to do everything in my power to make you as happy as I know you'll make me."

She felt tears of joy forming in her eyes and drew in a ragged breath. "Oh, Ty. If you were going to ask me, why make me worry? Why act as if you didn't even want to be friends anymore?"

He gripped her hands more tightly. "No, my love. No, I'm so sorry. I was just nervous that you'd turn me down."

Her skirts rustling around her, she dropped to her knees and took his face in her hands. "How could you ever think that?" She stopped and gave her head a sharp shake, realizing she'd been imagining crazy things, too. "I thought maybe your parents wanted you to marry someone else."

"Someone else?" He pulled away. "Why would you think that?"

"Because of who you are, who I am. I'm no one. An orphan. A servant girl. All that stuff you said about duty. I figured you'd decided you had to marry someone better suited to being a princess and a queen." Her entire body trembled at the thought of the huge responsibilities she faced, but a huge smile spread on Ty's face and calmed her.

"Hey," he said. "You still haven't answered."

"Yes, silly! Of course, yes!"

He held her for a moment and then took out a simple but beautiful ring. After slipping it onto her finger, he turned her hand to press his lips into her palm. "I was so afraid you'd say no. I figured you liked me better when you thought I was a servant. You've never seemed very keen on the idea of marrying a prince."

Joy bubbled up inside her and burst out in a short laugh. "That's true. The royal family can be pretty stuffy, I've heard."

"Stuffy, huh?"

"Very formal. Very serious. Very pretentious."

"Like this?" He reached forward to tickle her, and she rose to her feet. He reached for her again and then chased her to the edge of the terrace.

But she had no real intention of getting away. He caught her by the waist, spun her, and gave her the most wondrous kiss.

The stars high in the night sky flared, burned more brightly, and as Ty lifted her off the ground, she had to check to make sure they weren't floating. Never had she felt so completely and utterly free. So completely and utterly herself.

Cinderella.

Princess.

Ty's wife.

For the rest of their lives.

Together their magic was stronger. Together their love was stronger. Together she was stronger, and together they would live happily ever after.

Answers

There are eight possible routes through this book:

1, 2, 4, 6, 7, 9

1, 2, 4, 6, 8, 9

1, 3, 4, 6, 7, 9

1, 3, 4, 6, 8, 9

1, 2, 5, 6, 7, 9

1, 2, 5, 6, 8, 9

1, 3, 5, 6, 7, 9

1, 3, 5, 6, 8, 9

Become enchanted again with
another title in the
Twisted Tales series!
Will Sleeping Beauty be able to
save her village from vampires?
A thrilling twist on a classic!

sneak preview
SLEEPING BEAUTY ✦ VAMPIRE SLAYER

S unlight streamed through the floor-to-ceiling windows lining the
western-facing wall of the palace's reception room. On a raised platform
at its north end, Queen Catia of Xandra, two months shy of her
eighteenth birthday, sat on her throne with her husband, King Stefan. Between
them, their baby girl lay asleep in her fur-lined glass cradle.

Since the baby's birth, the palace staff had worked around the clock to make
the room beautiful for the princess's naming ceremony. Bright tapestries and
banners decorated the glistening marble and glass walls. Ribbons of silver and
gold hung from the vaulted ceiling, waving and dancing in the light summer
breeze blowing in from the open skylights. The royal guard, in their scarlet,
gold, and blue uniforms, lined the room—no fewer than ten on the throne
platform alone.

Yet the young queen's shoulders were as tense as a mountain lion ready to
pounce. At least there were no vampires, she said to herself.

Diplomacy demanded that the Queen of Xandra entertain the leaders
of other kingdoms, but all those assembled could sense the young
queen's discomfort.

The queen turned to her sweet, raven-haired baby girl, who so clearly took
after her tall and extravagantly handsome father. Even at this young age, the
princess's cheekbones were sharp, and her jaw defiant. Her big, electric-blue
eyes flashed intelligence and mischief from under long, dark lashes and strong
brows that commanded attention.

The fairy delegation hovered near the platform, their translucent wings acting like prisms as they passed through beams of sunlight. The fairies would grant a wish for the newborn based on what their queen saw in the child's future. They'd been known to grant wondrous gifts, but they'd also been known to bestow gifts more akin to a curse.

The fairy queen, the smallest of the group and dressed in a shimmering ice-blue dress, flew forward until she was hovering over the cradle. Holding her hands over the baby's head, the fairy queen closed her eyes and nodded, seemingly in a trance, and her entire body sparkled even more than it had before.

Suddenly, the fairy queen flew back from the cradle so quickly that a rush of air caught the tendrils of Queen Catia's hair.

Everyone gasped, and Catia's eyes widened in fear.

King Stefan leapt from his throne and strode down the steps toward the fairy queen. "What is it? Tell me, what did you see?"

Still hovering in the air, the fairy queen's body paled to the point where she was nearly translucent, then she laid her hands on his shoulders. "Stefan, King of Xandra, my friend and descendant of my old friends now passed, I see many shadows in your young daughter's future. Loneliness, darkness, and danger."

Queen Catia rose, lifted her baby from the cradle, and, holding her tightly, went to stand at her husband's side. "Darkness? Danger? What do you mean?"

Color had returned to the fairy's skin and she radiated pale blue. "My young queen, the danger's source isn't clear, nor its duration." She turned to the king. "I was planning to grant this child grace of movement, but I'm changing my gift." The fairy raised her hands above the baby.

"To symbolize light," the fairy said, "I grant this baby girl the name Lucette. May this name lead the princess out of the darkness she will encounter."

Queen Catia pulled the baby back from the fairy queen. "We're naming her Rose." Rose, for Catia's favorite flower. Rose, for the acres of gardens her husband had planted as a wedding gift last year. Rose because it was a beautiful bloom that could also protect and defend itself. Given the name Rose, her daughter would be both beautiful and strong.

King Stefan laid his hand on his wife's arm. "Darling, Lucette is a lovely name." He leaned down and whispered, "And it's not smart to decline a fairy queen's gift." Growing up in the country, his young queen had much to learn about other cultures.

The queen opened her mouth to protest, but before she could speak, a shadow fell, as if the sun had been covered by storm clouds, and an icy cold rushed into the room. The king wrapped his arms around his wife and child.

One of the wall-sized windows at the side of the reception hall shattered.

Everyone screamed and ducked as shards of glass burst into the room. Natasha, newly crowned Queen of the Vampires, burst into the room through the broken window. Nearly six feet tall, the vampire queen's rich red hair flowed and her skin shone as if it were cast from porcelain, providing a stark contrast to the shiny black stone that hung at her throat. Turning toward the royal couple, her yellow-flecked eyes flashed hatred. Crossing the room, Natasha's hair flowed around her, as if she held the wind at her command.

"But—it's daytime," Queen Catia blurted. "How can this vile creature walk in the daylight?"

What the young queen did not know was the black stone at the vampire's throat was magic and granted its wearer many powers beyond those of a normal vampire. The vampires of Sanguinia had stolen the Stone of Supremacy from the fairies over a thousand years ago.

Queen Natasha stepped forward and the satin of her low-cut red dress swished around her legs, flowing over the floor like pools of blood spreading across the marble. "Handsome as ever, Stefan," she said to the king.

"Hello, Natasha," King Stefan said. "I was saddened by the news of Vlad's death." King Vladimir had mysteriously died just weeks earlier, many suspected at his own wife's hands.

"Thank you, Stefan," the vampire queen said. "I wanted to invite you all to the funeral." She gestured around the room. "But in deep mourning, I couldn't bring myself to entertain guests." The vampire stepped up and leaned in to embrace him and peered over the king's shoulder toward his young wife. She bared her fangs dangerously close to the king's neck, but instead of biting, she turned and kissed King Stefan on the mouth. A small cry burst from his young wife, but she remained frozen in fear.

Natasha stepped away from the king and continued to leer at Queen Catia, her eyes filled with hatred.

"Go away!" Catia yelled. "You're not welcome here! You weren't invited!"

King Stefan spun toward his wife. "Catia?" The king's shock and hurt were obvious in his voice and expression, for his wife had lied and claimed the vampire delegation from Sanguinia had declined to attend, when in fact she'd burned their invitations.

"Please accept my apology, Natasha," King Stefan said. "I'm sure it was an oversight." He looked at his wife with pain in his eyes, then turned back to the vampire and continued, "But how fortuitous you arrived before the naming ceremony. We were just about to begin."

"Lovely." Queen Natasha smiled and her fangs showed between blood red lips. "But not before I offer my gift."

"No need for a gift," the king said, his voice strong and deep. "Especially not after your invitation failed to arrive."

"Do you think me that petty?" the vampire queen asked. "It is tradition for all reigning monarchs to offer gifts to new members of the other royal families."

"You are most gracious," King Stefan said.

The young queen tensed, because she knew that the vampire queen was not gracious at all. More like vengeful and desperate for power.

Many believed Queen Natasha had killed her husband for his power, and that she wouldn't stop there. They believed the newly crowed vampire queen coveted the kingdom of Xandra's gem-rich mines, its fertile farmland, its vast coastline, its fine fleet of ships. Her quest for power would not stop at controlling Sanguinia, the land of the vampires, she wanted to rule over the humans, too.

"What are you naming the child?" the vampire queen asked.

"Rose," Queen Catia blurted before her husband could speak.

"What a fitting name." Natasha stepped back and her skirts swirled around her. "A flower with fangs. I like that. Now, if you will hand me the babe"—she bared her fangs— "I will bestow my gift."

"Never!" Queen Catia retreated, hugging the baby to her chest. "I will never let you touch my child."

Natasha snatched the baby from the young queen's arms, and leapt to the empty orchestra balcony, high above the room. The assembled crowd screamed in shock and dismay.

The iron- and protein-rich vampire diet made vampires notoriously strong, but none had seen one jump so high.

"Get her!" Queen Catia screamed. "Someone! Save my baby!" The guards raced for the stairs.

Stefan stepped forward and called up. "Natasha, what are you doing? Please don't hurt my daughter."

"Hurt her?" The vampire queen held the child high above her head, and a stream of sunlight burst through the darkness and struck the babe. "Nonsense.

I'm only offering my gift."

She set the baby down on a planter of flowers on the balcony railing, then addressed the crowd. "To punish her rude mother, this child's blood will bring a curse upon the Kingdom of Xandra."

The entire room gasped, knowing such words might lead to war between Sanguinia and Xandra, after so many centuries of peace—so many years during which the necks of the Xandrans had not been at risk of vampire bites.

"Here is my gift." Natasha glared down at the assembled crowd of royalty and other dignitaries. "One day the princess will prick her finger, and the instant her blood is shed, she shall never again wake while the sun is in the sky. Every morning, as the sun breaks above the horizon, the princess will fall into a deep sleep, waking only as night falls." The vampire queen smiled. "And every other citizen of Xandra will suffer the opposite fate. They will fall asleep each night at dusk, leaving the princess alone in the darkness."

The vampire queen picked up the princess, and Queen Catia screamed, "Save my baby." The guards reached the balcony, but the vampire queen leaped onto the railing, balancing on the toes of her black stilettos.

She expelled a cackle that filled the room and shook the crystal chandeliers. "This child and the people of Xandra will pay for their young queen's rudeness and deceit!" She licked her lips, flew into the air, and vanished.

Sunlight once again streamed through the windows, and everyone shaded their eyes against the sudden onslaught of brightness.

"My baby!" Queen Catia ran toward the window as soon as she could squint her eyes open. "She's taken my baby!"

"No, she's here!" King Stefan yelled.

The queen turned to see her husband standing next to the cradle between their thrones. When he picked up the child, her little hand poked out from her blanket and her tiny fingers wiggled.

Queen Catia ran to join her husband and fell into his arms. "I've changed my mind," she cried. "Our daughter will need all the light in her life we can offer. Let's accept the fairies' gift and name her Lucette."

SLEEPING BEAUTY ♦ VAMPIRE SLAYER
ISBN-13: 978-1-60710-256-4
available now